And from

CAROL[YN DAVIDSON]

"Davidson wonderfully captures gentleness
in the midst of heart-wrenching challenges,
portraying the extraordinary possibilities
that exist within ordinary marital love."
—*Publishers Weekly*

"Carolyn Davidson creates such vivid images,
you'd think she was using paints
instead of words."
—Bestselling author Pamela Morsi

"From desperate situation to upbeat ending,
Carolyn Davidson reminds us
why we read romance."
—*Romantic Times*

KATE BRIDGES

"Bridges is comfortable in her western setting,
and her characters' humorous sparring
makes this boisterous mix of romance
and skullduggery an engrossing read."
—*Publishers Weekly*

"Dual romances, disarming characters and a lush
landscape make first-time author Bridges's late
19th-century romance a delightful read."
—*Publishers Weekly* on *The Doctor's Homecoming*

"Ms. Bridges is in a class all her own."
—*Old Book Barn Gazette*

ANA LEIGH

During her career, Ana has written twenty-four novels, won many awards and appeared on the *New York Times* and *USA TODAY* bestseller lists. Although her base has been in historical romance, Ana's first contemporary novel, *The Law and Lady Justice,* was published by Silhouette in June 2003. Ana lives in Wisconsin with her husband, Don, two sons, a daughter and five grandchildren. She loves to hear from readers and can be reached at P.O. Box 612, Thiensville, WI 53092.

CAROLYN DAVIDSON

Reading, writing and research: Carolyn Davison's life in three simple words. At least, that area of her life having to do with her career as an author. The rest of her time is divided among husband, family and travel—her husband, of course, holding top priority in her busy schedule. Carolyn welcomes mail at P.O. Box 2757, Goose Creek, SC 29445. Watch for Carolyn's new Harlequin Historical novel *Colorado Courtship* in February 2004.

KATE BRIDGES

is fascinated by the romantic tales of the spirited men and women who tamed the West. Growing up in rural Canada, Kate developed a love of reading all types of fiction, although romance was her favorite. She has been a neonatal intensive care nurse, then moved on to architecture and television production, before she began crafting novels of her own. She lives in Toronto, and she and her husband love to go to movies and travel. In December 2003 look for *The Surgeon*, Kate's upcoming Harlequin Historical.

Ana Leigh
Carolyn Davidson
Kate Bridges

FRONTIER
CHRISTMAS

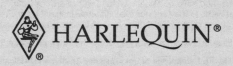
HARLEQUIN®

TORONTO • NEW YORK • LONDON
AMSTERDAM • PARIS • SYDNEY • HAMBURG
STOCKHOLM • ATHENS • TOKYO • MILAN • MADRID
PRAGUE • WARSAW • BUDAPEST • AUCKLAND

ISBN 0-373-83547-7

FRONTIER CHRISTMAS

Copyright © 2003 by Harlequin Books S.A.

The publisher acknowledges the copyright holders of the individual works as follows:

THE MACKENZIES: LILY
Copyright © 2003 by Anna Lee Baier

A TIME FOR ANGELS
Copyright © 2003 by Carolyn Davidson

THE LONG JOURNEY HOME
Copyright © 2003 by Katherine Haupt

CONTENTS

Dear Reader,

Probably other than "Merry Christmas" and "Happy New Year," most heard over the holiday season is the repeated phrase "I'm going home for Christmas."

Have you ever wondered why adults with homes and children of their own still carry in their hearts that "going home" means returning to their parents', their hometown—their roots—on this most sentimental of holidays?

You readers who have followed the series know full well that the meaning of *home* is the Triple M to any MacKenzie. But can it possibly become the same to a widowed sheriff struggling to find a home for his three children?

The MacKenzies: Lily celebrates family love and carries the Christmas message of hope. I'm grateful to Harlequin Historicals for giving me this opportunity to bring these MacKenzies back to you readers, and I hope Lily and Grady's story will carry that Christmas message to all of you.

May you and those you love have happiness and good health in the coming year.

Ana

THE MACKENZIES: LILY
Ana Leigh

This book is dedicated to my loyal MacKenzies readers in gratitude for their kind words and continued support. I cherish our friendship.

CHAPTER ONE

Lamy, New Mexico, 1899

THE HULKING BRUTE SHUFFLED closer, his thick lips contorted in a leering grin. Tiny black eyes gleamed from a burly face pitted with pockmarks and a heavy growth of dark whiskers.

"Give me a kiss, cutie, and I'll pay ya," he said. His voice rumbled from the depth of a barrel chest and sounded more like grunts than words.

Lily backed up to the wall. There were no other customers in the restaurant, not that anyone would willingly take on the gargantuan bully even if there had been. Certainly not the two Harvey Girls who huddled and watched with frightened expressions could do.

She was on her own. A quick kiss to the man's fleshy cheek might resolve the situation, but it would be a cold night in hell before she'd let him put those slobbering thick lips on hers. *Besides, Lily, you're a MacKenzie, and you don't mess with a MacKenzie. Right?* She'd heard that reminder often enough from her brothers and cousins when they were growing up together on the Triple M. *What would you do, Dad? Uncle Flint? Uncle Luke?*

Her charismatic father had always told her a person could get out of any predicament using the three C's—a cool head, common sense and cunning. She figured the fact that he stood four inches over six feet wasn't exactly a detriment either. Of course her uncle Flint's advice had been that it only took one C—a Colt—to get out of any mess; whereas her uncle Luke opted for a compromise between the two. He always claimed that if your *common sense* told you to pull your *Colt*—then pull it. Well, she had neither a cool head, cunning nor a Colt at the moment. What she had was the beady black eyes of this hairy ape leering at her—and her common sense told her she was in deep trouble.

Maybe she should try and knee the bully in the groin as Em and Rose had taught her. According to those two former Harvey Girls, now married to her cousins, they'd had to resort to it a time or two. Of course if she failed, it might turn this colossus into a raging bull.

Her vulnerable situation was interrupted by the tinkle of the bell above the door. They all turned their heads toward the doorway where the sheriff stood with a drawn C—*as in Colt*—in his hand. He obviously was of her uncle Flint's school of persuasion.

"Let her go," Sheriff Delaney ordered.

Even though she was at odds with the sheriff, Lily had never been so glad to see anyone in her life. She heaved a sigh of relief when her attacker dropped his arms and smirked at the lawman.

"It ain't no crime to admire a pretty gal, Sheriff."

"Admiring and molesting are two different things, stranger. What's your name?"

"Jake Banner, and I ain't touched her. Did I, sister?" he said, turning to Lily.

"Didn't look that way to me," the sheriff said. "You want to tell me what happened here, Miss MacKenzie?"

"Mr. Banner owes seventy-five cents for the dinner he ate and has refused to pay it unless I kiss him," Lily said. Banner gave her a dark glare.

"Pay her what you owe her, Mr. Banner," the sheriff ordered, and slid the Colt back into the holster on his hip. To Lily's thinking, *that* was a mistake.

Banner snorted and advanced toward the sheriff. "I don't figure you're gonna shoot me over six bits."

"Maybe not, Mr. Banner, but a night in jail will teach you that as long as I'm sheriff, women are safe in this town. Let's go."

"You ain't lockin' me up, either."

Banner swung a balled fist at the sheriff. The lawman ducked and delivered a blow to the bully's solar plexus. Grunting, Banner's beefy jaw dropped and he doubled over, clutching his stomach. The sheriff followed through with an uppercut to the jaw that sent Banner staggering backward, but he stayed on his feet.

With a feral growl Banner lowered his head and

charged forward like a snorting bull. He clasped his mammoth arms around the sheriff, and both men toppled to the floor. Pinned down by Banner's weight, and his arms locked in the viselike grip of the huge man, the sheriff could not break the hold the brute had on him. Banner began to squeeze the breath out of the sheriff.

Lily was not one to stand by idly. She looked for a weapon, spied a nearby pitcher of ice water and, without hesitation, picked it up, rushed over to the two fallen men, and dumped the icy water over Banner's head.

He let out a yelp of shock and loosened his hold on the sheriff. Before Banner could do more than raise his head, Lily delivered the coup de grâce—she conked him on the head with the heavy glass pitcher. Felled by the blow, Banner lay outstretched.

The sheriff got to his feet and stared down at his adversary. Banner's hair and face dripped with water and chunks of ice were scattered over him and the floor.

Hesitantly Lily asked, ''He's not dead, is he?''

''No, Miss MacKenzie, but one would have to say that you knocked him *cold*.''

A distracting, wide grin that changed the sheriff's usually grim look into a boyish one rocked her back on her heels. Darn the man. As annoying as he was, he did this to her all the time. Well ha! It might work on those other giggling girls standing in the corner, but not on her. Between her brothers and male cousins, she'd had to withstand engaging grins her whole life.

"That should teach Mr. Banner that you don't mess with a MacKenzie," Lily declared. She hoped the sheriff got the message, too: Lily Angelica MacKenzie does not fall prey to any appealing grin.

"I've come to learn that, Miss MacKenzie," Sheriff Delaney said. He cuffed Banner's hands behind his back and got the dazed man to his feet. "Thank you for your assistance, ma'am. Ladies," he added, with a nod to the other girls. Then he tipped a finger to his Stetson and departed.

The other Harvey Girls rushed to the window. "Oh, isn't he wonderful," Alice exclaimed. "And he's so courageous."

Clara nodded. "And so handsome, too."

Lily moved to the doorway and watched the sheriff haul his prisoner to the jail. "And so stupid! Easy to tell he's not from Texas."

Appalled, Alice stared at her. "Lily, how can you say that? Sheriff Delaney just saved you from that horrible man's vile clutches."

"Vile clutches! Alice dear, you've got to stop reading those ridiculous Beadle's Dime Novels."

Incredibly sweet, the young girl was from a small farm town in Illinois. Although her blond curly hair and green eyes attracted the local bachelors like a magnet, she was a naive romantic who passed up the real men who tried to woo her to instead spend her every free moment reading fictitious exploits of Western heroes from ten-cent novels.

On the other hand, dark-haired Clara was a direct contrast to Alice. She'd fallen in love and became engaged to the son of the local banker. They were to wed in less than two weeks.

"Why do you say the sheriff's stupid, Lily?" Clara challenged. "He did get you out of a bad situation."

"Maybe so, but he had the guy on the wrong end of a Colt and didn't take advantage of it. Texas mamas don't raise their sons to be that dumb."

However, Lily had to admit to herself that since his arrival in Lamy, Sheriff Grady Delaney had had his work cut out for him. Unfortunately, the town always attracted drifters and troublemakers passing through on their way to the thriving city of Santa Fe, only eighteen miles away; and he was doing a pretty good job of keeping the peace.

But even though Sheriff Delaney had his hands full with this unlawful element, Lily had her own problem with him—his neglect of his three children. Since he and his children's arrival the month before, she had confronted him time and time again with this issue. Raised on the Triple M, where every child was nurtured with loving care, Lily felt an ache in her heart every time she thought of the three motherless children.

"Lily MacKenzie, if you're so fond of Texas why

did you ever leave it?'' Clara asked, her blue eyes
flashing with merriment.

That was a question Lily had been asking herself
ever since she left the Triple M.

"It's this way, ladies. My brother Cole is married.
My cousins Kitty, Josh and Zach are married, and
six months ago, my sister Linda married the last remaining handsome bachelor in Calico. That left me,
my cousin Sarah and my brother Jeb the only single
MacKenzies on the Triple M. Jeb went off and joined
the Texas Rangers as soon as he recovered from the
wounds he sustained in Cuba. Sarah has declared
from the time she learned to talk that she never in-
tends to sell herself into the slavery of marriage, and,
as for me, ladies, I'm twenty-two years old and tired
of bouncing my siblings' and cousins' offspring on
my knee. The only prospects for a husband in Calico
are forty-eight-year-old Ezra Wilkins, a widowed
hog farmer with seven children, or the funeral direc-
tor, Silas Pritchard, who has to have been the pro-
totype for Mr. Washington Irving's Ichabod Crane.
So I decided as long as I was doomed to spinster-
hood, I'd have some excitement in life. My cousins
Josh and Zach married former Harvey Girls, and after
I listened to Em and Rose relate their experiences
working for Mr. Harvey, I decided it was the very
excitement I needed.''

"Well, you can't say it's not exciting,'' Clara said.

Lily sighed. "Yes, it certainly has been.'' But
what she had come to realize in the past six months

was that it really wasn't excitement she was seeking—it was a husband and a family. Since she hadn't found that man of her dreams, she had decided to go home.

There was just a skeleton crew here in Lamy. In a week this Harvey House would close permanently and Mr. Harvey was moving them to the larger one in Santa Fe. But she was so homesick for the Triple M that it would be a logical time to quit and return home. Trouble was, she had wanted to go home with a husband. She wouldn't find him in Calico, Texas—that's for sure.

Lily snapped herself out of the musing and closed the door. "All right, ladies, let's get this place in order. The train will arrive in thirty minutes."

In keeping with the tradition of pious young women, excellent cuisine and gracious elegance—the hallmark that had earned the Harvey Houses a reputation for helping to tame the West—the three women immediately set to work putting white tablecloths, crystal glasses and fine silverware on the tables in preparation for the thirty passengers due to arrive on the next train.

Dressed in their crisp uniforms, the three Harvey Girls were in front of the restaurant waiting to greet the arrivals when the train pulled into the station. After seating the diners they hustled efficiently about serving thirty dinners of tomato consommé, baked salmon fillets, wild rice and freshly baked hot rolls. Coffee, tea or milk was offered as a beverage, or a

glass of white wine to the more bon vivant. A sump-
tuous dessert of a meringue shell filled with lemon
pudding topped off the meal, and by the time the
train pulled out forty minutes later, every diner had
been properly fed.

As soon as they finished cleaning up for the day,
the rest of the crew departed. Lily was about to lock
up when she looked out the window and saw the
three Delaney children approaching the Harvey
House. Eight-year-old Andy and seven-year-old
Betsy were each holding a hand of their younger
brother. A grayish yellow mongrel trailed at their
heels. The two older children were appealing enough,
but it was three-year-old Mit who tugged the most
at her heartstrings. The little tyke had his father's
dark hair, brown eyes and engaging grin.

She went to the back door to greet them. Their
threadbare clothing and scuffed shoes were in the
same state as the children's soiled faces and dishev-
eled hair.

Mit's face split in a wide grin as soon as he saw
her. He ran up to Lily and hugged her around the
knees.

"Hello, sweetheart," she said, and picked him up.
The youngster never spoke but would cling to her.
Lily held him as she smiled at the other two children.
"How are the two of you today?"

"Okay," Andy said, kicking up puffs of dust that
succeeded in adding a fresh coat to his already
scruffy shoes.

"What about you, Betsy?"

The girl looked at her with a glimmer of resentment in her blue eyes. "I'm okay."

Lily couldn't understand what she had said or done to warrant Betsy's dislike, but the young girl always appeared hostile toward her.

"And how are you doing, Brutus?" The hound wagged its tail in anticipation. The dog knew what to expect as well as she did.

"We was wondering if you had a bone left over for Brutus," Andy said.

Lily smiled tolerantly. The youngsters had gotten in the habit of coming there for something to eat, and Andy always used the same excuse. To spare his pride, she went along with the ruse, but at her request, the chef always made a little extra for them. No child would go hungry as long as there was breath in Lily MacKenzie's body.

"Matter of fact, Andy, there's a nice big bone I've been saving for him. Are you children hungry?" Lily asked. "We have some salmon left over from tonight's dinner. I hate to see it go to waste."

"Don't 'member eating salmon before," Betsy said. "Is it a bird?"

"No, dear, it's fish. I'm sure you'll like it."

"We like catfish," Andy said. "But I reckon we can try it."

Lily nodded toward a backyard pump. "Tell you what—the three of you go over to the pump and, after you clean yourselves up, we'll sit down and have something to eat.''

It was a ritual they knew by rote. They grabbed the towel and brush she handed them and returned a few minutes later free of dust and grime, their hair neatly brushed.

Lily gave Brutus a bone and the dog stretched out on the back stoop to gnaw on it. For the next thirty minutes Lily sat down with the children and watched with pleasure as they gobbled up the food. Suspecting they did not get a decent meal at home, Lily made a point of seeing they got a balanced one there. In addition, from the condition of their worn clothing, she doubted the children had too many occasions to sample the extravagance of desserts at mealtime, so she always made certain they got a dessert to eat with the glass of milk she made each of them drink.

When they finished, Andy and Betsy thanked her politely. Little Mit gave her a hug and kiss. Lily's smile lingered as she watched the three children trudge down the road, Andy and Betsy once again each holding a hand of their little brother as the dog followed.

Her smile faded when she saw the sheriff approach the children. She was too far away to hear what was being said, but it appeared the children were getting a tongue-lashing from him. He picked up Mit and the other two hurried after him.

Lily wanted to race down the street and tell him what she thought of his actions. Life was so unfair, not only to those poor motherless children, but to her, too. What she would give to have such adorable children. How she would love and nurture them if they were hers. While their father…he just neglected them.

"OKAY, YOU KIDS WASH UP and get into your night-clothes," Grady said a short time later. "As soon as I finish up in the kitchen here, I'll read to you."

Grady grinned as he watched them scamper off. They were such good kids, and he was so proud of them. "And, Andy, make sure that Mit is clean behind the ears," he called out.

He'd just sat down when Betsy came running back. Dressed in a nightgown and her cheeks scrubbed to a rosy glow, she handed him a hairbrush and then held out her hands for his inspection.

"Very good, pumpkin," he said. "A lady must always keep her fingers and nails clean and neat."

Betsy beamed under his approval. "Yes, Daddy."

"Did you brush your teeth?"

"Yes, Daddy." She looked at him with an adoring smile that always tugged at his heartstrings.

"That's my gal," he said, and kissed the tip of her pert little turned-up nose. Then he began to brush her tousled hair, making sure he didn't pull too hard on the curly snarls. By the time he finished, the boys had joined them and he did the same to them.

Thirty minutes later, Grady closed the book he'd

been reading to the children and laid it aside. "Time to go to bed."

He picked up Mit, who had fallen asleep in his lap, and carried him to the bed. For a long moment Grady stared down at the sleeping child, then bent over and kissed him on the forehead.

Andy crawled in on one side of his sleeping brother and Betsy on the other.

"You children really had me worried when I came home to make your supper and found you gone," he said as he tucked the blankets around his eldest son.

"We were just out for a walk, Dad," Andy said.

"I've told you I want you kids to come straight home after school. You're the eldest, Andy. I depend upon you and Brutus to take care of your sister and brother. This town is wild and you never know what could happen."

"Not as long as you're sheriff, Daddy. You're the best sheriff in the world," Betsy declared.

"We can't stay in the house all the time, Daddy," Andy said. "If this town is so bad, why did you come here to be sheriff?"

"Because the pay's good, son." Grady clasped Andy's hand between his own. "I know it's not a pleasant life for you kids. And you've got more responsibility than a boy your age should have. Just one more year, Andy, and I'll have enough saved to put down on a ranch."

"With horses and chickens?" Betsy asked, her eyes bright with enthusiasm.

Grady walked over to her and sat down on the edge of the bed. "You bet, pumpkin. We'll have chickens and a couple horses. And you can have a garden, too."

She reached up and hugged him around the neck. "I love you, Daddy."

"I love you, too, sweetheart." He kissed her and tucked the blanket around her. "Now get to sleep."

"Dad," Andy said.

"What is it, Andy?"

"Miss Jenkins told me to tell you that she doesn't want Mit to come to school with me anymore. She says he's too young and disruptured."

"Disruptive, Andy," Grady corrected. "Is he?"

"Is he what?"

"Does he cause a disturbance during school?"

"When he gets tired of drawing pictures, or needs to go to the privy."

"I'll talk to Miss Jenkins tomorrow." He kissed Andy on the cheek. "Good night, kids. Pleasant dreams."

Brutus jumped up on the bed and stretched out at the feet of the children. "Take care of them, pal," Grady said, patting the big mutt on the head. The dog remained motionless except for its wagging tail.

Grady returned to the jailhouse and sat down at his desk. His misery felt like a lead weight suspended over his head by a thin rope that had begun to unravel. He was at his wit's end. He didn't know what to do about the children. He had to leave them on their own so much, and their welfare was constantly on his mind. They had barely touched their supper again. Granted it was the third night in a row he had served them soup, but he couldn't afford to waste it.

Since his arrival in Lamy he had tried to find someone willing to look after them during his working hours, but so far had been unsuccessful. The town attracted the worst element and the streets of Lamy were no place for young children. But the job paid well, and he needed the money if he hoped to ever be able to give them a decent upbringing.

Since Kate's death, he had tried to be both mother and father to them, but had failed miserably. Poor little Mit had never known his mother's soft voice or tender touch because she had died giving birth to him; but Andy and Betsy had, and he'd often heard them crying themselves to sleep because they missed her. At those times he wanted to join them, bawl his insides out. But tears wouldn't bring Kate back.

He closed his eyes and tried to conjure up the sound of her voice…her laughter. It was becoming harder and harder. He could see her in his mind's eye, but he couldn't hear her.

Don't leave us, Kate. We need you more than ever. He opened his eyes when the door suddenly burst open.

No! Not again!

CHAPTER TWO

"SHERIFF DELANEY, I'd like to speak to you."

Lily MacKenzie closed the door and strode over to his desk, determination gleaming in those sapphire eyes of hers. He had to admit that physically she was a beautiful woman with those incredible eyes and soft-looking hair that made a man itch to reach out and curl one of her dark ringlets around a finger. He shook the provocative thoughts aside. What in hell was he thinking? He must be more tired than he thought. Miss Lily MacKenzie had the tongue of a shrew and was using it to whip him bloody with unfair accusations—allegations that his children ran wild and unkempt, and he let his children go hungry.

Granted their clothing was old and threadbare. He couldn't afford to keep them in new clothes; they had to pass the clothing down from one to the other. But her claims that they were dirty were untrue; he always checked to make sure his children were clean and neat when they went off to school. He never heard such complaints from the schoolmarm. And his kids didn't run around like wild little heathens either.

Well, maybe the MacKenzie woman hadn't accused them of being that bad, but she'd come mighty close. He'd taught them manners, and to always be respectful to their elders. Furthermore, he might not be the best cook in the world, but he sure as hell made sure his kids had a hot meal in their bellies. Why didn't the woman just go about her own business and let him handle his?

Grady took a deep breath and prepared for the worst. "What can I do for you, Miss MacKenzie?"

She squared her shoulders and jutted that pert little chin of hers in the air. "It's not what you can do for me, sir. It's what you can do for your children."

He couldn't understand how a woman with the face of a saint could be so damn irritating. "Miss MacKenzie, we've had this discussion before and I have repeatedly told you, ma'am, I don't know what you're talking about."

"Exactly!" she declared with a triumphant smirk. "That is the problem, sir."

"What is, Miss MacKenzie?" he asked wearily.

"Your reprehensible disregard for the welfare of your children."

His head was pounding, his body was aching from the earlier tussle with Jake Banner, and he was too weary emotionally to go through another bout with this meddlesome female—no matter what she looked like.

"Ma'am, no one is more aware of the unfortunate conditions of my children's lives than I." He walked to the door and opened it. "It's quite late, would you like me to see you safely home?"

"I got here on my own. I certainly can get back the same way."

"As you wish. You are one stubborn female. If you'll excuse me, I have work to do. Remember to close the door on your way out." He grabbed his Stetson off a hook and departed.

Remember to close the door on your way out! She remembered all right—Lily slammed it as hard as she could on her way out.

She was mad. Downright, bull-stomping mad! How dare he just walk out and leave her standing there. Oh, the man was so rude! Her intention had been to have a calm, intelligent conversation with him—possibly try to work out a solution that would benefit the children—until that overbearing attitude of his blew away all her noble intentions.

Why had she even expected anything better from him? The man was so self-absorbed it was a wonder he didn't look in a mirror every time he passed one. In addition to which, he walked around as if he were carrying the weight of the world on his shoulders. Did he actually expect her to feel sorry for him? The ones she felt sorry for were those three neglected children of his. But he made it clear that he did not want to be reminded of them.

Well, Sheriff Grady Delaney had not seen or heard the last on the subject from her. A MacKenzie hadn't been born who'd ever turn their back on a child in need.

As she walked up the street, she glanced back and

saw that the sheriff had fallen in about a half block behind her. He obviously was making sure she got back safely. It made her angrier. No matter what she said, there was no changing his mind.

As soon as she got to her room, Lily undressed and went to bed. Unfortunately, she couldn't fall asleep and tossed restlessly in bed. She couldn't get the children's plight out of her mind, her heart heavy with the worry of what would become of them when she left Lamy in a couple of weeks. And to her further distress, those sorrowful brown eyes of Grady Delaney kept intruding on her misgivings.

THE NEXT MORNING as the breakfast train arrived, Lily's thoughts were still on the previous night's confrontation with Sheriff Delaney. Try as she might, she couldn't put this latest incident out of her mind. Her preoccupation was suddenly interrupted when she was grasped from behind and lifted off her feet in a bear hug.

"Hi, Lily," a husky voice said at her ear.

Delight surged through her. "Cole, put me down," she ordered. She turned around to greet her handsome brother. At the sight of him she felt a rush of homesickness. It was so good to see a face from home. Six months was a long time.

"What a surprise. What are you doing here?"

"I got stuck going to St. Louis on some Triple M business and I promised Mom I'd stop to make sure you were okay."

"Of course I'm okay. How is everyone back home?"

"Doing just fine. They all said to say hello."

"And how is my godchild?"

"Getting big, Lil. The little scamp's into everything."

"Oh, I miss her."

"Maggie thinks she's expecting again."

"I know, I just got a letter from her. I'm happy for you, Cole."

"You're coming home for Christmas, aren't you?"

"Of course. We'll be closing up the Harvey House in a week. I've decided to come home for good."

"That's great news. Mom and Dad will be glad to hear it." He grinned at her, a familiar devilment gleaming in his eyes. "Coming back alone?"

"Yeah. Why do you ask?"

"Couldn't find a husband, huh?"

Lily blushed in annoyance and put her hands on her hips. She wanted to groan aloud. Her brothers and male cousins would never let her live it down. "Who said I was looking for one?"

"Maggie and Sarah."

"That's the last time I'll ever confide in your wife or our dear cousin, Sarah."

"Sarah will be happy you're coming home to stay, and she's announced *she* has no intentions of ever getting married."

"Sarah's married to the Triple M—we all know

that. Sit down. While you have breakfast you can tell me the news from home.''

She hung on avidly to every word he had to say, but too soon it was time for the train to depart, and as they walked outside Cole slipped his arm around her shoulders.

''Tell everyone hello for me and give that daughter of yours a big hug and kiss from her aunt Lily.''

The departing train sounded a final warning whistle. ''Sorry I couldn't stay longer, Lil.'' He gave her a big hug and kissed her cheek. ''Be good.''

''I always am,'' she said, beginning to choke up as she watched him board the train. She felt an urge to climb on after him.

With a whistle and a spurt of steam, the train began to pull away. ''Ever think that might be your problem?'' Cole called out. ''Loosen up, gal.''

''Darn you, Cole, I'll get even with you for that.''

He grinned and waved. ''Luv ya.''

She waved back and stood on the platform until the train was out of sight. ''Luv ya,'' she murmured. Then she brushed aside the tears that had mysteriously appeared on her cheeks. Shoulders slumped, she went back inside.

GRADY WAS JUST APPROACHING the Harvey House when Lily came out of the restaurant with a tall stranger who had his arm around her. He stepped into a doorway where he could watch them unobserved. They were obviously close friends and, after they spoke a few words, the guy hugged and kissed her then boarded the train. She remained on the platform until the train was out of sight, and then dabbed at her eyes and went back inside.

It was clear to him that the two were more than just friends. He couldn't recall ever seeing the guy in town. So she had a sweetheart—or maybe the man was her husband. If she was married, she didn't wear a wedding ring. What the hell difference did it make to him anyway? He had more to worry about than Miss—or Mrs.—Lily MacKenzie's love life.

He'd intended to apologize to her for his rudeness last night, but instead, he turned around and headed back to the jail. Besides, if her sweetheart had just left town and she was feeling down in the dumps, he'd be the last person she'd want to see.

AS SOON AS THEY FINISHED work, Lily and the other girls went to the dressmaker's for a final fitting on their gowns for Clara's wedding, and then she went back to her room and wrote a couple letters. Cole's visit had been so short, it had just made her more homesick than ever. When she finished, Lily felt too restless to stay cooped up in her room, so she picked up the letters and left to post them.

On her way back from the post office, to her delight Lily saw Betsy Delaney peering in the window of one of the stores. Much to her surprise, the young girl was neatly groomed.

"Hello, dear, how are you?"

"Okay," Betsy said. She went back to staring pensively into the window.

"Where are your brothers, honey?" It was unusual to see her without the other two and Brutus.

"They're waiting for Daddy at the jail."

The girl's rapt attention remained on a frothy, ruffled gown of white organdy displayed in the window. The dress was much too fussy for Betsy, whose youthful, patrician beauty would best be complimented by a softer fabric and less frills, but to the seven-year-old, the dress probably looked like something out of a fairy tale.

"Isn't it beautiful, ma'am? I bet it's the most beautifulest dress in the whole world," the awestruck girl said.

"It's very lovely, dear."

"Boy, if I had a dress like that for the school play, I'd really look like a fairy."

"You're in the Christmas play! Betsy, how wonderful. What part do you play?"

"I'm a Christmas fairy. Miss Jenkins made a crown for my head and a wand to carry."

"How exciting. When is the play?"

"Friday night."

"Well, I'll be sure to come to see it. Here comes your family now," Lily said when she saw the three approaching figures.

As soon as Mit saw her, he broke free and ran to her. Lily picked him up and kissed him on the cheek, then smiled at Andy, and tousled his hair.

"Sheriff Delaney," she acknowledged.

"Miss MacKenzie," he replied with a nod. "Let's go, Betsy."

Her heart felt heavy in her chest as Lily watched them walk away. Then she entered the store.

The next day was Thursday and throughout the day she kept a watchful eye for the children. When it became apparent they were not coming that day, and with the school play scheduled for Friday, Lily picked up the dress box and headed for the small house the town provided for the sheriff and his family.

To her regret Grady Delaney opened the door in response to her knock. At the sight of her, his look of displeasure was embarrassing to her.

"I'm sorry to disturb you at home, Sheriff Delaney. Is Betsy home?"

"No, she's at school practicing for the Christmas play they're presenting tomorrow night."

"Yes, she told me all about it." She handed him the box. "Will you give this to her when she gets home?"

"What is it?"

"It's a dress she was admiring in the shop window."

"You mean you bought it for her?" he asked.

"I couldn't resist it, Sheriff Delaney. She said she was playing a fairy princess in the play and—"

He shoved the box back at her. "I understand. I

suggest you return it because I will not let Betsy accept your charity, Miss MacKenzie.''

"But, Sheriff, it's just a dress—and if you could have seen the longing in her eyes—"

Once again he interrupted her. "My daughter does not have to accept your charity, Miss MacKenzie. She has a dress that will do fine.''

He was being so unreasonable she wanted to scream. "Can't you understand what it means to a little girl to yearn for something beautiful, and then, like a miracle, she gets it?''

He snorted. "Like Cinderella at the ball.''

"Yes, exactly. Then you do understand," she said, relieved.

"You bet I understand, and I want it to end right *now*. If you've got a fairy godmother, lady, count your blessings, but don't try and play one to my kids. I learned a long time ago there's no Santa Claus, Easter Bunny or Tooth Fairy, Miss MacKenzie, and as for the Thanksgiving turkey, it ends up in a roasting pan.''

"Oh, you are a nasty individual, Sheriff. Do you take pleasure in being this unpleasant? You sound no better than that brute Jake Banner you locked up for using his strength to molest women.''

"Maybe I should start locking up a certain woman for using her accusing tongue to molest men.''

"Are you referring to me?''

"If the shoe fits, lady.''

Lily shook her head in utter confusion. "I can't

understand your hostility, Sheriff Delaney. Do you really see me as such a menace? I adore your children. I mean them no harm.''

"I'm proud of how my children accept the circumstances of their hard lives, Miss MacKenzie, and as well-intentioned as your charity may be, it's only fleeting, and more of a reminder of what they don't have. Even now, as much as they've grown to love you, you'll be leaving soon and they'll have to deal with another disappointment. So why prolong it? I prefer you stay away from them for your remaining time here.''

His words took all the fight out of her. In truth, she felt closer to tears. How could he be that cruel?

Swallowing a sob of despair, she raised her head. "Sheriff Delaney, there are events in life that can cause some people to turn bitter and cruel. Then there are those who are born just downright mean. I think you are an example of the second and won't be satisfied until you turn your children into the first.''

For what it was worth, this time Lily had the pleasure of walking away, but she could feel his stare right smack on the middle of her back as she continued up the street, dabbing at the tears stinging her cheeks.

She spent a very miserable night fretting over the sheriff's words and came to one conclusion: despite his wishes, she would not avoid the children for the few days she had remaining in Lamy.

The next day the Harvey House served its last

meal prior to moving to Santa Fe, and in another
week, following Clara's wedding, Lily would be
leaving Lamy for good. It was too bad Sheriff Grady
Delaney had to make this final week so unpleasant
for her, because with the idle time on her hands she
could have spent time with the children. It gave her
greater cause to really dislike the man.

That evening she attended the school play. Although the gown Betsy wore was clean and starched,
the dress showed its wear. Nevertheless, white fluffy
gown or not, Betsy performed brilliantly and Lily's
heart swelled with pride as much as any mother's in
the audience.

She admitted painfully to herself that she wasn't
Betsy's mother, and after a word of congratulation
to Lamy's little Christmas fairy—with the child's father standing nearby like a watchful sentinel—Lily
went back to her room.

CHAPTER THREE

THE NEXT MORNING Lily had an inspiration. A Christmas tree! She'd be willing to bet her best pair of boots that Grady Delaney had no intention of putting up a tree for Christmas. Well, whether he liked it or not, they were going to have one. Lily grabbed her coat.

Andy and Brutus answered her knock on the door. It helped to see that the sight of her brought a wide smile to the boy and a wagging tail to the dog.

"Andy, I have a great idea. Are your sister and brother home?"

"Yes, they are, Miss MacKenzie. What do you want with them?" Grady Delaney said, suddenly filling the doorway.

Drat the luck! He would have to be home. He left them on their own any other time. "Good morning, Sheriff Delaney. I thought it would be a pleasant outing to take the children and find a Christmas tree."

Betsy and Mit came running to the door. Mit squeezed through his daddy's legs and reached out his arms to her. Lily picked him up and kissed him. "Good morning, little love of my life."

"Oh, can we, Daddy?" Betsy pleaded.

Grady looked at Lily as if he'd like to strangle her on the spot. "It will soon be Christmas, Sheriff. Even you have to admit that a Christmas tree has nothing to do with Santa Claus. It's a symbolic celebration of the holiday."

"Have you ever chopped down a tree, Miss MacKenzie?"

"I personally haven't, but I've certainly observed others doing it back home. I always loved going to help pick one out."

"It's not as easy as it looks," Grady said. "And they are very heavy to carry."

She gave him her sweetest smile. "We'll pick a small one."

"Daddy, why don't you come with us?" Andy asked.

"Yeah, Daddy, you're so strong I bet you could chop down the biggest tree in the forest if you wanted to," Betsy said, looking up with adoration at her father.

By this time all three children were pulling on his hands or pants leg and pleading for him to come along. "I just bet you could, Sheriff Delaney," Lily said, with a challenging smile that she knew would only aggravate him more.

"All right," he relented, "but we can't take all day. I have to be back to work in three hours. You kids put on your coats and hats while I get a wagon from the livery."

"I'll make sure they dress warmly, Sheriff,"
Lily said.

He snatched his gun belt off a wall peg. "I'm sure
you will, Miss MacKenzie." A spark of humor
warmed his brown eyes as he buckled it on. "You
have an affinity for heating people up."

Lily's amused gaze locked with his. She couldn't
hold back her grin. It might be that under that som-
ber, Ebenezer Scrooge mien of Sheriff Grady Delaney, there lurked a school of pathetic little humor
cells floundering frantically for survival in their effort
to spawn. Just like salmon swimming upstream.
"God bless 'em," she murmured. They'd need all
the help they could get.

As soon as Grady arrived with the wagon, Lily
and Mit climbed up next to him and the two elder
children and Brutus hopped into the back of the
wagon. Lily, Andy and Betsy sang Christmas carols,
Mit clapped his hands, Brutus howled and Grady grimaced. It was a noisy but fun ride despite how hard
Grady tried to act as if he wasn't enjoying it.

He pulled up at a pine grove about five miles out
of town and as soon as he tied the horses to a tree
the children started to scatter.

"Get back here. No going off in all directions. I
want you to stick together."

His word was law to them, and they went from
tree to tree until they found one that pleased them
all. It stood about six feet tall, but Grady had to peel
off several lower rows of boughs to enable him to

put an ax to it. Then with Lily's help, they carried
the tree back to the wagon while the children gathered up the discarded boughs.

"See those pinecones on the ground?" Lily said.
"Gather them up, kids. You can use them to decorate
the tree."

The children ran off to do as she said, and when
Lily started to follow, she stepped on a large rock,
turned her ankle and, with a cry, fell backward into
Grady's outstretched arms.

He swooped her up and for an interminable moment they stared wordlessly into each other's eyes,
his face so close she could feel the warmth of his
breath. Her mind spun in confusion as a new and
surprising warmth surged through her from the
strength in the arms holding her. A gasp of surprise
slipped past her lips, and he shifted his gaze to her
mouth. Lily closed her eyes, parted her lips and
braced herself for the kiss.

"Did you hurt yourself?"

She opened her eyes and felt the hot blush staining
her cheeks. "No, I'm fine."

Lily felt so foolish that she wished she could disappear. Surely he must have guessed she thought he
intended to kiss her. What a fool she'd made of herself.

He put her down, her back against a wagon wheel.
"Sit still and let me check your ankle. You might
have sprained it."

"No, it feels fine."

"Lily, please sit still."

There was general concern in his voice, and he'd called her by her first name, which was a shock in itself. She was too mortified to offer any resistance, and leaned back.

Grady knelt on one knee and slipped off her shoe. Cupping her foot in the palm of his left hand, he traced the ankle and foot with the right one. His fingers felt warm and gentle as he searched for any break or swelling.

It always amazed Lily how gentle the touch of a big man could be. Raised in a family of tall men, she had discovered this phenomenon as a child. Grady's touch was just as gentle, but differed in the excitement it generated. The sensation was too pleasing to ask him to stop. His head was bent over her as he continued his examination. She fought the urge to reach out and feel the dark hair. Then it became too late to consider, because he finished, raised his head and smiled.

"Nothing seems broken."

"Does that mean you don't have to shoot me, Sheriff Delaney?"

He chuckled. The sound was so pleasant and unexpected that she was caught off guard by its vibrancy. "That doesn't stop me from wringing your neck, though. If you hadn't hatched this scheme, you might never have hurt your ankle."

"My ankle is fine," she declared. To prove the point—and get away from those disturbing brown eyes of his—Lily stood up. Fortunately, the wagon was there to support her or she might have fallen again. After several tentative steps, she tried it without a support and walked off the numbness just as the children came running back, with Brutus dogging their heels. Their pockets and hands were full of pinecones.

"We can't carry any more," Andy said.

Lily heaped them in the wagon. "Looks like you've got plenty."

"Time to get going, kids," Grady said. "I have to go to work."

They climbed up on the wagon and headed back to Lamy. When they reached the edge of town the sound of gunfire rang out.

Grady tossed Lily the reins. "Get the children inside."

He jumped down from the wagon and drew his Colt. As he ran toward the sound of the shots, four riders came running out of the bank. Seeing Grady, they fired several shots at him.

"Get down," Lily yelled. She grabbed Mit and rolled into the back of the wagon, covering the huddled children with her body.

As soon as the gunmen rode past them, Lily lifted the children out of the wagon. "Run home, and don't stop for nothing," she ordered.

"But Daddy's hurt," Betsy cried.

"Betsy, don't argue. Get going, children." She

thanked God that they were used to obeying an order. Hand in hand, they did as told.

Lily ran down the street to where a small crowd had gathered around Grady. The doctor had arrived already and was examining him. To her horror, she saw that Grady was bleeding and unconscious. Blood was oozing from a wound on his brow, and his shirt on his left shoulder was already saturated.

"Is he—"

The doctor shook his head. "He's still breathing, but it doesn't look good. Let's get him home."

"Dr. Preston, his children are home. Do you think they should see him like this?"

"If it turns out to be as bad as I fear, it won't much matter, Miss MacKenzie. Couple of you men help me get him to his house," he ordered.

Lily ran ahead of them and opened the door, then shooed the children into their bedroom and closed it after them. She hurried and pulled down the counterpane on Grady's bed and the men laid him down.

"Okay, everybody out. Miss MacKenzie, I'll need some hot water," Dr. Preston ordered.

"I'll put some water on the stove at once, Doctor."

As soon as she had put a kettle on to boil, Lily went into the children's bedroom. All three of them were crying.

"Is Daddy gonna die?" Andy asked through his sobs.

Lily sat down on the side of the bed and opened

her arms. The children cuddled together in her embrace.

"The doctor is examining your father now, and we'll know more as soon as he finishes his examination. Your father's been shot twice, but he's breathing, children. We just have to pray that he'll pull through this. He's a strong man, and if anyone can do it, he can."

"Daddy would want us with him now," Betsy said, swiping at the tears running down her cheeks.

"I'm sure he would, honey, but the doctor doesn't want anybody in the room until he's through fixing him up. I have to take the doctor some hot water now, but I'll be back as soon as I can. In the meantime, you children say a prayer for your father. I believe he's going to be all right, my darlings, and you must believe the same. Never give up hope or belief in the power of prayer."

"Daddy says we shouldn't hope 'cause we'll only be disappointed," Andy said, his young face a picture of despair.

"Andy, I'll never give up hoping. I've done it all my life. Just try it. All of you…just try it," Lily said, with less conviction than she felt.

She slipped out of the room and closed the door softly. Glancing heavenward, she murmured, "Please, God, don't take away the only thing those children have to cherish."

GRADY HAD NEVER FELT so strange. His whole body seemed too heavy to lift from the bed. He tried to open his eyes, but the lids felt weighted down. After a few seconds he tried again and succeeded. He became aware he was in his own room, but his head was throbbing so painfully that he lay still, hoping the ache would pass. What in hell had happened? There'd been a bank holdup, a gunfight and a flash of pain... Good Lord, he must have been shot!

His groping hand sought the source of a burning ache and encountered a bandage wrapped around his left arm. Raising a hand to his head, he felt another bandage at his temple. Grady groaned aloud and closed his eyes. *My God, his head, too!*

Gritting his teeth against the pain, with sheer willpower, Grady sat up and shifted his legs off the bed, only to be struck instantly by a wave of nausea and dizziness.

''What are you doing?''

The shout pierced his throbbing temple like a knife thrust. No, it couldn't be. What would she be doing here in his house—his bedroom? He must be having a nightmare. That was it. He was dreaming this whole thing. Lately she'd been popping up frequently in his dreams—and they weren't nightmares. But there was no accounting for what a man might dream when he was feverish and shot full of lead.

Grady closed his eyes, took a deep breath and willed himself awake. Then he opened his eyes again and his nemesis was now looming over him like a specter from purgatory.

"Lie back, you mustn't get up," Lily ordered.

She must have the strength of Samson, because he felt weightless when she put a hand on his chest and shoved him down.

"You've lost a lot of blood, Sheriff. You've got to remain in bed."

That same hand, which felt as if it could wield an ancient broadsword, moved to his head and strangely enough it now felt cool and soothing on his fevered brow. It felt damn good.

"You're still running a fever. The doctor said to send for him as soon as you regain consciousness, so please lie still until then."

She wasn't going to get an argument from him. Everything was becoming too complicated to analyze. He just wanted to sleep. Grady closed his eyes.

As soon as Lily stepped out of the bedroom she was met by the worried countenances of the three children who were seated at the kitchen table.

"Good news. Your father is awake, children. Andy, will you go and fetch Dr. Preston?"

Andy took off on a run and Betsy shoved back her chair and headed for the bedroom. "Wait, Betsy," Lily said. "Let's make sure the doctor says it's okay for your father to have visitors."

The young girl paused with her hand on the doorknob. "How come you can go in and see him, but I can't? He's *my* dad."

From the anger in Betsy's eyes, Lily realized she'd trod once again on sacred ground to the young girl.

It seemed that for every stride forward with the child, she fell back two steps.

"Tell you what, honey. As soon as Dr. Preston gives us the okay, you can go in and feed your dad some of that soup we cooked up."

"You mean it!" Betsy exclaimed.

"I bet he'll be good and hungry by then. Honey, why don't you put Mit down for a nap while I clean up these lunch dishes? It will probably take the doctor a while to examine your father."

"Okay." Betsy grabbed Mit's hand. "Just remember, I get to feed him."

"I'll remember," Lily said. She'd made the impulsive promise without consulting the doctor and hoped she wouldn't have to disappoint the child.

Within minutes Andy returned with the doctor and by the time Lily washed and dried the lunch dishes, Dr. Preston joined her in the kitchen.

"It would appear the worst is over," he said. "Fortunately the bullet only grazed his temple. Grady's in good physical condition, but he's lost a lot of blood, and must remain in bed to regain his strength and prevent those wounds from opening."

"I hope you told him that, Doctor, because he tried to get up earlier."

The doctor nodded. "No doubt. I'm afraid your work is cut out for you."

"How long will he be laid up, Dr. Preston?"

"If he doesn't disturb the wounds, it shouldn't be more than five or six days."

Five or six days! Good Lord, how could she tolerate the unpleasant man for that length of time? Her thoughts must have been reflected on her face because the doctor asked, "Are you relinquishing the duty, Miss MacKenzie?"

"I'll do all I can for the children's sake, Doctor."

"I appreciate that, Miss MacKenzie, because he does need nursing. I've changed the dressings on his wounds, but I recommend you change them this evening. I left some aspirin tablets and instructions for administering them on the dresser. It's a new product and combines an analgesic and antipyretic for treating both pain and fever. If he has any relapse, send for me."

"Ah, Dr. Preston, can he eat?"

"Just something light at first."

"Is vegetable soup okay?"

"That should be fine."

"Can he have visitors, Doctor? His children are anxious to see him."

"Keep the visits short. Sleep is the best medicine for the next couple days." He picked up his black bag and headed for the door. "You're doing a fine job, Miss MacKenzie. Keep up the good work."

Andy and Betsy had listened quietly to the doctor's instructions. As soon as he left, Andy asked, "Can we go in and see him now?"

"Yes, dear, but you heard the doctor. You mustn't stay too long."

Betsy was already at the bedroom door. When they

went in, Grady was asleep. The two children stood
at the side of the bed staring fretfully in silence at
him. Lily's heart went out to them. They'd been so
frightened that they'd lose him. At least the doctor's
words must have been comforting to them.

"I guess we better let him sleep," she whispered.

Betsy pressed a kiss to the hand of her sleeping
father, and then the children followed her out of the
room.

An hour later Lily checked on him and Grady was
awake and trying to sit up. She hurried over and
helped him.

"How are you feeling?" she asked, and began to
plump up the pillows.

"Fine."

"Uh-huh," she said. "Are you hungry?"

"I could use a cup of coffee."

"I have a pot on the stove. And I made soup. I'll
heat it up and as soon as it's hot, we'll get some
down you."

"Just coffee."

"The hot soup will do you good."

Grady definitely had his mind made up. He may
be wounded, feverish and bedridden, but he wasn't
going to tolerate this termagant's orders. When he
felt like eating—he'd eat.

"Miss MacKenzie, nobody's going to spoon-feed
me," he declared. "When I'm well enough to feed
myself, I'll eat." He folded his arms across his chest
and winced from the pain of it, but was too stubborn

to drop his arms. He had a point to make with this woman.

He looked and sounded like a petulant child, and despite the seriousness of his illness, Lily was hard-pressed to feel sympathetic.

"You hear me and hear me well, Grady Delaney, I was raised with a whole passel of the most bull-headed men you better hope you never encounter, so another mulish-minded member of that species isn't going to scare me off. There's a frightened little girl in the other room who spent the night crying and praying that her daddy wouldn't die. Now she wants to feed him some soup, and you're going to let her or I'll pour that damn soup down your throat."

"You're as meddlesome at nursing as you are at minding other people's business," he groused, then almost had to duck when she gave the pillow a final whack that was damn near enough to scatter the feathers.

Lily walked to the door. "I'll send in your children."

Why hadn't she said that she meant for Betsy to feed him? Of course he wanted to see his kids. The woman was an irritant. Beautiful but irritating. He was grateful that Lily was looking after his kids while he was laid up, and he'd tell her as much when he felt better. But right now he just wished she'd leave him be. He knew how to take care of himself. He'd been doing so for most of his life. The thought was instantly shoved to the back of his head and he broke into a grin when Andy and Betsy entered the room.

With a face crunched in concentration, spoonful by spoonful Betsy fed him the soup while Andy held the cup of coffee to his lips for Grady to sip from it.

"I think your daddy needs to rest now," Lily said as soon as they had finished feeding him. She shooed the children out of the room, and they left with a promise to bring Mit in when their little brother woke up from his nap.

Lily wasn't going to get any argument from him either. The mere act of eating had sapped him. In addition to which his head ached, his shoulder hurt, and he could barely keep his eyes open.

"Do you need anything else right now?" she asked as she adjusted the pillows so he could lie back.

"No, I'm fine. Thank you, Miss MacKenzie. I may not show it, but I do appreciate your help." He closed his eyes and was asleep before she even reached the door.

CHAPTER FOUR

LILY SPENT ANOTHER night sitting in a chair, stealing short naps while keeping a watchful eye for any change in Grady's condition. He had a relatively restful night, so in the morning she sent the two older children off to school.

With Mit and Brutus sitting on Grady's bed, Lily perched on the nearby chair and watched the stubborn man struggling to feed himself.

"Are you sure you don't want my help?" she asked.

"No, thanks. I'm doing fine." He winked at Mit. "Aren't we, son?"

Mit's childish laughter was delightful. Since he never spoke, it was always a pleasure to hear him laugh, and was comforting to know that at least the youngster was capable of making a sound. She believed from the bottom of her heart that when Mit was ready, he'd speak.

Since seeing the children with their father, Lily had to admit she'd been wrong about his relationship with them. All three of the children worshiped him, and it was plain to see that he adored them. Even Brutus held the same affection for the man—the dog's tail wagged a mile a minute every time the sheriff spoke to him. And there was no fooling a dog; they had an irrefutable sense about people.

Lily hadn't realized she'd been smiling until Grady said, "Penny for your thoughts, Miss MacKenzie. Your smile's as wide as the Mississippi."

"I was just thinking about dogs. My father always said the country should let dogs elect the politicians. A smooth-talking drummer can get a lot of people to swallow the snake oil he's peddling, but a dog'll give it a sniff and trot away."

His chuckle was infectious and she responded with light laughter.

"Yeah, your father's right about that," Grady said. "And they're loyal, too. Having Brutus around gives me a lot of peace of mind. Nobody's gonna hurt the kids if he's near." He finished the soup and handed her the bowl. "You sure make better tasting soup than I do."

"Well, thank you, Sheriff Delaney, I enjoy cooking." She did not understand why the polite compliment should give her so much pleasure, but it did.

"Did you learn how to cook working for the Harvey restaurants?"

"I learned how to cook long before I became a Harvey Girl—right at my mother's stove. She's been teaching me recipes for as long as I can remember."

"She taught you well, Lily." He'd said her name again. Their gazes met and held, his usual and very familiar impatient look now replaced by one of warmth and tenderness. In the brief exchange, something passed between them that she'd never experienced with any man. Confused by her quickened heartbeat, she lowered her eyes.

"Come on, Mit. We better let your daddy rest." She picked Mit up and hurried from the room, fighting the temptation to look back at the man in the bed.

By evening Lily was exhausted—not from working so hard. She was used to hard work. She was downright sleepy. For the past two nights, she had sat up in a chair in a bedside vigil. Granted she had dozed off in an occasional catnap, but now with the crisis over, her body ached to stretch out in her bed. However, she didn't dare leave Grady alone with only the children, who were sound asleep themselves. He still had a fever and could suffer a relapse.

Well, since there was no bed—or even a couch to lie on—she had to do the next best thing. Lily stretched out on the parlor floor on a makeshift bed of pillows and quilts that Alice and Clara had brought her. Lord knows she had slept enough times under the stars or in a line shack on the Triple M when she'd gone out with the fellows during roundup. This wasn't any worse. Question was: how in the name of creation did she find herself in this house, sleeping on the floor, with a wounded man and three children depending on her? But her last waking thought before drifting into sleep was her confusing reaction to those brief seconds when she and Grady had looked into each other's eyes.

LILY WOKE WITH A start and sat up. The room was in darkness and it took her several seconds to collect her thoughts. Then she heard the sound that had awakened her—an outcry from Grady's bedroom. Bolting to her feet, she raced to the door.

Grady appeared to be in the throes of a nightmare and was thrashing and mumbling aloud. She put her hand on his brow. Just from the feel of it she knew his fever had risen.

Suddenly he grasped her hand and cried out, "Sweetheart, please don't leave us."

The sudden move caught her by surprise and it took her several seconds to realize he was still asleep.

She nudged him gently. "Grady, wake up." He opened his eyes. They were glazed from fever. "I'm sorry to wake you, but it's time for another dose of your medicine."

He tried to chuckle, but the sound caught in his throat. "Seems crazy to wake a man up to take medicine to make him sleep."

Lily couldn't help smiling. "I suppose it does. Sounded like you were having a bad dream though."

"Yeah, I was dreaming of Kate—my wife." The pain he was suffering reflected a much deeper and older wound than the recent ones he had sustained.

"I understand. Andy told me about his mother." Lily sat down on the edge of the bed. "Would you like to talk about it, Grady?" Strange how his name slipped so easily past her lips. "My mother always told me grieving takes a long time, but keeping it bottled up inside of you only cuts it deeper."

"Guilt takes longer. It's my fault Kate died."

"I don't understand. Andy told me his mother died when Mit was born."

"Yeah, Andy was only five then, Betsy four. Kate and her folks had been neighbors, we grew up together."

"Where was that, Grady?"

"Hope, Arizona. When Kate and I were growing up, we used to call it Hopeless. It was just a hole-in-the-wall little town about five miles from Holbrook. My mom died from snakebite when I was eight, and my dad died four years later. He'd been sheriff of the town and a drunken gunfighter passing through shot him in the back. Kate's folks ran the local general store and took me in."

"I'm sorry, Grady." The thought of losing her father and mother even now was heartrending. What if they'd died while she was younger?

"Nine years ago, when I turned seventeen, I decided to strike out on my own," Grady said. "Kate was sixteen then. I told her as soon as I got settled, I'd come back and marry her. Before I could leave, an epidemic of cholera hit the town bad. It wiped out her family and a good part of the other folks, too. So Kate and I got married and tried to keep the store going, but there were only enough folks left for us to barely eke out a living.''

Lily was afraid he was tiring, but she didn't want to stop him. He was a private person—a lonely one—and for the past three years he must have kept this all bottled up inside. She was no doctor, but she agreed with her mother. It would be better to let him get it all out now rather than keep chewing at his insides.

Grady was deep in reverie now, his voice husky with poignancy. ''Kate was tiny…couldn't have weighed more than ninety pounds soaking wet—with long black hair as shiny as a raven's wing. It hung to her waist when she let it down. And she had blue eyes that were always glowing with warmth. I swear she kept sunshine bottled up in them to offset the rain. And the Lord knows there was enough of that in her short life. She was always a frail person—doctor called it asthma. It was a miracle she hadn't fallen victim to the cholera when it hit. The doctor warned us after Betsy was born not to have any more children. After a few years, when she missed having a baby to rock in her arms, she wanted another child. She begged for us to have just one more. I should have stood my ground and listened to the doctor. Couple of weeks before the baby was due, she had a bad asthma attack and had to take to bed. Shortly after that she went into labor. It was a long labor and bad delivery. She was so weak she…'' His voice trailed off and for several seconds he stared into space. "I should have listened to the doctor."

Lily's heart ached for him. Forgotten were their numerous confrontations. This was a side of Grady Delaney she had never suspected existed. For the first time in her trouble-free, twenty-two years of existence, she could see what a struggle life can be for those less fortunate. Grady was only a few years older than she, yet his life had been one loss after another. First his parents, then his wife, now the hardship of raising three children alone. How she had misjudged him. He had tremendous strength of character and she, whose fortitude had never been tested, had dared to criticize him. She was consumed with shame.

"Grady, you can't blame yourself for Kate's death. She wanted another child."

"And I should have said no. I knew the risks—"

"And so did she." Lily gentled her tone. "Don't you see, Grady, she knew the risks, too, but her heart made the decision for her—as did yours. And now you have that dear child in return. That's her gift to you, Grady."

"But why did I have to lose one to gain the other?"

"I don't have the wisdom to answer that, but I would think it should make the gift that much more precious." She got to her feet and had him swallow another aspirin and glass of water.

"Now go back to sleep, Grady. The more rest you get, the quicker you'll recover."

Returning to her makeshift bed on the floor, Lily lay in the darkness thinking about their conversation. She was so confused and didn't understand her own feelings. Somehow in the past couple of days she had developed as much concern for the father as she held for the children. It had to be because he'd come so close to dying. What other reason could there be?

THE NEXT DAY, after Andy and Betsy went to school and Grady was sleeping soundly, with Mit in hand and Brutus at their heels, Lily slipped away to the general store and bought some food supplies—many of which Grady would consider entirely unnecessary. In addition, she purchased an ornamental star for the Christmas tree, a bolt of bright red ribbon, a ball of string, a package of balloons and a can of gold paint and several artist brushes.

Grady would have a fit if he knew what she had done, but he was flat on his back, and by the time he found out it would be too late to do anything about it.

She hated to conspire against him, but there appeared to be no compromise in the man when it came to what he believed to be charity. And it appeared anything he didn't earn or pay for himself was charity to his way of thinking.

They were there and back before he was even the

wiser and for sure her two conspirators, Mit and Brutus, were not about to say anything.

Betsy came home from school alone. When Lily asked her about Andy's whereabouts, the girl looked guilty and said he had to stay after. Lily figured Andy must have misbehaved in class. Well, she wasn't about to condemn him for that. She couldn't help smiling. The Lord knows well enough how mischievous her brothers and cousins had been in school when they were younger. The poor teachers who had to cope with Zach, Cole and Jeb together had had their hands full, and all of the boys at one time or another had spent time after school denouncing their misdeeds on the blackboard.

Her mouth shifted into a poignant smile thinking of those days growing up together on the Triple M. How embarrassed she and Linda, Kitty and Sarah had been over their brothers' and cousins' misdeeds, but often more than not the girls would join in with them just the same. There were no bounds to their loyalty to each other. It was always one for all, and all for one.

She felt the pang of homesickness in her breast. It was good she was going home soon. She missed them all so much.

GRADY AWOKE to an almost forgotten smell of baking cookies. He raised himself up and saw through the open door that Lily and the children were grouped around the kitchen table decorating cookies. What had that cost?

He flopped back down. He was too weak to argue about it. Besides, it was already done, so he lay back and enjoyed watching and listening to Lily leaning over them, complimenting each of the youngsters on their creative decorating. The sight and sound of it was more healing than any pill he could swallow.

Later she came to his room with a plate of cookies and a cup of coffee for him.

"You're really patient with the kids, Lily."

"They're wonderful children, Grady. You must be very proud of them."

"I am. I hope for their sake I can get something started that will offer them more security than they have now."

"How do you expect them to feel secure with the job you have? My goodness, Grady, you almost were killed. What if you had been? Who would take care of them?"

He chuckled. "You for one, that's for sure."

"It's not a laughing matter, Grady. You can offer them the biggest house in the world, but as long as your life is in danger they'd never have a sense of security."

"I know that, Lily, but there's nothing else I can do. I don't have the knowledge or experience to do anything besides that or ranching. And no one's going to hire a hand with three children. Besides, this job of sheriff pays three times more than any other job. I figure I can save enough in the next year to put down on a small spread.''

"I understand your motive, Grady, but it doesn't make the situation any less risky." She smiled and lightened her tone. "You need a miracle, Sheriff— like striking a bonanza or finding that pot of gold at the end of the rainbow."

"Yeah, I sure do. Believe it or not, I used to think I could. That my big break was just around the next bend or maybe a day away."

"Maybe it is, Grady. You've got to keep hope alive within you. I know I have no right to criticize, but you're raising your children not to have hope either. That's wrong. Children need it in their lives. My dad always told us that Mr. Hope is the greatest motivator there is." Lily giggled. "Mom always corrected him and said it was Mrs. Hope. The thing is, Grady, hope is faith. And faith is believing in a power greater than one's self. You can't do it alone." Lily stood up. "Time I let you get some sleep." She blew out the lamp. "Good night, Grady."

"Good night, Lily."

"HOW COME you're dipping that string into that sugar water, Lily?" Andy asked the following night.

"We're going to wrap it around those balloons you children blew up. Then when the string dries, we'll pop the balloons and have sparkling round string ornaments to hang on the tree."

"What makes them sparkly and round?" Betsy asked.

"The sugar."

Andy was still perplexed. "But what makes it stay round?"

"The sugar water causes the string to stiffen when it dries. That's why we're putting it around the balloons—to shape it. You'll see, honey. Now as soon as we're through here, we'll get to painting those pinecones with gold."

Betsy clapped her hands. "The Christmas tree is going to be so beautiful."

"You bet it is," Lily said.

"Who taught you how to do this, Lily?" Andy asked.

"My folks. I remember how we did all this when I was growing up."

"Did you string popcorn, too?"

"We sure did." She winked at them. "Trouble was, we ate it faster than we could string it."

Once again, after the house had quieted, Lily went in and sat at Grady's bedside. It had developed into a ritual they both seemed to enjoy. As they drank coffee and chewed on cookies, she was beginning to learn and understand more and more about Grady Delaney. She found out the wisdom of that old adage about judging a book by its cover. For in truth, Grady was a deeply caring person who loved and cared about his children more than he'd led her to believe.

"Which of the children resemble Kate the most?" she asked.

"Well, Mit has her shy smile, Andy the way he holds his head when he's deep in thought, but Betsy..." His voice deepened with poignancy. "Betsy's the walking image of Kate. Same dark hair, pug nose, delicate chin. The kids were lucky enough to get the best of their mother's looks and not their dad's."

"I don't know about that. Andy has your features and Mit has your brown eyes." She stood and began to gather up their cups. "When they get older I bet they'll be real lady-killers."

THE FOLLOWING MORNING Grady would have no more of lying in bed. He got up and with Andy's help was able to dress. At first he felt pretty weak, but he took it easy and mainly sat with Mit on his lap watching Lily moving about in the kitchen. Often their glances met, and whenever that happened, Lily would drop her eyes and turn away.

With Grady up and around, his wounds healing and his fever broken, there was no reason for her to remain. Besides, the day after tomorrow was the wedding, and Lily had packing to do before leaving Lamy.

That evening she cooked them their final meal together, made red velvet bows, and then they decorated the Christmas tree. Grady put the star on the top of the tree while Lily and the children draped strings of popcorn on the boughs, hung golden pine-cones, then popped the balloons and hung round, sugar-coated ornaments or bright red bows on the ends of the branches.

The children stared awestruck at the end result and even Grady admitted how nice it looked.

That night, after the children went to bed, Lily didn't go into Grady's room for their late-night chat. She lay on her makeshift bed trying to imagine what it would be like without them, dreading what tomorrow would bring.

Lily got up early and slipped four wrapped packages under the tree: a book for Andy, a locket for Betsy and a little wooden toy for Mit. Her gift to Grady was a small needlepoint with the words ''Hope Is Eternal'' to hang on his bedroom wall.

When the time came to say goodbye to the children, Lily sank to her knees and pulled the crying children into her embrace. The ache was so severe that surely her heart was splintering into pieces, and she fought to hold back the tears that threatened to escape.

''Now, I'll write you and you have to promise to write me back.''

''We will,'' Andy said.

Sobbing, Betsy flung her arms around Lily's neck. ''I love you, Lily. I love you so much. I'm sorry I was bad to you.''

''Oh, sweetheart, you were never bad to me.'' She hugged and kissed her, then did the same to the two boys. "I love you all so much. Be good, my darlings. I'll keep you in my prayers every night."

Lily hugged and kissed each of them again, then stood up. Tail wagging, Brutus trotted over to her, and she leaned down and gave him a farewell pat on the head. "Take care of them, boy."

"I'm going to walk Lily home," Grady said. "You kids stay here until I get back." He picked up the small satchel she had brought containing a change of clothing.

Lily was relieved that Grady didn't say anything as they walked up the street. It gave her time to compose herself before having to say goodbye to him.

When they reached her room, she drew a deep breath and turned to face him.

"I guess this is goodbye. I'm sure you'll be relieved not to have me in your hair anymore."

"No, I kind of got used to that itch. I don't have the words to tell you how much I owe you for what you did for us, Lily. The kids couldn't have made it through without you. Just saying thank-you doesn't seem enough."

"What you do for love, Grady, doesn't need a thank-you. The satisfaction is in the doing."

"You're a remarkable young woman, Miss Lily MacKenzie. I'll never forget you. And with a little more of that coaching, you might have made a believer of me. So you're leaving soon."

Lily nodded. "The morning after Clara's wedding. I'm taking the early train back to Texas."

"The kids are sure gonna miss you."

Lily sucked in a breath to choke back a sob. "And I'm going to miss them, too. I can't tell you how much. I hope when school is out for the summer, you'll let them come and visit, Grady. It would mean so much to me."

He nodded. "I reckon I owe you that much for all you've done for us. You quitting the Harvey Girls for good?"

"Yes. I only became a Harvey Girl to add some excitement to my life, but I've discovered excitement isn't what I'm really looking for."

"What is?"

She shrugged. "I really don't know. I figure I'll recognize it when I find it."

"Just around the next bend or maybe a day away," he said, with a tender smile that threatened to rip whatever heart she had left right out of her breast.

"Or maybe it's right at my fingertips and I didn't reach for it." She couldn't bear another moment of the agony. "Goodbye, Grady." She turned away and entered her room. Her whole body was trembling and she leaned back against the door.

For a long moment there was silence, then she heard the sound of his footsteps as he walked away.

CHAPTER FIVE

BRIGHT SUNSHINE HELPED to reduce the December chill in the air on Clara's wedding day. The three women spent the last few hours together chatting and preparing for the ceremony. The next day they would be going their separate ways: Clara on a honeymoon, Alice to the Harvey House in Santa Fe, and Lily returning home to Texas.

In late afternoon they dressed for the wedding. The bridal attendants' matching gowns of red silk velvet were simplistic but feminine, and purposely made to embrace the holiday season. The fitted bodices were trimmed with white lace that flowed into double tiers of fluttering sleeves that hung to the elbow. A woven band of white roses and red velvet ribbon adorned their hair, elbow-length white gloves partially covered their arms, and they carried small bouquets of white roses and bright green holly leaves intertwined with red velvet ribbon.

The marriage of the banker's son drew the attendance of the respectable local citizenry and the reception room soon began to fill after the church service.

The evening had passed swiftly and Lily had just

stepped back to watch the newlyweds dancing when Alice rushed up to her. "Doesn't he look divine?" she whispered.

"Yes, Ted is very good-looking. I was just admiring what a handsome couple they are."

"Not Ted, the sheriff," Alice said. "He's over by the door."

Lily's heartbeat quickened when she saw Grady Delaney standing in the doorway. His eyes swept the room and halted when they met hers. She held her breath in the endless seconds their gazes locked, and then he nodded and turned his head away.

She had to admit he did look handsome, indeed, in a black suit, white shirt and black string tie. Easily the best-looking man in the room. But she could no longer fool herself into denying she was attracted to a lot more about Grady than just his good looks.

It was a good thing she had a sensible head on her shoulders or else the combination of the attraction she felt for him coupled with the appeal of his children would be too great a temptation for her to ignore. Well, come tomorrow it wouldn't be a threat any longer. She would be on a train back to Texas. However, deep down, the thought of never seeing him or the children again was tearing at her heart.

"I'd like to know who's watching his children," Lily murmured to cover up her delayed response.

"How can you look at him and think about his children?" Alice said. "He's so handsome and courageous. It's a wonder some woman hasn't snatched him up in the past couple years.''

''I don't think the sheriff is interested in remarrying, Alice. He's still mourning the loss of his wife. Or maybe he just hasn't met a woman he'd want to marry.''

''Then he's a gorgeous fool, because you would make a wonderful wife for him. You're already in love with his children.''

''Which, my dear Alice, doesn't necessarily make me *in love* with the children's father.'' Lily couldn't look Alice in the eye after that blatant lie. She was so crazy about him she wanted to shout it out.

''Why don't you give the poor man a chance, Lily? He can't be as bad as you make him out to be. And I think he's sweet on you.'' Alice giggled. ''Furthermore, didn't one of those poets say something about the lady protesting too much?''

Before Lily could utter a denial, Alice glided away. The little twit turned her head and winked, her mouth wreathed in a smile not unlike the proverbial cat with a mouth full of canary feathers.

''Sweet on me, indeed!'' Lily murmured. Grady Delaney was the last man who'd ever be sweet on her. That would be too much to hope for. Besides, it was obvious he was still in love with his dead wife. If she believed for a moment he cared for her, she'd swallow her pride and admit her true feelings for him.

She cast a fretful scowl in his direction. Furthermore, just because Sheriff Grady Delaney was tall and god-awful handsome, whatever gave Alice the idea she'd welcome his advances? She sucked in her lower lip between her teeth. Oh dear, were her feelings for him that obvious to others, or did the girl read too many of those Beadle dime novels that promised happy endings? Grady had made a point of telling her there are no happy endings in real life.

"Miss MacKenzie, may I have this dance?"

Smiling, she offered her hand to the gray-haired gentleman who had approached her. "I'd be delighted, Dr. Preston."

As the doctor led her to the dance floor, she glanced in Grady's direction. His back was to her, and he was deep in conversation with several men. *Very well, Grady Delaney. If you intend to ignore me, I'll be glad to oblige you.*

She flirted outrageously, laughed gaily and danced every dance, but he ignored her. *The whole evening!* Why she had commiserated over leaving this man was beyond reason. Mistook a feeling of sympathy for one of love. She was a lovesick fool who confused the true depth of love with a mere physical attraction. Rather than be angry with him, she should thank him for not encouraging her.

Tomorrow morning couldn't come soon enough.

The crowd had thinned by the time the band struck up the final waltz for the night, the haunting melody "After the Ball."

Grady suddenly appeared before her and without

a word he extended his hand. For the stunning length of her drawn breath, Lily looked into his eyes and knew everything she had told herself all evening was for naught—she loved Grady Delaney with all the depth and passion her heart could hold.

The essence of him closed around her as he took her in his arms and they moved to the music. She let her mind savor the moment—a moment that would have to sustain her for the long days that lay ahead without him. Overcome by the thought, she couldn't contain her tears. She broke from his arms and rushed out a nearby door. The cool night air hit her at once and she began to shiver. She would have run all the way back to her room, but his hands on her shoulders stopped her. He turned her to face him.

Removing his suit jacket, he slipped it around her shoulders. It still held the warmth of his body, which only unnerved her more.

"Tears, Lily?"

Pride prevented her from blubbering out a confession of love. She brushed aside her tears and resumed walking.

When they reached her room she unlocked her door and then, with a forced smile, turned to him and handed him his jacket. "I guess this is goodbye. I'm sure you're glad to be rid of pesky me once and for all."

"Why the tears, Lily?" he questioned again.

"It's silly. Just a woman thing. I can't help thinking how my experience here in Lamy parallels the song. It's all been like a magnificent ball, but now the ball is over and just like the words of the song—'' she looked up at him ''—I'm left with an aching heart.''

Grady cupped her cheeks between his hands, his thumb brushing aside a recalcitrant teardrop. ''Lily, I'm…oh, God, Lily.''

The warm slide of his hands curved her neck and he pulled her to him. He dipped his head and his mouth covered hers, his lips firm and moist, surprisingly gentle yet hungry for a response. Emotions whirled within her with a wild and heady passion that swirled through her mind and being. She felt her knees weaken and slid her arms around his neck, her need as demanding as his. This was what she had yearned for and she wasn't going to let the moment pass.

The kiss deepened into another, and then another, the probe of his tongue exploring the chamber of her mouth sending jolts of delight spiraling through her with a feeling so thrilling she gasped with pleasure.

His touch became a sensual massage. She savored it. Gloried in the exciting tension that knotted her stomach and titillated the very center of her womanhood. She made no effort to stop him when the warmth of his hands caressed the slope of her bare shoulders and shoved off the flimsy sleeves of her gown. The bodice fell with them. He filled his hands with her breasts and when his mouth and tongue joined the erotic impetus she whimpered in ecstasy.

The sound broke the mood. He raised his head and stepped back. Appalled, he fumbled with her gown and pulled it up. "Oh, my God, Lily! I'm so sorry. I didn't mean to…that is… I guess I must have drunk too much of that spiked punch. Please forgive me."

Lily couldn't get her body and mind to function together. Her body was crying for him to go on and her brain was trying to comprehend that he was saying something about spiked punch. She had no idea of the passage of time as she stared dumbfounded at him until the meaning of his words finally sank in.

"Are you saying the only reason you kissed me is because you had too much to drink?"

He had the decency to look contrite. "It's a poor excuse, I know, and—"

"That you're drunk?" she cried, now mortified beyond restraint. "That you would have done the same to any woman?"

"I know there's no excuse for my actions, Lily. I got carried away."

She felt numb. Betrayed. The reality that there was no emotion behind his actions was more appalling to her than how close she had come to surrendering her virginity to him. "I guess we both did." She groped for the handle of her door. "Goodbye, Grady."

"Lily, please—"

She closed the door, cutting off his words and the sight of him. Then she leaned against the door and let the hot tears flow. When she had cried herself out, she undressed and went to bed.

Long past midnight she lay awake still pondering her situation. When she left home she'd had such great expectations: an exciting job as a Harvey Girl, and eventually finding a husband and then return to settle down on the ranch.

Instead, the whole experience had been a disaster from the start. Her life as a Harvey Girl had been more terrorizing than exciting and she soon had lost her enthusiasm for the job. She had lost her heart to three motherless children she now had to leave behind, and she had almost lost her virginity to a drunken sheriff—the same person she'd been stupid enough to want for a husband.

Once she got back home, she'd never set foot off the Triple M again.

Unable to sleep, she got up at dawn, packed her remaining items in her bags and left for the depot to board the train early. She feared the children would show up for another goodbye, and she was too heartbroken to go through it again with them.

She was glad she had thought to do so when the children appeared ten minutes before the train was due to depart. Grady was with them. Lily dodged back where they couldn't see her but she was able to watch them. How she would miss them. She felt as if she was deserting them, and her heart wrenched at the sight of Mit standing there looking sad and confused. If only she could take him—all of them—with her.

Finally she looked at Grady. As much as she

wanted to, Lily couldn't hate him. Seeing the tall figure, her breath caught in her throat. Despite the outcome between them, she realized what her heart had recognized from the beginning: no matter how hard she tried, she could never hate Grady Delaney. But her aching heart cried out, *Will you ever forget him?*

With a blast from the whistle and the grind of metal against metal, the train lurched forward then puffed slowly out of the station. Rain began to splatter the windows, and she pressed her face against the pane for a final look at the four desolate figures who remained on the platform as the rain poured down on them.

It continued to rain all the way into Texas. When they reached Lubbock, the train was halted and would be delayed overnight because a section of the track ahead had washed out.

A norther was sweeping across the Panhandle, the bitter wind changing the rain into shards of sleet. That's all she needed to add to her misery. Lily was chilled to the bone by the time she reached the hotel. After renting a room, she ate a hot meal in the hotel's dining room and dispatched a telegram to her family to tell them of the delay. She then returned to her room, took a bath as hot as she could stand it and settled into bed with the dime novel Alice had given her to read.

She refused to sink deeper into morose. As far as she was concerned this was just another bump in her rocky road of life—a life doomed to maidenhood and bouncing other people's children on her knee. She read ten pages of the book, cast it aside and cried herself to sleep.

LILY AWOKE to an incessant knocking on the door and sunlight streaming through the window.

"Miss MacKenzie, are you awake?"

She sat up in bed. "Yes, who is it?"

"It's Mr. Holloway, the hotel manager, Miss MacKenzie. The railroad has informed us the repairs are completed and the train will be departing at eight o'clock."

"Thank you, Mr. Holloway."

Lily glanced at the clock. She had less than an hour to get ready. In fifteen minutes she had dressed and groomed herself and checked out of the hotel.

Sometime during the night, the sleet had turned to snow, and the ground was now covered in a blanket of white. The sun was shining brightly, and despite the strong wind everything looked fresh and clean. The air was sharp but invigorating, and as she ate a bowl of hot oatmeal and drank a cup of coffee, she reflected that at least there was another good thing about the day—maybe she was one day closer to getting over Grady Delaney.

Her positive thinking lasted until the train pulled out of the station. True she was one day closer to forgetting him, but every turn of the train wheels took her farther away from him and the children.

Lily slumped down in the seat in despair and reached for the dime novel.

The heavy cowcatcher attached to the front of the engine pushed the snow off the track as the train chugged along slowly. It took three hours to go the remaining seventy miles before they finally pulled into Calico at noon.

Lily glanced out the window and saw the tall figure on the platform. Her eyes gleamed with pride and adoration at the sight of her father. He was nearing his mid-sixties, and the lines at the corners of his eyes and mouth reflected the many years he'd spent in the ruggedness of the outdoors, the gray on his temples and mustache the years of maturity. Neither had diminished the handsomeness of a face that women still couldn't pass without casting a yearning second glance. Tall and lithe, he carried the broad shoulders and slim hips of a man half his age, and his step was still as brisk as the lively gleam in his sapphire-colored eyes.

Spying her, he grinned and waved—and the day became a little brighter.

FROST-CRUSTED SNOW crackled beneath the runners of the sleigh as it skimmed along the road. "You warm enough, honey?" her father asked. He gave the reins another flick to encourage the team to a faster trot. "I didn't think you'd want to get on the back of a horse on a day like this."

Lily snuggled deeper into the warmth of the bearskin tucked around her. "I'm fine, Dad. I hope the snow lasts through Christmas."

He glanced skyward. "From the look of those low-hanging clouds, I figure we'll probably get some more snow." His mustache and eyebrows glistened with frost, and his breath hung on the chilled air like puffs of smoke.

"I love a white Christmas. I just hope it warms up a little more. My butt is freezing," Lily said.

"You learn that talk in Lamy, young lady?"

"No, Daddy. I believe my brother Cole taught me that."

Cleve laughed. "Just as feisty as ever, aren't you, Lily Belle?"

"Daddy," she groaned. "You promised you'd never dredge up that horrible name again."

Chuckling, he shook his head. "It's hell when a man's kids grow up."

"Did Jeb make it home for Christmas?"

"Yesterday. He has to go back the day after Christmas." He paused momentarily before asking, "You planning on staying for good, honey?"

"I bet you've been dying to ask that since I arrived."

"So what's the answer?"

"Yes, I'm home to stay. A team of wild horses couldn't pull me off the Triple M again."

"Sounds like you've brought a broken heart home with you instead of that husband you planned."

How did he do it? Ever since she was a child, he

always could tell when something was bothering her. "I never can fool you, can I?"

"Well, there's always been a special bond between us, honey. You want to talk about it?"

"There's really not that much to tell. I kind of took a liking to this sheriff, but apparently the feeling was one-sided. Anyway, nothing serious really happened between us."

"Just a liking or are you in love with this man, Lily?"

Lily drew in a painful breath. "I'm in love with him, Dad, but one thing's for sure—he's not in love with me, so...no husband. Don't tell Mom. If she thinks I'm depressed it will spoil her Christmas."

"You know, honey, the course of love rarely runs smoothly. Some people need a lot more convincing than others."

"You mean like Grandpa holding a rifle on you to *convince* you to marry Mom."

He broke out in laughter. "You're a real brat, you know."

She looked at him and grinned. "Luv ya, Dad."

"Luv ya, sweetheart." He flicked the reins again and the jingle of the sleigh bells played a warm tune on her heart.

CHAPTER SIX

THE NORTHER THAT HAD blistered the Panhandle with stabbing cold and a blanket of snow in its wake had moved on. The chill bite of winter still crisped the air, but the bright sunshine that glistened on the snow-crusted earth gave the promise of a warming. In a few days only isolated patches of snow would remain as evidence of the storm's passing, but for now young and old alike would have the white Christmas they had wished for on this day before Christmas.

The train puffed into the station and lurched to a stop. Grady picked up Mit in one arm and the heavy suitcase with his other hand.

"You two be sure to stay close," he cautioned Andy and Betsy as they disembarked from the train.

He glanced around at the town of Calico. It didn't appear to be more than a whistle-stop. When he saw a boarded-up hotel with a Closed sign on it, he put Mit down. "Betsy, hold your brother's hand, and Andy, make sure Brutus doesn't take off on a run."

"You know Brutus don't run, Daddy, even after jackrabbits," Andy said.

Grady walked over to the ticket window followed

by the three children and the dog. "Excuse me. Is there a hotel in town to stay at until morning?"

"We ain't got no hotel, mister. Closed up 'bout five years ago," the stationmaster said.

This was something Grady hadn't figured on. Now where could they go after they spoke to Lily until the train pulled out in the morning?

"Could you give me the directions to get to the ranch of Cleve MacKenzie?"

The man gave him a long look. "Ain't seen you around before. You ain't MacKenzie kin, are ya?"

"No."

"Got business with him, have ya?"

"Could be."

"The Triple M borders the town, but to get to the house you gotta go 'bout ten miles up the road from here."

That was another serious setback. He couldn't expect the kids to walk ten miles in the cold. "Is there a livery here where I can rent a buckboard?"

"Nope. Livery closed up two years back." He took off his hat and scratched a bald pate wreathed in white hair. "Reckon Silas Pritchard might rent you the use of his buggy seein' as how you're headin' out to the Triple M."

"Where can I find this Mr. Pritchard?"

"At the funeral parlor." At Grady's shocked look, he added, "Ol' Silas is the undertaker."

"Thank you."

"If you want to get your kids out of the cold, they

can come in here and toast their toes by the pot stove till you get back.''

"I'd appreciate that very much," Grady said.

"Is that hound housebroke?" the man asked.

"Yes, he is."

"Reckon he can come in then, too. Hate to see a dumb animal left out in the cold."

"Brutus ain't dumb, mister," Andy declared.

"Brutus isn't dumb, Andy," Grady corrected as they entered the small office.

"That's what I said," Andy replied.

The rush of heat from the stove was a blessing, and as soon as he got the children settled in, Grady sought out the undertaker. After a short negotiation, for two dollars and the promise of returning it no later than tomorrow morning, Pritchard hitched up the covered buggy to an old swayback mare that looked to Grady like he'd have to carry the horse the last five miles.

They all squeezed into the seat, and Brutus stretched out on the floor at their feet. Grady tucked the carriage robe securely around the children, then headed down the snowcapped road at a slow pace—not that the horse would have been capable of going much faster even if the road were clear. Dog and children were all sleeping by the time he saw a pointed arrow marked Triple M. Directly next to it was a sign that read MacKenzie. He turned onto the road and after about another half mile came to a cluster of at least eight or nine houses and several other buildings. Neither Lily nor the stationmaster had mentioned a town named MacKenzie, although it was not unusual to name one after the original settler. At least there were people out and about here, which was far different from Calico.

A couple men came over to the buggy. "Can I help you?" one asked.

"I'm looking for the Triple M ranch," Grady said.

The two men exchanged amused glances. "You're on it, mister. I'm Josh MacKenzie, what can we do for you?"

"I'm looking for the home of Cleve MacKenzie."

The other man stepped forward. "Can I help you? I'm his son, Cole."

Grady recognized him as the man he'd seen with Lily at the station in Lamy. His spirits almost soared through the top of his hat—the man was Lily's brother, not her sweetheart. He offered his hand. "Glad to meet you. Name's Grady Delaney." They shook hands and Grady said, "Actually, I came to see Miss MacKenzie—Lily that is."

"What about?" Cole MacKenzie asked.

"It's a private matter," Grady said, beginning to feel increasingly uncomfortable.

"And apparently none of your business, cousin," Josh MacKenzie said, amused.

"Hey, Dad, can you come over here for a minute?" Cole yelled to several men standing near the open door of a barn.

Grady watched with interest as one man started toward them trailed by the others.

"Problem?" the man asked when he reached them.

So this was Cleve MacKenzie—Lily's father. Grady took a long look at the man.

He certainly appeared formidable—they all did. The one thing that stood out immediately was the height of the men. Grady stood four inches above six feet in his stockings, and from what he could tell, these Texans stood that tall if not taller.

"This is Grady Delaney, Dad."

Cleve shook his hand. "Pleased to meet you. How can I help you, Mr. Delaney?"

"Actually, sir, as I already mentioned to your son, I came to see your daughter, Lily."

"That so." MacKenzie regarded him with curiosity. "Delaney…hmm. Are you the sheriff of Lamy, New Mexico?"

"I was, sir. I resigned as sheriff yesterday."

"What business do you have with my daughter, Mr. Delaney?"

"Private business, Dad," Cole interjected.

Cole's remark drew soft laughter from the other men in the group and a faint smile from Cleve MacKenzie. He glanced at the three children who had been awakened by the talk and were now sitting up staring unabashedly at the men surrounding them. Even Brutus was sitting up with perked ears on his cocked head.

"I suspect you'll find Lily in that third house from the end, Mr. Delaney. And if you just drove in from Calico, I'd get those children inside out of this cold."

"Thank you, sir." Grady turned the buggy around and drove back to the house Cleve had pointed out to him. By the time Grady reined up in front of it, Cleve and Cole MacKenzie had already reached the house on foot.

"Let me give you a hand with those children," Cleve said. He lifted Betsy into his arms. "Hi there, honey."

Betsy returned his smile but said nothing. Andy jumped down and Grady picked up Mit. "Just leave it in the buggy," he said, when Cole reached for the suitcase.

"But, Dad, Lily's gift is in it," Andy said.

"That's right. I forgot." Grady grabbed the suitcase.

"Isn't this Silas Pritchard's rig?" Cleve asked.

"Yes, I rented it for the day."

"I'll take care of the horse," Cole said.

"You better take that hound with you, son. Find him a warm spot in the barn. Your mother's got the house all decked out for Christmas and she's already announced she doesn't want any dogs underfoot right now."

Grady handed Cole the reins. "Go with him, Brutus," he ordered. The dog jumped back into the buggy.

"Best wipe your feet," Cleve cautioned before entering the house, "or Adee will get after us with a broom."

The house smelled of pine and freshly baked apple pie. Of aromatic candles and the stuffed turkey roasting in the oven.

Wide-eyed and mouths agape, the children stared around with awe. Garlands of pine woven with the bright red berries and shiny green leaves of holly were strung in hallways and on the mantel over the fireplace, where a clove-encrusted ham rotated on a spit. Wreaths adorned with pinecones and red velvet bows hung in the windows.

Presents wrapped in holiday paper were piled under a ceiling-high balsam set in the corner of the room awaiting the Christmas Eve ritual of decorating it when the whole family was assembled. Grady remembered overhearing Lily telling that to the children.

"Adee, we've got company," Cleve said. He paused under the mistletoe hung in the doorway of the kitchen. "Ho, ho, ho! Caught you under the mistletoe." He placed a kiss on Betsy's cheek, resulting in a bright blush and girlish giggle from the youngster.

The woman who stood at the sink turned her head when Cleve called to her. Grady sucked in his breath at his first glimpse of Lily's mother—the same willowy figure, dark silken hair and delicately carved face that glowed with the lustrous bronze of her Spanish blood. He felt as if he'd been given a glimpse into the future of the ethereal beauty Lily would possess in her maturing years.

Curiosity mingled with warmth in her brown eyes when she looked at Grady. "Mr. Delaney and his children came here to see Lily."

"She and Linda were just here a few minutes ago. They must be in her room."

Cleve put Betsy down. "I'll go check."

"Please sit down, Mr. Delaney," Adee said. "My, what a lovely family you have. How would you children like a nice hot cup of cocoa to warm up your stomachs?"

Andy and Betsy looked at Grady, hopefully. "We don't want to inconvenience you, ma'am. I can see you're busy."

"Nonsense!" Adee exclaimed. She rushed over and took Mit from him. "You want some cocoa, don't you, sweetheart?" Mit studied her face with a wide curious stare, and then he reached out a hand and touched her face.

Adee kissed his little hand. "Oh, he's so precious."

"I think he sees how much you and Lily resemble each other."

"Is that right, honey?" she said to Mit.

"I'm afraid he doesn't talk, ma'am." At her stricken look, Grady added, "He can hear and laugh or cry, but he just doesn't try to speak."

"Really?" She smiled at Mit. "Sweetheart, tell Adee how old you are." Mit held up three fingers.

"Oh, you're a sly little one," she said, and sat Mit down at the table. Then she reached for Betsy's hand. "And you must be Betsy, and this handsome lad with you is Andy."

"Yes, ma'am," they said in unison.

"Lily has talked about nothing else but you three children since she got home yesterday. I'm so glad for this chance to meet you. Now why don't you all sit down at the table with Mit while I make the cocoa, and I bet I can find some sugar cookies, too, if I try. Mr. Delaney, would you prefer cocoa or coffee?"

"Coffee's fine, ma'am, if you've already got a pot on the stove."

"Mr. Delaney, in this house there's always a pot on the stove. My husband lives on it."

"Jeb said Lily went over to Linda's," Cleve said, rejoining them. "He ran over to get her."

"We sure didn't mean to cause all this trouble, sir," Grady said.

"It's no trouble, Mr. Delaney," Adee assured him.

"Name's Grady, ma'am."

"Then Grady it shall be," Adee said.

At that moment the front door slammed and Lily called out, "Mom."

"We're in here, honey."

Breathless from running, Lily came into the kitchen. "Mom, what's wrong? Jeb said—" Her words were cut off by her gasp of surprise when she saw the children. Then her worried expression changed to surprise and finally incredulous joy.

The reaction from the children was instantaneous. Squealing with happiness, the three jumped up and rushed over to her. Lily sank to her knees and opened her arms. They huddled together, hugging and kissing.

"I can't believe this. How did you get here?" Her eyes were misting. She looked up and saw Grady standing in the corner.

"Hello, Lily," was all Grady could get past the lump in his throat. She was so beautiful and the realization of how much he loved her was a stabbing pain in his chest. He wanted to hold her so badly, to feel her in his arms. To kiss her and admit his love for her and the reason he came. Now he didn't dare. Not because there were others present—but because now he knew, more than ever, that she was beyond his reach.

Lily stood up. "Hello, Grady. This is a surprise."

He turned away quickly and for want of an excuse opened the suitcase and pulled out a flat package wrapped in brown butcher paper tied with ordinary white string. "The children wanted to give you this." Andy came over and took the package from him.

"Merry Christmas, Lily. This is for you from me, and Betsy and Mit," Andy said solemnly.

"For me! Oh, I love surprises." She sat down at the table and the children gathered around her, waiting with eager anticipation as she untied the string and unwrapped the paper.

"Oh my, how lovely!" she exclaimed at the sight of the white handkerchief within. One of the corners had been embroidered with tiny pink flowers.

"Mr. Baker paid me a nickel a day to sweep out his store so's I could pay for it," Andy said. "We made one for Daddy, too," he whispered in her ear.

"And I embroidered it," Betsy said proudly. "I made the French knots just like you taught me."

"And Mit held his finger on the string so's we could tie the bow, Lily," Andy said.

"Oh, thank you, my darlings. It's so lovely. I shall cherish it forever." This time Lily couldn't restrain her tears. "I love you all so much," she sobbed.

Adee ran from the kitchen, dabbing at her eyes with the hem of her apron. Cleve looked at Grady, shrugged helplessly and then followed her out.

"Thank you for bringing them, Grady," Lily said when she regained control of herself.

"It was the least I could do since it was so important to the kids."

He felt awkward and didn't know what else to say. Under the circumstances the wisest thing was to leave. "Well, kids, I...ah...think it's time we get going."

"Oh, no, Grady. You just got here. Please don't leave so soon. Can't you stay a while longer?" Lily pleaded.

At that moment, Adee's tears now dried, Lily's

parents returned to the kitchen. "My goodness, I should be ashamed of myself," Adee declared. "I promised these children some cocoa and cookies." She began to fuss at the stove.

"Please don't bother, Mrs. MacKenzie, we have to leave now anyway. It's a long ride back to Calico."

"You got kin in Calico?" Cleve asked.

"No, but—"

"Then why leave, Grady? There's no train out until morning, and no place to eat or sleep in town. Where are you planning on spending the night?"

Grady had no earthly idea. He only wanted to get out of there as quickly as possible. He could see now it had been a big mistake to come there uninvited.

"You planning on holing up in Pritchard's buggy for the night?" Cleve asked, amused.

"I'm sure we'll be able to find some place to stay." Maybe that stationmaster would let them spend the night in his office.

Adee would not hear of it. "Nonsense, Grady Delaney. This is Christmas Eve. You and the children are going to stay right here. We've plenty of room."

"We can't do that, ma'am. Looks like you're planning a party and we'll only be underfoot."

"It's only family. Lily, while I make the cocoa, take the children into Linda's old bedroom. Grady can have Cole's." She smiled at him. "They're both married now and have their own houses."

Lily took Mit by the hand. ''Follow me.''

Grady picked up the suitcase. He felt like a jackass harnessed to a team of thoroughbreds. What in the name of sanity was he doing here?

CHAPTER SEVEN

WHILE LILY AND HER MOTHER fed the children, Grady stood with Cleve in the parlor enjoying a cigar and a hot mug of coffee. He liked Cleve and Adriana MacKenzie. They were forthright people governed by honest emotions that they didn't try to conceal, and he now had a better appreciation of why Lily had been so disturbed by what she thought was his neglect of his children. She'd been raised to care about people, so it had been against her inherent sense of decency to stand by idly and let it happen. He wondered if the rest of this MacKenzie clan held to the same principles.

Cleve's nudge drew him back to the present. "Would you like something to put a little kick in that coffee, Grady?"

"No, this is fine, sir. It's the best coffee I've ever tasted."

"Yeah, I think so, too. It's grown in Columbia and we have it shipped in from Dallas. We keep it stocked here year-round."

"Stocked, sir?" Grady asked.

"You see, son, we have a store—warehouse, you

might say— where we stock the kind of things we don't grow on the Triple M.''

"What kind of things, sir?"

"Oh…ah…things like sugar, coffee, some canned foods, condiments, general household items. Special things the ladies want like cold cream and such. Things that can't be grown, canned, or smoked right here on the Triple M.''

"How long has the ranch been in your family, sir?"

"Since 1835. It was just a couple thousand acres then. My dad died the following year at the Alamo. My brother Luke was only two at the time and my brother Flint was one year old. I wasn't born until six months later. Mom raised us alone. When we all finally married and settled down, we started to expand the ranch whenever money and land became available.''

"How big is the ranch now, sir?" Grady asked.

"Three to four hundred thousand acres. Closer to four.''

Grady almost choked on the sip of coffee he'd just swallowed. "Did you say four hundred *thousand* acres?''

"Give or take an acre or two," Cleve said.

"My God!" Grady mumbled, too astounded to say more.

"I know what you're thinking, son. Sometimes it boggles my mind, too. Fortunately, between my brothers and me, we've never had to hire too many hands. The ranch is practically entirely manned by MacKenzies, or those married to a MacKenzie.''

Grady snorted. ''Sounds like there'd be more chiefs than Indians.''

''Not at all, everyone has some kind of specific responsibility. It's never been a problem.''

''Maybe for a MacKenzie, but I'd think those guys who married into the family would be considered the runt of the litter.''

''Not so, Grady. My niece Kitty's married to Jared Fraser, a retired army officer turned writer. He has a home in Dallas, but chooses instead to live on the Triple M because he enjoys helping with the round-ups. My daughter Linda's husband used to be the local schoolteacher. Bob's set up a school right here on the Triple M for the children.''

''I don't want to sound disrespectful, sir, but I've gotten used to the name Delaney. I don't think I'd cotton to being called Mr. MacKenzie,'' Grady said. ''No offense intended.''

Cleve chuckled. ''And you think that would happen if you married one of the owners' daughters?''

''Well maybe not to my face.''

''Grady, Jared Fraser was awarded the Congressional Medal of Honor for bravery. Bob Fellows was offered a position to teach at the University of Texas. If you'd met them you'd know that both are confident and accomplished individuals who could function successfully wherever they chose. No one's gonna call them 'Mr. MacKenzie' behind their backs.''

"I'm not that accomplished, sir, and I have to admit these last couple years sure haven't added much to my confidence, either.''

"Lily doesn't think so. She said you've done a remarkable job of cleaning up Lamy in the short time you've been sheriff.''

"I liked the job, but it's more for a single man. My kids need me more than the town. I only took the job because the pay was good.''

"Do you love Lily, Grady?''

The sudden question took him by surprise, but he had the good sense not to try and deceive this man. "Yes, sir. Very much.''

"And I know she loves you,'' Cleve said.

Grady jerked up his head. "Did she tell you that?'' he asked anxiously.

"Yes, the same as you just told me that you love her. Seems to me the both of you would be better off telling each other instead of me. You might not have this problem then. In my day, two people in love was enough to overcome any obstacle. Mind telling me the real reason you came down here?''

"I planned to ask Lily to marry me.''

"So what changed your mind?''

"I've got nothing to offer her except three children and a few hundred dollars in the bank that I've been saving up to put down on a small ranch.''

"I'm sure she's aware of that. So that's not enough of a reason to keep you apart."

Grady glanced over to where Lily and her mother were sitting at the kitchen table with his children. "When I fell in love with Lily I thought she was a working girl. I didn't know her family owned one of the largest ranches in Texas."

"Lily *is* a working girl," Cleve said. "Has been her whole life. Sure we're a wealthy family now, but we haven't always been. Furthermore, everyone on the Triple M carries his or her own weight. Our sons and daughters work side by side with any other hand on the ranch. That's why it's been successful. Traditionally, all of the men in the family have served as lawmen at one time or another, and all have left home as well to test their wings. But they've always been drawn back to the Triple M. And when my brothers and I pass on, each of our children will legally own a portion of the ranch — just as my brothers and I did when we lost our parents. There's three generations of love and loyalty here, son."

"I can see that, sir."

"So you intend to leave," Cleve said. "Where are you heading?"

"I thought I'd try up north. Couple towns in Wyoming are advertising for sheriffs."

"Thought you wanted to be a rancher."

"I do, when I can afford it."

"You got any particular place in mind for that ranch?"

"I haven't given it that much thought. Some place warm for sure. Figure I've got a year to make my mind up."

"You know, Grady, I have a solution you might want to consider. Last month our neighbor Bert Hubbard died and his wife Cassie wanted to sell their ranch so she could move to California to join her daughter. We bought her out. It's a small spread adjoining the east end of the Triple M between here and Calico. Plenty of good graze and water. I'm sure if I talked to my brothers I could convince them to let you homestead it for a while. I'm not talking charity, Grady. It'll cost you a mite, but we're not hard to do business with."

"Sounds too good to be true," Grady said.

"Cassie sold off the stock, but there's always some strays you could round up to get you started. Give you a chance to see if you really take to ranching before sinking every cent you've got into it. Ranching's a hard life, son—cold in the winter, hot in the summer, and come rain or drought, the work goes on. Then, if you find you like it, you can make us an offer."

"Why wouldn't you want to hold on to it yourself?"

"Heck, Grady, we've got more land now than we know what to do with. We only bought the Lazy H because the Hubbards have been good friends and Cassie wanted out."

The look in Cleve's eyes challenged him. "And

Cassie kept a trim house, so it doesn't need much in repairs. And while you're working, your children can come here for their schooling. Couple of the boys' wives help Bob out at the school, so your children will get proper schooling and they'll have plenty of schoolmates to keep them company.''

Grady pondered the offer. Was Cleve MacKenzie a devil or saint? Whatever, the man was dangling a temptation damn hard to resist. ''Why would you offer this to me, sir? We've just met.''

''It's not my way to play a heavy hand in my children's lives now that they're adults, but I pride myself on being able to judge a man's character. I like what I see in you, Grady. And I'm proud that my daughter sees it, too. I'm a fatalist. I'd like for you to hang around for a while so we could get to know each other better and see what kind of hand is being dealt here.''

Cleve MacKenzie couldn't hold back a grin. ''And I've got to be honest with you, Grady. Since you're too proud to live on the Triple M, it'd be nice having my daughter living right next door at least. And who knows, we MacKenzies might grow on you and you'd decide to stick around here permanently. What do you think?''

''I'd be a fool to turn it down, sir. I have three children to consider.''

''I figure there's a couple others with stakes in the game, too.''

''You mean Lily and me.''

Once again Grady's glance sought and found Lily. He watched her kiss Betsy on the cheek and then walk away. How he yearned to have this woman to love and cherish. Dare he harbor the dream that it could become a lasting reality and not just a wistful thought?

His mind wandered back to the vision of her moving about in his kitchen at night. How she hummed as she washed the dishes or set the dough to rise for the next day's bread—the waking to the smell of that bread baking the next morning. He recalled the sound of her voice—her laughter—as she sat at his bedside nursing him back to health, or held his son in her lap as she read to his children.

Even now the fragrance of Lily teased his sensibilities. His arms could still feel her softness, his lips the taste of her. The rush of excitement from a shared kiss.

Was it all within his grasp, or just another swift kick in the ass fate would mete out to him?

"In Texas a man's handshake is his bond," Cleve said. "Do we have a deal, son?"

Grady dragged his gaze away from Lily and looked at Cleve MacKenzie. He reached out and grasped the hand offered to him.

"A deal, sir. Just remember, no charity."

"I'll hitch up the sleigh and drive you over to look at the place. It's not more than five miles from here. We can be there and back before we're even missed." He offered a crooked smile. "Or would you rather have Lily drive you? I figure the two of you have a lot to talk over.''

"Yes, we do, but I want to get it straight in my head before I try. Could be she might not cotton to the idea, so I'd appreciate it, sir, if you don't mention it to her right now.''

"If that's the way you want it, Grady. In the meantime, you and your family can stay here until you get settled in. There's furniture and the like in the house, and we can spare a wagon and team, too, but you'll need to stock up on food and firewood before moving in.''

"That's very generous of you, sir, but I'm not going to impose on your and Mrs. MacKenzie's hospitality any more than I have already. They're my kids—my responsibility. I'll take them with me, and we'll make out okay.''

Cleve gave him a long look. "Pride's a noble virtue, son, but it won't win you the pot in a poker game.''

"Your point being, sir?''

"Life's just like poker, Grady. You can play the cards dealt you, throw them in, or try to draw to a better hand. But if you keep betting on a bluff, more often than not you're gonna lose.''

"I don't equate pride to running a bluff, Mr. MacKenzie. In my opinion if you have to depend on charity to stake you in that game, you have no business sitting in on it.''

"Then you should have considered that before you

tossed in your ante when you had those three kids. How old are you, Grady?''

''Twenty-six, sir.''

''Well, I'm twice as old and then some, and I've sat in on more games than I care to admit. This isn't the time to fold—try drawing to a better hand, son.'' His eyes suddenly lit with merriment. ''Besides, Grady, I can tell you from my own experience, you're not dealing the hand any longer. Take a look for yourself.'' He nodded toward the kitchen table where Adee was sitting with Mit on her lap.

''Lily's mother's been pining for a slew of grandchildren for a long time. She's not gonna let those kids put one foot out in that cold. Try taking them out of here, Grady, and you'll end up battling a she wolf protecting her cubs.''

Grady couldn't help chuckling. ''So Lily inherited those headstrong, nurturing instincts of hers from her mother.''

Cleve cocked his head with pride. ''She's her mother's daughter, son. I'll hitch up that sleigh.'' He winked and walked away.

When he joined Cleve in the barn, Grady whistled for Brutus. ''I might as well take him with us.''

''Think he made other plans for the night,'' Cleve said. ''Cole told me he took off with Lulu.''

''Lulu?'' Grady asked.

Cole grinned. ''Our resident bitch. One of these days we're gonna have to have that gal spayed or she'll have this ranch overrun with pups.''

"Merry Christmas, Brutus," Grady said, leaning back and chuckling. "The kids will sure be disappointed, though. They've never spent a Christmas Eve without him."

"Well, son," Cleve said profoundly, "it's been my experience that sometimes a pat on the head just ain't enough to do it for you." They both erupted into laughter.

Ten minutes later they were on their way to the former Lazy H Ranch. Before leaving, Cleve had insisted upon loading up the back of the sleigh with a few staples from the warehouse such as coffee, sugar and some canned items.

As they rode along, Cleve talked freely about the MacKenzie family. It seemed, with the exception of a few, most of the couples had had tumultuous relationships before they married. It was comforting to know that he and Lily weren't the only ones. But one undeniable fact that came across was the deep love and loyalty they all felt for each other.

The house was more than Grady had anticipated. Apparently the original structure had been nothing more than a large room that served as kitchen and living area, a bedroom and a loft. Two more bedrooms and a parlor had been added to the structure, and the fireplace rebuilt so that it now opened into both parlor and kitchen.

With the exception of a few sentimental keepsakes, Cassie Hubbard had left everything behind from linens to pictures on the wall. And Cleve had not exaggerated about her housekeeping—even a month of standing deserted had not tarnished the condition of the well-kept house.

"How many children did these Hubbards have?" Grady asked.

"Two," Cleve said. "A daughter who married and moved to California about five years ago, and a son who'd enlisted in the army and was killed in Cuba last year. They were a good family—real fine folks. Couldn't have asked for better neighbors. Are you satisfied with the house?"

Grady laughed. "Mr. MacKenzie, this is better than anything I could have ever hoped for. The kids won't know how to act."

"Glad you like it. Want to take a look at the barn?"

The barn appeared to be as snug and fit as the house. There were even several piles of dry hay he could use to feed the horses.

"I figure I'm gonna wake up any minute," Grady said. "Maybe you ought to give me a good kick in the butt so I don't keep on dreaming."

"This is all well and good, Grady, but the worst is ahead of you. Like I said, ranching's no picnic. You have to work your ass off to make a go of it."

"I've never shunned hard work, sir. How much are you asking for homesteading it?"

"Haven't given it much thought. How about five dollars a month? Then if you decide you want to stay, whatever you've paid in we'll put toward the buying price.''

Grinning, Grady said, ''Reckon this calls for another one of those Texas handshakes, sir.''

''Name's Cleve, Grady,'' Cleve said as they shook hands. ''Let your tongue get used to the feel of it, boy, because I think you're gonna be around for a while. Now we best get back to the house before the women get too curious.''

''Do you think Mrs. MacKenzie would mind if I stay here tonight? I could get the place ready to bring the kids over in the morning.''

''Adee won't mind, but Grady, this is Christmas Eve. Don't you want to spend it with your children?''

''I know between Lily and your wife, the kids won't have time to fret that I'm not there. And when they see this place tomorrow, it'll be the best Christmas gift I could ever hope to give them. I'd like to have it all shipshape when they do.''

''Can't believe you'd swap all that good food Adee's been preparing for weeks for a can of pork and beans. But okay, son, although I don't think Lily's gonna take kindly to the idea.''

''Try not to tell her any more than you have to, sir. Tell her I'll explain it all tomorrow.''

''Okay, son, you're dealing. Merry Christmas.''

As soon as Cleve drove away, Grady returned to the house. He put a pot of coffee on the stove, and then built a fire. There was enough firewood piled up to keep it going through the night, but he'd have to chop some more in the morning before he brought the kids there.

He walked from room to room, studying the pictures, running his fingers over the tables. Reading the titles of the books that filled several shelves in the parlor. He found some sheets and quilts in a chest, and made up the beds. Andy and Mit would have to share a room, so he'd let them be the first to claim a bedroom.

Returning to the kitchen, he poured himself a mug of coffee, and then stretched out on the woven rug in front of the fireplace to think.

He still felt it all was a dream and couldn't believe that this would be his one day—that his kids would finally have a roof over their heads that they could call home.

And Lily. Was it possible she did love him as Cleve had said? If he made a go of this, he'd have something to offer her rather than a life of struggle and hardship. But it would take at least a couple of years. Would she be willing to wait? Could he bear to wait? Just seeing her earlier had started his loins aching again. Two years would be an eternity. He'd never be able to hold out that long without making love to her.

Granted she'd be near, which was better than not seeing her at all, but it was not the same as knowing she would be right there when he came home, that she would warm the house with the sound of her voice and laughter—as much as they warmed his heart. And having her near wasn't the same as Lily being in his bed—the last one he kissed good-night and the first one he kissed good morning.

Grady rolled over on his stomach, rested his head on his folded arms and closed his eyes.

Two years. Good Lord, two years would be a lifetime!

CHAPTER EIGHT

"GRADY, WAKE UP."

He opened his eyes to discover Lily bending over him.

"Wow! I must have fallen asleep." He stood up. "What are you doing here?"

"I came over to get some answers. I don't understand this, Grady," Lily said. "Your showing up here—now Dad tells me you're considering homesteading the Lazy H."

"Would that bother you if I did?" he asked.

"Don't try to weasel out of this. I think you owe me some straight answers."

"I reckon I do."

"Then let's begin with the real reason you came down here—and don't try to tell me it was only because the children had a gift for me."

"Are you sorry we came?"

"There you go again. You know I'm glad to see the children, and I love the handkerchief, but I know darn well you wouldn't spend the time and money just to bring it to me when you could have mailed it much cheaper."

"I also felt we need to talk, Lily."

"That's what I've been trying to get you to do, but you seem to keep dodging my questions."

Funny, he had no problem discussing it with her father, but now that the time had come to actually talk to Lily about it, he felt more nervous than ever. He picked up his coffee cup and walked over to the stove.

"Coffee?" he asked.

"No, I do not want a cup of coffee. I want answers."

Grady poured himself another cup and returned to the fireplace. "Sit down, Lily."

"I'd rather stand," she said.

Her impatience wasn't making it any easier for him. "Okay, but promise me you won't interrupt until I'm through explaining."

"I promise."

He took a long sip of the coffee. "I wasn't being truthful with you the night of Clara's wedding when I told you I had too much to drink. You see, I wanted to kiss you. I didn't think it would get out of control."

"So you came all the way here to apologize."

"Lily, you said you wouldn't interrupt."

"All right, go on," she said.

"The next morning the children and I went down to the station to tell you the truth."

"You told the children you kissed me!" she said, aghast.

"No, not that. When I got home the night of the

wedding, Andy and Betsy were still awake. They were heartbroken at the thought of your leaving and they confessed what they had done. The little devils had decided that Mit needed a mother, so when we moved to Lamy, they picked you out as a prospect, then devised a scheme to bring us together. They'd dirtied themselves up and went to you looking hungry and neglected. You'd clean them up and feed them, and then come and see me about it."

"You mean that was all an act?"

Grady nodded. "That's right. When they came home, they were cleaned up, that's why I never understood what you were talking about."

She couldn't help smiling. "Those devious little imps. But Betsy always appeared to resent me."

"Yes, she admitted that. As much as she wanted a mother for Mit, she was used to being the number-one female in my eyes and didn't want to be replaced. She was just plain jealous of you, Lily. But you won her over, and she came to love you as much as Andy and Mit do."

Lily's eyes were misting when she looked at him. "So they really do love me. It's not just because they wanted a mother."

"Lord no, Lily! All three of those kids worship the ground you walk on. They had this gift for you and wanted to tell you the truth, because they were afraid their scheme had backfired and you disliked me for neglecting them. The morning you left Lamy,

I brought them to the station but we couldn't find you.''

"I saw you, but my heart couldn't bear another farewell with them, so I remained out of sight," Lily said.

"Well, when the train pulled away, it made me take stock of myself and my priorities. I'd been concentrating so hard on saving up to buy a ranch that I ended up ignoring the one certainty that could bring more happiness to us than owning a ranch—that's you, Lily. And I'd been too blind to see or admit it. So I resigned as sheriff, packed us up and came down here intending to ask you to marry me.''

That was like taunting a bull, and the explosion came instantly. "Well, aren't you the noble one, Grady Delaney. You've got to be about the most noblest person I've ever met," Lily declared. "Rather than stand in the way of your children's happiness, you'd make the big sacrifice and even go so far as to marry *me*. Well, thank you, sir, but no thanks. When and if I ever decide to marry, it will be to a man who loves me—and not one who's merely looking for a mother for his children.''

"Will you cool down, Lily, and let me finish the way you promised you would?''

"I've heard about all I want to hear, because if you're hanging around hoping to convince me otherwise, you're wasting your time." She spun on her heel and made a beeline for the door.

"I said I *intended* to ask you. I changed my mind as soon as I got here."

It was enough to halt her with her hand on the doorknob. She turned her head and looked back. "And why was that?"

"I had no idea your family was so wealthy. As soon as I saw the Triple M, I knew I'd be a fool to expect you to give up all this when I had nothing to offer in return."

"Of course you would think that. That's your problem. You don't understand why people marry." She strode back in anger. "Do you think the reason Maggie O'Shea married my brother Cole, Bob Fellows married my sister Linda, Emily Lawrence married Josh, Rose Dubois married Zach, or Jared Fraser married Kitty—just to name a few—was because they were MacKenzies and their parents owned a big ranch?" Her head bobbed angrily. "I don't think so."

Grady folded his arms across his chest, leaned back against the mantel, and crossed his legs. Just the stance raised her ire more. Any second he expected to see smoke come out of her nose and ears.

"What do you figure the reason might have been, Miss MacKenzie?"

Lily mistook his amusement for smugness. Those sapphire eyes of hers had turned black in anger. "Because they were crazy in love, that's why!" Arms akimbo, she declared, "Do you think any of them even cared who or what their parents were? They could have come from a different planet for all that it mattered. That's what love between a man and woman is all about, Grady Delaney. It's not picking and choosing who can protect you or provide for you the best. Heck, if that's all that mattered, most of us might just as well stay with our folks. But love is knowing in your heart that he or she is the one person you need the most and—"

"And want to be with every breathing moment for the rest of your life," he said.

"That's exactly right," she declared. "Furthermore…" She looked at him, bewildered. "What did you just say?"

"Kind of describes the way I feel about you," Grady said, walking over to her.

She was still too stunned to trust her quickened heartbeat. She backed away. "Furthermore, Mr. Delaney, what's so bad about marrying a MacKenzie? Despite all our posturing—and I'll admit we've been known to do so on occasion—we're a family most folks take a liking to."

"I'm finding that out," Grady said.

"And one more thing, I'd…" She suddenly paused and looked at him, more confused than ever. "Please repeat what you said?"

"I said, I'm beginning to find that out," Grady replied. "Your family is very likable."

"No, I mean before that."

"Oh, you mean after you pointed out to me that love is knowing in your heart the one person you want to be with the most, I said that it describes the way I feel about you."

"I don't understand," she said. The raging bull had changed into a bewildered little lamb. At the adorable sight, his defenses collapsed, and he couldn't keep his hands off her.

Grasping her shoulders, he pulled her to him. "You precious little fool, I'm so crazy in love with you that I can't even think straight anymore."

He covered her mouth, devouring its sweetness. The moment his lips touched hers, hot blood surged through him, licking at his loins with a heat that consumed him. His lips roamed her face and neck, only to return to redeem the sweetness of her mouth.

"I love you, Lily. I love you," he repeated in a breathless litany as he rained kisses on her upraised face.

His sudden move caught her unexpectedly and, confused, she struggled to try and control the mounting excitement that threatened to overpower her ability to reason. With her last remaining vestige of resistance, she shoved him away.

"Is this when you offer the apology that you drank too much spiked coffee?"

"I couldn't admit the truth to you that night. I was in love with you, but you were determined to leave.

I figured you were anxious to get back to the guy I saw you with at the train depot.''

''Whatever are you talking about?''

''Well, it doesn't matter now because I've since found out it was your brother Cole and not a sweetheart.''

''If you would have asked, I'd have told you,'' she said.

''You sure would have. If I'd have asked, you would have told me it was none of my business.''

''You don't know that,'' she snapped.

''Just the same, at the time I figured I had no right to make love to you.''

''What makes you think you have the right now?''

''Because now I believe that you love me, too. Will you marry me, Lily?''

''Why? Because your children need a mother?'' She turned away from him.

''Because *I* need you. Honey, that was just a stupid, pride-saving excuse I made up in case you slammed the door in my face.'' He turned her to face him. ''I know I've acted ten times the fool. I had my life all figured out, and falling in love wasn't part of it. Then this determined little termagant came along with a pair of sapphire eyes that curled around a man's mind and never let go. Lord, how I tried not to fall in love with you. Tried to convince myself what a pain in the rear you were.''

She smiled sheepishly. ''I guess I was.''

"Yeah, you sure were—a big pain in my heart, in my head and in my body, too. The more I fought you, the more I wanted you." He cupped her cheeks between his hands. "The real truth is that I love you, Lily. I want to marry you."

Her heart was pounding The Anvil Chorus against her ribs, and she feared it would break through her chest. She wanted to shout out her love for him, but still harbored one doubt. She knew Grady was an honorable man—that fact was indisputable. But what if he only *thought* he loved her? Had convinced himself because of his concern for his children's happiness?

"Look me in the eyes, Lily, and tell me you don't love me."

She lowered her eyes. "I can't do that."

He tucked a finger under her chin, forcing her to look at him. "Why?"

"Because I do love you, Grady. I'm just not certain you love me."

"Sweetheart, I swallowed my pride and came down here to ask you to marry me. I wouldn't have done so if I didn't love you. I don't know what more I can say or do to convince you."

He looked so sincere that she couldn't doubt him. Her heart swelled with love and overflowed into her eyes. Slipping her arms around his neck, she giggled impishly.

"You've said yourself how stubborn I am. I guess

you're going to have to try some more of that convincing, Grady Delaney.''

With a smothered groan he crushed her to him and their lips met hungrily. Whispered expressions of love and desire passed breathlessly between them, but mainly he communicated with the touch of his mouth, his hands and his tongue. The erotic sensation took her beyond reason or physical restraint.

Driven by instinct rather than worldliness, she responded with fevered kisses and exploring caresses, her straining body quivering with an intuitive excitement of what was yet to come. And she knew the longer she waited, the better it would be.

And when their bodies merged and he entered her—in that ecstatic moment of climax—she knew she had discovered the wisdom of that promise.

The room glimmered with the glow from flickering candles and the fire crackling on the hearth. There was a dreamy intimacy to their kisses as they lay talking—reaching out to touch each other—neither willing to let the moment end.

''I figured we could wait to marry until I had a chance to build up this ranch,'' Grady said.

She rolled over and raised her head. ''I want to help you build our future, my darling, not sit back and wait until it's done.''

''Baby, it's hard work and—''

''I know that, but I'm strong, Grady. I can help you.''

He laced his fingers into her hair. "I don't think we could keep apart until then anyway."

"Grady, my beloved, in case you didn't notice, we didn't. I suggest the sooner we wed, the safer we'll be."

"Well, it's too late to get married today."

"There's always tomorrow."

"Tomorrow's Christmas," he murmured.

"And what better gift could we give the children?" she said.

"Or each other." Rolling over, he sealed it with a kiss. And then another. And then another...

BY THE TIME they returned to the Triple M, dusk had fallen and the house was filled with people. Lily and Grady took her parents aside and told them that they were getting married.

"I knew that the moment I saw the two of you together," Adee said. "But tomorrow? Honey, don't you want a big wedding with a bridal gown and all the trimmings?"

"Mom, Grady and I decided the sooner the better. It will make it easier on the children, too. And besides, everybody's home right now and can attend. Those are the only people important to us. Grady doesn't have any family."

"Tomorrow's fine, Adee," Cleve said. "Jim and Sally are coming to dinner, aren't they? We'll just tell him to bring his Bible. Let him earn his meal for a change," he added, with a wink at Grady.

"Give us time to tell the children," Lily said, "then you can make the announcement, Dad."

They rounded up the three children, took them into Lily's bedroom and closed the door. Grady and Lily knelt down and encircled the three in a hug. "Kids, Lily and I have something to tell you," he said. "We're getting married tomorrow."

At first the children appeared not to understand. When his words finally sank in, they began to cry with joy—and cry they did, between hugs and kisses. Whether Mit really understood that Lily was going to be his mother was not important. Seeing everybody else's tears of happiness were enough to make the youngster shed his own. And by the time they left the room, even Grady's eyes were misty.

As soon as the announcement was made, the couple was swamped with kisses, handshakes and well wishes. Of course poor Jeb and Sarah had to take the joshing of which one would be the next to bite the bullet, but soon the excitement settled back down to normal—that is as normal as they can be with a house full of celebrants.

A hum of voices and laughter rose from among the people gathered in small clusters or moving about holding infants in their arms. Grady looked for his children and spied Mit sitting on Adee's lap. Andy and Betsy were sitting on the floor in a corner playing a game with a set of identical dark-haired twins named Becky and Jenny.

Grady was proud of himself for remembering the names of the girls, because since they returned he'd been bombarded with names such as Uncle Flint, Aunt Garnet, Jeb, Zach, Rose and Em. Somewhere among them was an Aunt Honey, an Uncle Luke, a Josh and a Cole, as well as a Linda, a Sarah, a Jared and a Kitty—and he was sure there'd been a Maggie in there and a Bob, too. There were babes in arms and several toddlers. Names and faces floated through his head, but it would be a month of Sundays before he would be able to place all of the right names with the proper faces. He couldn't even remember who among them were MacKenzies and who were daughters- or sons-in-law, because no matter how Cleve had tried to convince him to the contrary, they were all MacKenzies now.

But now he knew he could live with that. He liked these MacKenzies; they were a part of what made Lily the loving and caring person she was. And if she could embrace his family with her love, he sure as hell could embrace hers.

And when his three children stood side by side with the other young children who had been called forward to join the traditional ritual of each family member hanging an ornament on the tree, the memory of the glow of happiness on his children's faces would warm his heart forever.

Later, after everyone had feasted on the multitude of food prepared for the occasion, Grady was standing talking to Lily's uncle Luke when his lovely wife, Honey, came over and joined them. He now was able to place together the names and faces of at least another couple, in addition to Adee and Cleve. And if his memory was correct, Luke was the eldest of the three brothers.

"Grady," Honey said, "Adee told me Mit never speaks. Is that true?"

"Yes, no matter what we do or say, he'll nod or shake his head, but he never says a word."

"Sounds familiar, doesn't it, Luke?" she said.

Luke nodded. "We had the same problem with Josh. He didn't speak until he was six. Now we can't shut him up."

"Don't listen to him, Grady," Honey said with a loving glance toward one of the tall men across the room. "Do you have any idea why Mit doesn't speak?"

"No. As I told Adee, he laughs or cries, but that's about all."

"According to the doctor, Josh's problem was that he'd withdrawn, that he no longer trusted people. You see, Luke went off to war right after Josh was born, so he never got to know his father. Then when he was only two years old, he witnessed his mother and grandmother being raped and murdered by a band of Comancheros who raided the ranch. Fortunately, a Mexican who worked on the ranch managed to escape with Josh. He took the boy to Mexico and when Luke returned from the war and finally tracked them down two years later, the poor child was once again taken away from the only person he knew.''

"So you aren't Josh's real mother," Grady said.

"Don't try to tell her or Josh that," Luke interjected. "You'll get an argument from both of them."

"I didn't meet Luke until Josh was six. I fell in love with the child the moment I saw him. I think that's the real reason I married this stubborn lout," Honey said.

"Here all this time I thought it was so I'd let you out of jail," Luke said, slipping an arm around her shoulders. "You're under the mistletoe, Jaybird."

"Why do you think I came over here, cowboy?" Honey asked, raising her head to his. He pressed a light kiss on her lips.

The whole banter between them was confusing to Grady, but what was evident was the love between them. It was so tangible he could almost reach out and touch it.

"How did you finally get Josh to speak?" Grady asked.

Honey shrugged. "It was a miracle. He just started talking one day."

"No offense, Aunt Honey, but I've never cozied up to believing in miracles."

"I'm telling you, Grady, that's how it happened,"

Honey said. "One day Luke was about to shoot a stray dog that had been seriously hurt in an accident. When Josh saw what he was about to do, he cried out to him to stop."

When Grady appeared unconvinced, Luke said, "She's telling it straight, Grady. That's what happened."

"And it will happen with Mit, you'll see," Honey said. "Just like it did with Josh. All it takes is a miracle—and they happen all the time."

At that moment Betsy came up to them, leading a tearful Mit by hand. "Daddy, Andy told Mit there's no Santa Claus."

Seeing the child in tears, Adee rushed over to them, and upon hearing the problem she picked him up in her arms.

"Oh, sweetheart, of course there is."

"Adee, I've tried to encourage the children not to have false hopes or belief in someone who doesn't exist," Grady said.

"Shame on you, Grady Delaney. Hope is a measure of faith, and what would life be like without faith?"

She called all of the children together and had them sit down on the floor at her feet. "Darlings, I want you all to listen to this beautiful Christmas message that I'm going to read to you."

Adee began to read them an editorial dated September 21, 1897, that had been clipped from the *New*

York Sun newspaper. Written by an editor named Francis P. Church, the editorial was addressed to an eight-year-old girl named Virginia O'Hanlon in response to her letter asking if there is a Santa Claus.

Children and adults alike listened with rapt attention—even the wiser and non-Santa believers among them—as Adee read the author's eloquent words of assurance that Santa Claus exists as long as such things as love and generosity exist, poetry and romance exist, and the childhood faith in Santa Claus that lights the world. And that even if you can't see him, there is nothing more abiding than childhood faith.

Lily slipped her hand into Grady's. "See, you old skeptic. And you tried to convince me there's no Santa Claus," she whispered. "You've just got to believe in miracles."

He raised her hand to his lips and pressed a kiss into her palm. "Guess I have to admit I was wrong, sweetheart. Christmas is a time for miracles. You agreed to marry me, didn't you? I could never hope for a greater miracle than that."

She squeezed the hand holding hers. "Oh, there'll always be another miracle, my love."

"'No Santa Claus!'" Adee read on as the article drew to a close. "'Thank God he lives, and he lives forever. A thousand years from now, Virginia, nay, ten times ten thousand years from now, he will continue to make glad the heart of childhood.'"

When she finished, the children clapped and jumped to their feet. Throwing their arms in the air, they danced around shouting, "Hooway for Santa Cwaus!"

Mit came running over to them, his body trembling with excitement. Then with his eyes glowing with happiness, he lifted his little arms high and cried out, "Hooray for Santa Cwas!"

Dear Reader,

Christmas is my favorite time of year, partly for the memories I hold dear, but mostly because it provides the people who surround me with an opportunity to share our love and appreciation for each other. We give gifts and send greetings, eat more than we should and visit folks we never see at any other time during the year. And through all of that celebrating and joy, we band together, if only for a few days—soaking up and disbursing enough happiness to hold us until another December rolls around. My wish is that this story will help each of you to recall some poignant memory, some Christmas morning, perhaps, when your world was overflowing with the wonder and awe that this holiday instills in each of us. Honey and Zachary became very real to me, although they were purely figments of my imagination. My hope is that the love they shared will spill over into your Christmas celebration and somehow make this holiday season a bit more meaningful to you and yours.

With all good wishes,

Carolyn Davidson

A TIME FOR ANGELS
Carolyn Davidson

To every angel, shepherd and wise man
who ever appeared in a Christmas pageant—
including those of my children whose acting
careers began and ended with such endeavors—
I dedicate this story. To each child whose
childhood included hours spent in learning
their lines for that magic moment, when they
stood before parents and friends to tell the
age-old story of the Bethlehem babe. And to
the man who shared evenings with me after our
little ones were sound asleep, with me reading
the instructions as he wielded screwdriver and
pliers, putting together toys and then hiding
those gifts in closets, I dedicate this effort.
He has given me a sense of Christmas each day
of our long years together. I love you, Mr. Ed.

PROLOGUE

Fort Collins, Colorado
July, 1897

"YOU'RE H. B. MORRIS?" His tone was dubious, his eyes narrowed in scorn as the tall banker eyed the young woman before him. Zachary Bennett glanced down at the loan application in front of him. And then he confronted the delicately formed young woman who sat in the chair on the other side of his desk.

"I assumed that the person asking for a loan was a man," he said, lifting the papers he'd been perusing and shuffling them neatly into a stack.

"Never assume anything, my pa used to say," the golden-haired female said curtly. "If you'll take a good look, you'll notice I'm not a man."

"Yes, I can see that." Zachary's gaze slid from the top of her bonnet to the tip of her toes, pausing almost imperceptibly as he noted the fullness of her bosom and the narrow line of her waist beneath the clinging dress she wore, a dress that might have fit her several years ago.

"You made certain I'd notice, didn't you?" he

added, lifting a brow as his eyes paused to note the work boots she wore. She'd ruined the effect, he decided, her boots worn and shabby, unsuited to the picture she presented with her figure emphasized by her snugly fitting dress.

"I beg your pardon?" she whispered, her cheeks flushing as if she'd only now recognized his appraisal of her face and form.

He waved his hand, dismissing her query. "Let me just say this, Miss H. B. Morris. The property you want to place a lien against is already mortgaged. Apparently, your father borrowed money against the deed two years ago. In fact, he just made a six-month payment on his loan last month. The next is due January first."

"My father died on June twenty-fourth," she said quietly. "He must have paid on the note just before then."

"He died?" Zachary's hands tightened their grip on the paper he held. No one had informed him of the death of one of their customers, and as manager of the bank, he should have been made aware of that fact.

"I didn't know he'd borrowed money," the girl said, rising from the chair, her jaw clenching. "I assume this means there is no funding available for me?"

"My dear young woman," Zachary began. Aware of the vulnerable beauty of the woman, he deliberately hardened his heart against his more tender urges. "You have no assets."

And wasn't that the biggest lie he'd ever told? Even in her present state of despair, she had more physical assets than any other young lady he'd seen in a month of Sundays. And as her blue eyes filled with quick tears and her hands clutched at the small bag she carried, he realized, with a pang of regret, he'd put to death the hope she'd carried into his office. Now her lips pressed firmly together, her eyes blinked back the tears, and she turned away from him, ready to flee his presence.

His gaze traveled the line of her back, touching the curves that filled her worn dress. She had assets aplenty. Just not the sort that would allow him to lend her the two hundred dollars she needed. Perhaps—

"What do you need the money for?" he asked, lifting his pen, running his fingers along the length of it.

She turned back to face him, a bit of hope lighting the depths of glistening eyes. "I need a buggy for my use, and most important, the place needs a new well. I can fund both with an additional two hundred dollars."

"Perhaps, instead of investing in a new well, you should consider selling the farm." He circled the desk and opened the door for her. "I'm sure you could make a bit of profit from its sale and, in doing that, relieve yourself of a lot of responsibility."

"And then where would we live?" she asked, her voice breaking on the words.

We? "Perhaps we should talk this over," he suggested. "Will you walk with me to the hotel for some breakfast?"

She shot him a scornful look. "I ate at five-thirty this morning before I milked the cow and fed the chickens. It's almost time for dinner, and I have work to do."

"Maybe I could help you in some way, outside the boundaries of the bank," he said quietly. His business sense dictated that he not risk the bank's funds for her benefit, but his personal leanings might allow for a loan without rigid terms. "There must be some sort of solution to your problem."

Her eyes widened. "My mother warned me about men like you when I was sixteen years old. I don't believe we have anything to talk about unless your bank is willing to loan me the money I need."

"You're insinuating—" He broke his words off sharply as he recognized her meaning. His breath caught, shame causing him to recognize the fact that he'd been ready to put her in a position of debt to him personally, a position she'd had the good sense to refuse.

"I'm not for hire, Mr. Bennett. I know you haven't been living in Fort Collins very long, but if you had, you'd realize that decent women are the rule here, rather than the sort of females you left behind in the big city."

He watched her walk through the bank lobby, stunned at his own impetuous behavior—repenting his lapse in judgment. Even with her heavy boots, she carried herself with grace and dignity, her back straight, her shoulders squared. And as she crossed the threshold onto the city sidewalk, he felt a pang of regret that she'd escaped his presence before he'd had a chance to learn her whereabouts. Something about the woman touched him deeply, struck a chord.

Even with shabby garments and poverty as her companions, she'd brought to life within him a desire to know the woman herself, to find a meeting ground. And then she'd simply walked away.

He frowned and his breath caught as she disappeared. His movements brisk, he turned back to the finely furnished office he'd made his own. There were women aplenty available in Fort Collins. He was foolish to allow himself to focus on a farm girl, one who had so readily cast aside his impulsive offer of help.

Attempting to shed her image from his mind, his gaze brushed the nameplate on the door as he crossed the threshold into his office. The newly attached plate had a smudge on one corner and he paused, barely resisting the urge to shine the brass with his handkerchief. Yet, a jolt of pride touched his spine as he read his own name thereupon.

Zachary Bennett—Manager. His jaw tightened as he repeated the silent vow he'd taken the day the plate was screwed into place. His grandfather would never find reason to be sorry he'd given him this opportunity to run the bank.

"Problems, Zack?" the deep, resonant voice asked as his mentor approached from the back set of offices. The old man walked tall, his eyes penetrating and calculating, a habit, Zachary decided, considering the number of years Joseph Bennett had spent in this place. A place where he'd only of late made a position available for his grandson.

"No," Zack answered, shaking his head. "I just had to turn down a loan request."

The older man nodded in understanding and passed through the open doorway into the younger man's office. "It happens," he said. "A bank can't afford to give money away, after all." And then he settled down in the chair H. B. Morris had vacated only moments ago.

"I came in to talk to you, Zack," he said quietly. "I've stood by and kept an eye on things for the past two months, and I see no reason to spend any more time here. You've taken hold, my boy, and I find I can leave this place in your hands without a qualm."

Zack held his breath, aware that the next moments would make a decisive change in his life. And then his grandfather smiled, nodding slowly.

"I've decided to retire," he said, and as if she had never existed, all thought of the golden-haired woman disappeared from Zachary's mind.

"You're going to retire?" Zack repeated the words, stunned by their meaning.

"Yes. I'm making you president of the bank, Zack. It's time—past time—for me to do all the things I've put aside for the sake of my business." He cocked an eyebrow at his grandson and smiled. "I'm leaving it in your hands. Make me proud."

CHAPTER ONE

December 20, 1897

"BY YOURSELF? You're going out alone? In this snow?" His housekeeper looked askance at him as Joseph Bennett shrugged into his heavy topcoat and lifted a heavy canvas sack over his shoulder. "Won't you at least wait for Mr. Zachary? Perhaps—"

A wave of his gloved hand halted her words, and the elderly man shot her a look of aggravation. "I'm old, not senile," he said sharply. "I can handle the reins as well as any other man in town, and my grandson has accepted an invitation to a holiday party. He works hard, and I'm not going to interfere with his chance to celebrate a bit."

The housekeeper sniffed, lifting her head a bit higher, the better to look down her nose at her employer's choice of baggage. "At least let me put your packages into a box for you to carry," she said. "I'll have Homer load them into your sleigh."

Joseph reached for his hat and placed it jauntily upon his snowy white hair. "No need for anyone to put themselves out, Mrs. Hawkins. I'll be on my way to the orphanage before Homer can find his coat."

He was out the door and off the porch, his booted feet seeking purchase in the swirling snow as he made his way down the walkway to the street. The white gate opened at the touch of his hand and he lifted his canvas bag into the sleigh, following it in with only a small grunt of effort. His boots were warm, his gloves fur-lined, and his coat was made to fend off any sort of weather the Colorado winter could offer.

Mrs. Hawkins stood in the doorway as he took up the reins, and he lifted a hand in her direction, a silent farewell that she responded to by firmly closing the heavy portal. "As if a little snow ever hurt anyone," Joseph muttered, admiring the sound of his sleigh bells as he turned the corner, heading for the orphanage he helped to support. It sat four miles from town, nestled in the foothills of the mountains, a large brick building that held almost forty children. He'd be there in an hour, in time for supper.

In his bag were gifts for the smaller girls, his contribution to the party to be held there tonight. His fellow benefactors, all of them businessmen who had met with success in the past years, would join him, and together, they would play out this evening's festive celebration. That Zachary would quibble over his driving out alone was a mere inconvenience. Joseph Bennett was as strong and capable as he'd ever been in his life. His grandson tended to be overprotective, and Joseph usually bore it with grace.

But not tonight. Christmas for the orphans could

not be postponed. Not even a driving snowstorm could divert him from his purpose.

EVEN FIVE DAYS BEFORE Christmas, angelic beings were in short supply, Honey Belle Morris decided. If ever she'd needed a guardian angel, it was now. She wiped the foggy windowpane with her dish towel and peered out into the darkness. The falling snow gave an eerie glow to the night, yet fell in such abundance that it was almost impossible to see beyond the porch railing.

"Whatcha lookin' for?" Five years old, Hope was the image of what a cherub should be, Honey thought. She held out a hand to her small sister and attempted a cheerful smile.

"I was just wondering if the snow had slowed down yet," she said, then deliberately lightened her tone of voice. "If this keeps up we'll be able to make our own Christmas angels in the snow tomorrow morning."

"If we want angels, we'll *have* to make our own," Hope said bluntly. "They're like Saint Nicholas, just part of a story in a book."

Hope's disbelief in such things was a by-product of the disappointments that had overwhelmed the sisters during the past months. And yet Honey coaxed the child's good nature into existence, squeezing her fingers as if to impart her love in this small way.

"Sweetie, your guardian angel watches over you while you sleep. Remember Mama telling you? She even showed you pictures in the Bible of the angels.''

''I try not to think about Mama,'' Hope whispered, and then her chin lifted and her mouth turned down at the corners. ''I told you before, Honey,'' the little girl said with a wave of her hand. ''I don't believe in angels. If they were real, Mama and Papa wouldn't have died in the river.''

''Well, they exist, whether you believe or not,'' Honey said after a moment, unwilling to argue with the child, secretly admitting to herself her own loss of faith in the heavenly beings of late.

The rushing water in the riverbed, following a heavy summer rain high up in the mountains, had toppled her parents' buggy into the cold mountain stream and washed them into the narrow gulch to their deaths, leaving the sisters to fend for themselves on the small family farm. Only the horse had remained, standing amid splintered bits and pieces of the family buggy the next morning, the parents' bodies found downstream.

Five months had passed, months of hard, unending toil as Honey worked the rocky soil to hoe and weed the kitchen garden, only to see the tender plants dry up in the late summer sun, thwarting her hopes of a good harvest. She'd watered as best she could but had ceased, lest the well dry up totally, leaving them without precious water.

Managing to save only about half the expected crop of vegetables to put in canning jars and set aside for the winter months, she faced a shortage of supplies before spring. A new well was imperative, or next summer promised total disaster.

It was hard to be cheerful when the pantry shelves were almost bare and Christmas was about to take place, whether or not they were ready to celebrate. Mama had always said that Christmas was in the heart, but telling that to a five-year-old was a losing proposition. There were no gifts, and now the snow made it impossible to venture into the woods to look for a fir tree to decorate. Until the snow came to a halt, there was no way to get to town for supplies. And from the looks of the weather tonight, that was not going to happen before morning.

Honey turned away from the window. "Would you like some toasted bread?" she asked her sister. "We have lots of butter, and we can spare some sugar to sprinkle on top."

Hope nodded, apparently willing to be congenial. "I'm glad you made bread today, Honey," she said, offering a quick smile as if to apologize for her bad mood.

It was one blessing they shared, Honey thought. Neither of them could keep a grudge, their naturally sunny dispositions holding them in good stead. She lifted a loaf of bread from the shelf and sought out her knife, then cut thick slices and placed them on the oven rack. The cookstove heated the kitchen well. It was a cheerful room, and they spent most of their time there, leaving the parlor doors closed against the cold. A vent in the kitchen ceiling carried the heat into the bedroom upstairs where they both slept.

Wood was stacked against the outside wall to the left of the back door, a supply that should last for two or three days, if she conserved it, Honey decided. After that she'd have to go to the woodshed and fetch another load, cutting it to stove lengths on the chopping block near the porch with the smaller hatchet. The ax was heavy, but by next week, she'd have to use it to split the heavy logs she'd dragged from the woods before the first snow fell.

The scent of toasted bread wafted from the oven as she opened the door, and she stabbed the crusty pieces with a long-handled fork, then placed them on a plate. Settling down at the table, knife in hand, she was in the midst of spreading butter on them when Hope whispered a warning, her small fingers grasping Honey's sleeve.

"There's a man on the porch," the little girl said, her words breathless, her voice fearful. "He just looked in the window."

"Well, land's sakes," Honey said, rising quickly and glancing toward the frosted pane. "Let's see if he's all right. He must be half-frozen, out there in the snow." She moved quickly to the back door and opened it far enough to peer outside, looking quickly to her right where a figure caught her eye. Indeed it was a man, bundled in a long coat, a bulky canvas bag trailing behind him. Snow covered him in a blanket of white, obscuring his face save for dark eyes that squinted in her direction.

"Ma'am?" He reached out a hand toward her and then toppled headlong in her direction, his spectacles falling from his face to lie at Honey's feet. She stepped outside, the gust of wind blowing snow across her shoes, whipping her skirts about her legs and snatching the screened door from her grasp.

"Help me, Hope," she called back into the house as she bent to pick up his eyeglasses, placing them in her apron pocket. And then she turned to the task of dragging the man's prone form across the few feet to the door. "Hold the door," she told her sister, and then, with strength built by days of hard work, she lugged the man into her kitchen and deposited him on the floor.

"Maybe you oughta sweep him off with the broom," Hope suggested. "He's full of snow, Honey." She eyed the stranger dubiously, one finger tangling in a long, golden lock of hair as she scooted up onto a chair. "He's old, isn't he?"

"It seems so," Honey murmured, kneeling beside the unconscious gentleman, her fingers touching the pulse in his throat. "But he's alive, and that's the important thing."

His white brows moved as she spoke, and then his eyelids fluttered and he squinted up at her, his voice trembling as he whispered words of thanks, struggling to sit up. "I could have frozen to death, young lady, if you hadn't opened the door to me."

"Well, you're not going to freeze tonight," Honey said stoutly. "Let's get you off the floor and sitting in a chair by the stove, mister."

In moments, he'd shed his coat, and Honey placed it over a chair nearer the heat of the cookstove. "It ought to be dry by morning," she said. "And in the meantime, you need a good cup of tea to warm you up."

"Tea?" he asked, his face lighting as he spoke the single syllable. And then he rubbed his hands together as if in anticipation. "My wife used to fix tea for the two of us every evening before bedtime. Said it would help us sleep." His dark eyes squinted a bit as they followed Honey while she moved quickly around the room, bringing cups to the table, filling the teapot from the heavy teakettle on the stove, and then carrying it to where he sat.

"It won't take long," she told him. The sugar bowl from the kitchen dresser was old, one her mother had treasured, and she wiped it off a bit as she placed it before him. "We have fresh cream, too," she said, heading for the pantry where the pitcher sat next to an outside wall. "And I just toasted some bread. Would you like some?"

He nodded, peering at the buttered toast with interest. "That sounds wonderful," he said, looking up as she poured his tea. A plate appeared before him and he lifted a piece of toast to it. "I don't want to eat yours," he said.

"I can make more," Honey told him, slicing more

bread and placing it in the oven, enjoying the heat that enveloped her from the open door.

The old man reached for the milk pitcher. "Do you have a cow?"

Honey turned from the stove, and nodded silently, and Hope filled in the blanks. "Our cow is Bossy and we have six chickens, too. And Honey milks the cow every day, while I feed the chickens and gather up the eggs." Her small face lit with pride in her achievements as she boasted of the chores she was entrusted with.

"And where are your mother and father?" the old man asked kindly as he poured the thick cream into his tea. "Are they away from home?"

Hope's eyes filled with quick tears as she shook her head, and Honey spoke softly. "They aren't with us any longer. There was an accident last summer." Her lips pressed firmly together, holding back the futile tears she'd long since vowed not to shed in the presence of others.

"You young ladies live here alone?" the man asked, frowning as he watched Honey pour her own cup full of the fragrant tea. "Surely you have help."

"Yes," she answered quickly. "A neighbor came to cut the hay and helped me harvest the corn crop. He left half of each in the barn for me, so I have enough to feed my animals," Honey said quickly. "And another lady stops by on her way to town and takes my butter to the general store. I trade it out for flour and sugar."

"Don't you have transport?" he asked, his gaze sweeping the room as he spoke, his eyes gentle as they rested once more on Honey's face. And then he rubbed at his eyes, frowning. "I must have lost my eyeglasses in the storm."

"Oh. I have them," Honey said quickly, reaching in her pocket and lifting his glasses to the tabletop. She rubbed the lenses with a corner of her apron and held them out on her palm. "I was afraid they'd get broken, and then I forgot I'd picked them up from the porch."

"Thank you," he said, adjusting the earpieces and peering through the lenses. "My, that's better. Now, you were telling me…" He waved his hand, as if he urged her to continue with her explanations of the limited scope of their existence.

Honey hesitated, unwilling to vent her tale of woes on a stranger, but he leaned forward, as if caught up in her words. "Well," she began, "we have a horse, but the buggy was broken to smithereens when it got caught in the river. We were lucky the horse didn't drown, too," she said quietly, after a moment's pause.

"Your folks were drowned?" he asked softly, and at her nod, he reached to pat her arm, a gentle movement that drew her attention.

"It's all right," she said quickly. "We've really gotten along pretty well, sir."

"Is your place free and clear?" he asked. "I know it isn't any of my business, young lady, but perhaps it might be wiser to sell out and move to town. Maybe life would be easier if you were around other folks."

Honey shook her head. The dark cloud she'd been living under hung a bit lower as his query registered. "My father had placed a mortgage on it. I only found out when I went to the bank in July. The next payment on it is due the first of the year," she admitted, and then spread her hands in a gesture of acknowledgment. "I doubt we'd make much even if we sold the place, and we still wouldn't have anywhere to go."

"Surely you can find a position in town," he suggested, "and a place to stay."

She shook her head. "No, I'm going to try to scrape together enough to make the mortgage payment. I may be able to sell some of the hay, and I've been thinking of doing some sewing for folks." The words sounded hopeless to her ears even as she said them aloud, and she sighed deeply. Sometimes it seemed the load she carried was almost too much to bear. "I figure I'll worry about it after Christmas."

"Maybe we could arrange a loan from the bank," he offered, and she almost laughed aloud at his words.

"I told you, I've tried that. Way back in July," she said harshly. "And the gentleman there said he couldn't help me any."

"I don't recall seeing you in the bank," the gentleman said.

Honey shrugged. "I was there, all right." And then she glanced up at him. "Do you work there?"

"I did," he said after a short hesitation. "My name is Joseph Bennett, ma'am. I'm no longer with the bank on a regular basis, but I still have some influence."

"I doubt anyone could influence the man I talked to," she said glumly, and felt a surge of anger rise within her as she recalled the words of the man she'd faced across the wide desk over five months ago. *You have no assets.*

She would not take out her ire on this old man, no matter that he was in some way affiliated with that institution run by a gentleman with ice in his veins. "He made it clear that he couldn't do anything for me," she said quietly, swallowing the hasty words that would have repeated the final blow to her hopes.

"He did, did he?" One hand rose to stroke his white beard as the gentleman leaned back in his chair. "Young fella, was he?"

"Older than me," Honey said. "A lot younger than you."

"Everyone's younger than I am, dear girl," Joseph Bennett said with a smile. "I've come to a place in my life when I cherish every morning I wake up and find I'm still breathing."

"Mister?" Hope slid carefully from her chair and approached Joseph diffidently. "Do you know that when you put on your spectacles it makes you look like the pictures in my Saint Nicholas book?''

His smile was wide as she gazed up at him, her eyes scanning his features. "I do? Just like the pictures of Saint Nicholas? Well, what do you know about that?''

"It's just a story, Hope," Honey reminded her quickly. "Remember, we talked about the difference between—''

"I know, but he *does* kinda remind me…'' The child's words trailed off and she bit at her lip as she backed away. And then she sniffed disparagingly. "I don't really believe in pretend stuff though. Things like angels and Saint Nicholas.''

"Well, as it happens, I believe in Saint Nicholas," Mr. Bennett said quietly. "And I most certainly believe in angels.''

"Do you have a guardian angel?" Hope asked, her attention caught by his statement. Her eyes widened as if she could scarcely believe his words.

"Yes, indeed," Mr. Bennett said firmly. "How do you suppose I found your house when I lost my way in the storm?''

"I meant to ask where you were going on a night like this," Honey said. "Surely it must have been something awfully important to take you out in the weather.''

Mr. Bennett smiled wryly. "Well, it seemed important to me at the time. Now I wonder why I didn't take my housekeeper's warning more seriously and stay at home.''

"You got a housekeeper?'' Hope asked, wide-eyed. "Is that somebody that's gonna keep your house if you don't come back home?''

Honey laughed softly as she shook her head at Hope's theory. "A housekeeper is someone who tends to your house if you're a gentleman living alone,'' she explained.

"Don't you have a sister or a lady of your own to live at your house?'' Hope asked sadly.

"I had a wife, a long time ago,'' he answered, bending to look into the child's eyes. "It's sort of lonely there these days. And my housekeeper is talking about being too old to climb the stairs and take care of a big house anymore. I may be alone before long.''

"Don't you have nobody?'' Hope's big eyes filled with tears, as if she sorrowed for Joseph's lack of family.

"I have a grandson,'' he said. "But he doesn't live with me these days. He built a house of his own over the past few months.''

"All by himself?'' Hope asked, as if such a feat were too enormous to be believed.

"No,'' Joseph said with a smile. "He hired men to do it for him.''

"Won't anyone be out looking for you?'' Honey asked, aware that, surely, at least the housekeeper would be missing her employer by now.

"My grandson was to stop by this evening," Joseph said. He drew his watch from his waistcoat pocket and checked the time. "It's getting late, and I suspect he'll be dropping by to check on me anytime now. I hope he doesn't take it in his head to set out searching in this weather."

His gaze traveled to the window, where snow blew against the pane. "My horse is tied to a tree, just next to the porch," he said suddenly. "I forgot about him. Is there room in your barn for him to spend the night?"

"Of course," Honey said, her hand touching his as she rose from the table. "You stay right here with Hope, and I'll put on my boots and go out and tend to him. I have to milk the cow anyway, so I'll be a while."

"Just unhitch my gelding from the sleigh and he'll follow you without any trouble," Joseph said. And then with a sigh that might have been relief, he settled back in his chair and watched as Honey donned her boots and heavy coat. "Will you be all right out there?" he asked. "I don't want you to lose your way taking care of my horse."

"I have a rope tied to the porch post and running out to the barn," she said. "Pa always used to keep one strung out all winter long. Said you never could tell when you were going to need it. I'll put your horse and sleigh in the barn."

"Your father was a wise man," Joseph murmured, his eyes following Honey's slight form as she opened the back door. "We'll be fine," he said reassuringly as she turned back to him, and she nodded. As she crossed the threshold she heard him speaking to Hope, his words raising a question that was guaranteed to keep the little girl happy for the next half hour.

"Why don't you bring me your book about Saint Nicholas and we'll read it together?" he asked the child.

THE PAIL OF MILK sat in the narrow pantry, covered with a clean towel till morning, and Honey's coat was draped over a second chair near the stove to dry. She'd washed up the few dishes, banked the fire and turned down the lamp over the table.

"I'm not sure where you'll be able to sleep." The man looked tired enough to curl up on the floor, but that would be against all rules of hospitality should she suggest such a thing. And then she thought of a solution that would eliminate him having to climb the stairs to the second floor. "I have an extra feather tick upstairs I can bring down for you to use, if you don't mind the floor in here," she suggested.

His nod was courtly, she thought, and his words were warm as he accepted her hospitality. "That would be fine," he said. "I'll help you carry it down." His offer was well-meant, but Honey shook her head.

"It's not heavy," she countered, thinking that he looked as though a good strong wind would blow

him over. He'd been through a storm tonight, a wea-
rying process for anyone, let alone an old man. His
eyes looked tired, and his shoulders were stooped,
and she felt a pang of apprehension as she watched
him. "I have a couple of quilts that will keep you
warm, Mr. Bennett. You just wait right here. Hope
will lend a hand."

In fifteen minutes, the tick had been dragged down
the stairs, a quilt thrown over it and another placed
to one side. Her father's big pillow was fluffed up
and covered with a clean pillowcase, awaiting the
weary traveler's head. And Joseph Bennett looked
every inch a tired man, Honey decided.

"I'm sorry I can't do better for you," she told
him. "But the other rooms upstairs are too cold for
you to use."

He smiled at her and touched Hope's golden curls
with a wrinkled hand. "I have something in my bag
I'd like to give your little sister, Miss Honey. I have
gifts for the children at the orphanage with me, and
they won't miss it if Hope has a new doll to take to
bed with her tonight."

"A new doll?" Hope's voice lifted on a note of
wonder. "For me?"

"If those things are for the children at the orphanage, we can't let you—"

"Honey!" Hope's calling of her name was a cry
of anguish, and Honey bit her lip as the child
clutched at her sister's skirt.

"There's no problem," Mr. Bennett said quickly.

"I always take along extra gifts when I attend the party there. In fact, I'll warrant the other sponsors took enough presents along for all the children tonight. They probably didn't even miss mine."

"I doubt that," Honey said quietly. "But if you have something to spare, I know Hope will be pleased. There wasn't going to be anything for Christmas this year, I'm afraid."

Hope's eyes gleamed with pleasure as Mr. Bennett retrieved his bulging canvas bag and opened the top, reaching into its depths to lift out a pink-and-gold-striped box. "I think this will please you," he said, bowing deeply as he offered it to Hope.

She held it against her chest and her eyes filled with tears as she looked up at her sister. "Do you think Mr. Bennett could be my guardian angel, Hope? Maybe he isn't Saint Nicholas, but he could still be an angel, couldn't he?"

"I'd say so," Honey said, standing on tiptoe to touch her lips to the wrinkled cheek. "I'd say he qualifies for the job."

CHAPTER TWO

December 21

SUNLIGHT GLISTENED on snowdrifts and heavy branches bent low, laden with a foot of winter's bounty. But Zachary Bennett found little to admire in the beauty before him. He was intent on the road delineated by a tree line on either side of the narrow expanse of fallen snow. Any tracks made by his grandfather's sleigh had been long since covered and he was, at this point, going on sheer guesswork.

He'd driven his team out of the gates of the orphanage almost an hour ago, the place where he'd fully expected to find Joseph Bennett. His mouth set in a grim line, he'd left there in haste.

"I'm sorry, Mr. Bennett." Clara Pembrooke's words had carried genuine concern as she spoke of the aborted Christmas party of the night before. With the storm preventing the sponsors from appearing on their doorstep, she'd announced to residents that they would no doubt hold the celebration after the roads were fit to travel.

"I assumed your grandfather had stayed at home,"

she'd said, a frown telling of her distress. "I certainly hope he found shelter last evening."

With an abrupt nod, he'd left her and now he drove his team of mares across the pristine stretch of snow, seeking in vain for tracks that would point to Joseph Bennett's trail. Off to the right, up a steep grade and perched against a rocky abutment, stood a two-story house, outbuildings scattered to one side. Smoke came from the chimney, and the signs of occupancy bode well for the chance of information on a traveler who might have gone astray in the storm.

He drove his team up the narrow lane and around the side of the house, noting the unpainted shed and outhouse, the porch that needed repair and a screened door that had seen better days. No sleigh tracks were apparent, just a single set of footprints dimpled the snow leading to the barn.

He followed them, hearing a horse whinny a welcome from inside the building, and then his own mares answered the call, stomping their shod hooves and tossing their heads. Laying aside the lap robe, he climbed from the sleigh and attached a short line to the harness, then tied his team to a handy hitching post.

His hand was on the big, sliding door when it opened before him and a heavily bundled figure appeared. Blue eyes met his—startled blue eyes— strangely familiar eyes, he decided. He set that thought aside to be considered later, even as his gaze touched upon a small, straight nose and full lips that opened as if to speak.

"I beg your pardon," he began, doffing his hat as he recognized that a woman stood before him. "I didn't mean to frighten—"

She waved a hand dismissively as the blue eyes narrowed, as if in recognition of his identity. "You didn't," she said, her words a curt rebuff.

"I'm looking for my grandfather," he told her, at a loss as to her apparent bad temper. Perhaps the woman was frightened, alone here with a stranger at the door.

"Joseph Bennett? He's *your* grandfather?"

And somehow he felt certain she already knew it to be a fact, that her query was meant to insult him in some way. "Yes, he is." His mind swept over the past months, seeking some knowledge of where he'd last seen those eyes, and then as he watched, her hand lifted and the hood of her coat was pushed from her head.

Golden hair, turned almost to silver in the sunlight, wound in a braided coronet around her head. She eyed him warily yet defiantly, as if waiting his judgment, and then, with a small smile that tucked into one corner of her mouth, she spoke again. "He's in the house with my little sister. You can go in if you like. I'm almost finished here."

"Can I help you?" he asked, ever the gentleman—strangely lured by the mystery of blue eyes that dissected him and found him wanting, aware that somewhere, sometime, he'd seen her before. Then, as she turned away without reply, he recognized her, knew the proud toss of her head, the straight line of her spine as she walked into the depths of the barn.

"H. B. Morris," he breathed quietly, and as she halted abruptly, he realized she had heard him speak her name. "You're H. B. Morris," he said more loudly, striding to where she stood. "I knew I recognized you."

"Did you?" She stepped away, back to where a handful of chickens scratched in an enclosure at the other end of the barn aisleway. A bowl with several eggs in it sat atop a log and she lifted it, then returned to where he waited.

"You came in asking for a loan last summer," he said.

"And you refused me."

His shrug was slow and he spoke the words of agreement with regret. "I had no choice, Miss Morris."

Her head lifted, her chin jutting a bit. "I know. You told me. In fact, what you specifically said was that I have no assets."

Her accurate accusation stung, and his abrupt nod acknowledged her words. "You apparently have been able to get along, I see." His gaze swept over the walls and across the accumulation of tools and bits and pieces of barn equipment. "You even seem to have a nice-looking sleigh," he said, nodding toward a shiny specimen beneath the eaves.

Then he looked a bit closer and strode toward the vehicle. His hand touched the smooth surface and he swung his head toward her, his eyes resting impatiently on her stony expression. "This isn't your sleigh, is it?"

"I didn't say it was," she said simply. "It belongs to your grandfather. I only put it out of the storm for him last night." She tilted her head toward the second stall down the aisle. "His horse is there."

She bent to pick up a pail, over half filled with milk. Her hand had barely gripped the handle when he stepped to her side, reaching for it. "I'll be glad to carry that for you," he offered, unwilling to deny her the courtesy of his help.

"Never mind," she said, grasping it firmly, the bowl of eggs in the curve of her other arm. "Just pull the door closed behind yourself." And with that she set off, out of the barn and toward the house.

He followed, carefully shutting the door and making new tracks in the snow, her stride considerably shorter than his own. "If you have a shovel, I'll be glad to widen the path for you," he offered, passing her by in order to arrive on the porch in advance, reaching for the door.

"I got along just fine before you arrived," she said. "I'll still be managing on my own when you've gone."

And wasn't that about the neatest bit of sarcasm he'd heard lately? The woman was a challenge, and a wary attraction to her sharp tongue and wit struck him with the force of a strong west wind. He'd seldom been so impressed by a female, he thought, recalling his instant attraction to her months ago.

His grin smothered by a cough, he watched as she stomped the snow from her boots and entered the house. He followed her, glancing quickly around the room, a poorly furnished but nevertheless welcoming kitchen. A cookstove gave off an abundance of heat and the scent of coffee and something baking in the oven beckoned him closer.

"Zachary!" His grandfather waved an uplifted hand, his other hand holding a book on his lap, his index finger holding the place where he'd apparently been reading. "I figured you'd be making tracks in this direction once you realized I'd missed the gate to the orphanage in the storm."

"I was worried about you, Grandfather," Zachary said quietly. "I'm glad you found a shelter."

"I'd thought to set off for home this afternoon," Joseph told him. And then he turned to H. B. Morris, his eyes lighting as she shed her coat and settled her boots near the stove.

"Honey, this is my grandson, Zachary," he said, pride apparent in his voice as he made the introduction.

Honey? The endearment vibrated in Zack's mind. "Honey?" he repeated softly, disparagingly, his eyes fastening on the woman as he narrowed the space between them. His lips barely moved as he formed softly spoken words of derision. "You work fast, don't you?"

Her cheeks already flushed from the cold air, she reddened even more as she bit her lower lip, as if refusing to rise to his bait.

"Zachary? I'm sure I don't know what's going on here." His grandfather spoke a bit sharply and Zack stiffened, turning to face the implied criticism.

Bowing his head in a gesture of respect, he approached the rocking chair. A small hand lay on his grandfather's shoulder, and peeking over the back of the chair a pair of blue eyes that were familiar met his gaze. "Who's he?" a small voice asked.

"My grandson," Joseph said, imbuing the words with a harshness Zachary had seldom heard. "He seems to be laboring under a misapprehension."

"It's all right, Mr. Bennett," the young woman said quickly, catching Zack's eye as she spoke calmly. "Your grandson is only concerned for you. He doesn't want anyone to take advantage of your good nature."

"I don't need you putting words in my mouth, Miss Morris," Zachary said quietly, facing the woman. And then he glanced back at the little girl who sheltered behind his grandfather. "Is this your sister?"

Joseph touched the small fingers and drew the child from behind him. "This is Hope, a good friend of mine. She's been sharing her books with me." His look was a warning, one Zachary understood implicitly. *Don't frighten this child.*

Removing his gloves, he held out a hand to the girl. "I'm pleased to meet you, Hope," he said, his smile genuine, noting the china doll she held clutched to her breast.

As soft and warm as a fluttering baby bird, her fingers rested against his palm, and the child smiled tremulously up into his face. "I'm pleased to meet you, sir," she whispered, and then darted a look at her sister, as if for affirmation of her good manners.

"I suppose you've come to rescue your grandfather," Miss Morris said, drawing his attention away from the child. She held out a hand to her small sister and the girl stepped across the room and stood in her sister's wake. "I assure you, Mr. Bennett, we've kept him warm and fed and he's suffered no ill effects from his visit."

"I would assume such to be the case," Zachary said politely, even as Joseph grumbled beneath his breath. "I'll ready your sleigh, sir," he said, directing his words back to his grandsire, retreating from the chill of blue eyes that reflected wintry ice.

"Go on, then," Joseph said, rising from the rocking chair, motioning toward the door. He looked back at Miss Morris. "If you'll get my coat and hat, I'll get ready to leave, Honey," he said warmly. "We'll be seeing each other very soon, I predict. When you make your next trip into town, I'll expect to see you."

Honey. Again, the pet name stuck in Zachary's craw as he opened the door and stomped onto the porch. She'd obviously made an impression on a vulnerable old man. It was a wonder she hadn't coaxed her way into his life already. And from the sound of things, she was well on her way to achieving that goal.

We'll be seeing each other… His grandfather's words rang in his mind as he retraced his steps to the barn, his stride long, his hands impatient as he slapped his hat atop his head and pulled his leather gloves into place. The door opened readily and he sought out the horse in the second stall. Beyond it stood a mare, a chestnut beauty shaggy with a winter's coat, but well-groomed, nonetheless.

At least the woman had a horse, although there didn't seem to be a vehicle of any sort on the premises, save his grandfather's sleigh. The harness was at hand and he led the gelding from the stall and out the door. The sleigh came easily over the earthen floor, and he fit it behind the black gelding, fastening the buckles and readying it for travel.

From the house, he heard the opening and closing of the door, then a sound of snow crunching as Joseph approached, a bulging canvas bag over his shoulder. "I'll need to drop this off at the orphanage on our way to town," he said, lifting the bundle into the back of the sleigh before he climbed aboard. "Thank you for harnessing my horse, Zachary."

"I'm just thankful to find you alive and well,"

Zack admitted. "I've been worried since I found you still away from the house last night. I'd have come looking then, but I knew there was no point in getting lost in a snowdrift myself."

"You might know I'm capable of finding shelter," Joseph told him. "I haven't lost my senses yet."

"You missed the orphanage gate," Zack reminded him. "It was pure luck you found this place."

Joseph shook his head as he lifted the reins. "I don't think so, son. I don't believe anything happens without a reason. I feel certain that I was meant to be at this very place last night. I've never felt more of a Christmas spirit in my life, than I did in that house."

He turned with a thoughtful look to consider the farmhouse, where a small girl stood in the window, her finger tracing idly against the frosted pane.

"I gave Hope a doll from my bundle," he said. "I always have more than enough for the children, and she didn't stand a chance of having Christmas this year."

"They're that hard up?" Zachary asked idly, even as his practical mind reviewed the poor furnishings of the house and the circumstances of the two females who lived in it. "I expect the older one has something set aside for the child."

Joseph shook his head. "No, she told me there wouldn't be any gifts this year." He tugged at his beard. "I have something in mind, though."

"Don't be too softhearted, sir," Zachary said quietly. "I hope you won't be taken in by a pretty face."

"She's got more substance than you think," Joseph said. "Although," he admitted with a smile, "her face *is* downright beautiful, if you ask me." He shot a knowing look at Zachary. "You had to notice, unless you've gone blind from the snow."

"I noticed," Zack said, heading for his own vehicle. He waved a hand at his grandfather. "Go on ahead. I'll be right behind you." Untying his team, he turned his horses in the barnyard and climbed into the sleigh. From the house a movement at the window caught his attention, and as he watched, a slender hand touched Hope's shoulder and she was drawn from sight. And then curtains were pulled to cover the glass pane.

"Goodbye, *honey,*" Zack muttered beneath his breath. "Don't make any plans, sweetheart. You'll not be dealing with an old man from now on."

December 22

"CAN WE GO TO TOWN TODAY, Honey? The snow is melting a little bit." Hope smiled brightly at her sister, swishing her skirt, bouncing on her toes, her impatience showing as she awaited a reply. The promised trip was already two days overdue, but the weather and unexpected company had delayed things.

Now Honey faced telling the child that there was

no money for Christmas goodies, that the next month promised to be bleak and cheerless. Somehow the words remained unspoken as she surveyed her small sister. And then she fit her index finger into a trailing curl that lay on Hope's shoulder and tugged gently.

"We'll go," she said decisively. "I don't know how much we can spend for treats, but we'll see what we can do." There wouldn't be enough for the mortgage payment, no matter how far she stretched the money in the bank. Perhaps it would be a greater favor to Hope for her to have one last happy time to remember when the harsh winds blew in January.

The mare was saddled, her bridle put in place, and Honey led the creature from the barn. On the porch, Hope waited, her eyes wide with anticipation as the horse was led toward the house.

"I'll just get a sack from the pantry," Honey told her, "and then we'll be ready." A quick nod of approval accompanied by a flashing smile showed Hope's approval. Within minutes, they were together in the saddle, Hope perched on Honey's lap as the mare began the trek to Fort Collins.

The sidewalks were cleared of snow, the rutted street a mixture of slush and mud, and Honey had to search out a place to tie her mare. "Everyone is shopping today," she murmured as she lifted her sister from the saddle. She straightened the child's bonnet, smoothed down the collar of her woolen coat and reached for her hand.

And then looked up into the face of a man she'd

just as soon never lay eyes on again. He swept his hat from his dark hair and shot her a look that seemed to take in her appearance in one fell swoop.

"Good morning, Miss Morris," he murmured, bowing in an almost obscene gesture of courtesy.

She offered a nod. "Mr. Bennett." It was as brief a greeting as she could politely manage, and with a tug on Hope's hand, she stepped up on the sidewalk, intent on leaving his presence.

"I have a message for you," he said, falling in place beside her as she double-stepped toward the general store.

She ignored him, only slowing her pace when Hope dragged her feet in protest.

"You're makin' me run," the child said breathlessly. "Slow down, Honey."

"Yes. Slow down, *honey*," Zachary said nicely.

"I haven't given you leave to call me by my name," she said quietly, unsure what her response should be. All around them, townsfolk were coming and going, voices rising in greeting, an air of celebration seeming to be prevalent in the atmosphere. It would not do to be embarrassed by untoward behavior here in the middle of town.

"Your name?" he asked, his hand beneath her elbow as he drew her closer to a storefront. "I'm not sure what your name is, Miss Morris. I know my grandfather uses an affectionate term when he speaks to you..." His voice trailed off as he glanced down at Hope's upturned face.

"As does your sister." His pause was long, his mind obviously working out the solution to his dilemma. And then his eyes met hers and the bleak chill within them softened. "Your name is *Honey?*"

"No, not legally," she said, wishing his fingers would release her arm, aware of the warmth of those long digits seeping through the heavy fabric of her coat sleeve. "My mother named me Honoria Belle, but when Hope was small and began talking, she couldn't speak all the syllables and she shortened it."

"To Honey," he said, his voice seeming to linger as he spoke it quietly.

She tugged with futile strength, but his fingers tightened their grip as he refused to release her. "I beg your pardon," he said quietly.

"Please, Mr. Bennett, I'd like to go to the general store and do my shopping. I want to be back home before the weather changes."

He looked up at the sky. "Do you think we'll have more snow?" he asked.

"Please, Mr. Bennett," she repeated, feeling a blush rise to cover her cheeks. "People are looking at us."

"I don't mind," he said blandly. "I'm only here to deliver a message, Miss Honey. My grandfather asked me to drive out to your farm, and if I hadn't caught sight of you riding into town, I'd be on a fool's mission right now."

"Deliver your message, then," she said abruptly, her heart beating rapidly as she was drawn closer to

his tall form. Almost pressed against the front of the
newspaper office, she felt trapped as he stepped in
front of her, the better to keep them from the passersby.

"My grandfather would like to see you. Will you
stop at his home before you return to the farm?"

"Yes," she answered quickly. "Now, let me by.
I don't have time to dillydally, Mr. Bennett. I have
much to do today."

"Well, you'd better rearrange your tight schedule
to include an hour or so with my grandfather. He's
impatient to see you, thus my orders to ride out and
fetch you into town. I'm certainly glad I saw you
here. I'd rather stay in his good graces."

"Well, far be it for me to cause him to be upset
with you, now that you've managed to snag my attention," she said, unwillingly intrigued by his dashing good looks. Dark hair, and eyes like the elder
Mr. Bennett's, were set off by strong features, and
she felt a flurry in her stomach, as though butterflies
had taken up residence.

"What comes next?" she asked.

"I'm to ride to his home and announce your arrival in town, and he'll be awaiting your presence as
soon as your business is finished here."

"I'm not sure I like being ordered about in this
fashion," she said, her natural independence assert-
ing itself, and then watched as a crimson ridge appeared on his cheekbones.

"I'm truly sorry," he said. "I don't want to be in

trouble with both you and my grandfather. I didn't mean to be pushy, Miss Morris. I beg your pardon. I'm only following orders.''

She hesitated for a moment, then decided quickly in favor of pleasing the old man who had been so kind to Hope during his short stay in their home. ''All right,'' she said. ''I'll go to see your grandfather as soon as we've finished in the general store, Mr. Bennett.''

''Call me Zachary, please,'' he instructed, waiting patiently as she caught a deep breath, and then smiling into her uplifted face as she looked at him. ''My name is Zachary,'' he repeated, and paused until she gave him a nod of agreement. He stepped aside then, his fingers releasing her, and she bent to Hope, touching her shoulder and guiding her down the sidewalk.

''Are you mad at the man?'' Hope asked innocently. ''He smiled at me, Honey. I think he's nice.''

''Yes, I suppose he can be,'' Honey replied, intent on reaching the general store and completing the shopping as soon as she could. What the elder Mr. Bennett wanted with her was a question she wasn't willing to address, she decided. Hope's pleasure would have to come first, and it seemed that spending some of their sparse supply of money would be a part of that undertaking.

Sugar was the first item she purchased, three pounds to be used for baking, Hope dancing excitedly as they discussed cookies and icing. She had not planned well for this shopping trip, she realized, forgetting the weight of their purchases, and so she revised her plans. Lard could only be purchased in a large bucket today, and Honey decided that butter would have to be her choice for shortening. She would need room to carry home the most important items, once she finished itemizing the foodstuffs needed.

"Baking powder?" she asked, and at Mr. Sanders's nod, she scanned her list. "Maybe a piece of bacon or ham?" It would make the soup more festive to have bits of meat with the vegetables, she decided. "And cornmeal, too. Three pounds, please." That would have to do. Already she was going beyond the amount of money she'd planned to spend. And the most important items were yet to be purchased.

"Hope?" She bent close to speak in her sister's ear. "Would you like to look at the candy and see if Mr. Sanders has any Christmas canes for our tree?"

Hope's eyes grew even more excited. "A tree? We're really going to have a Christmas tree?"

"We'll go out in the woods and see if we can find one tomorrow," her sister promised. "Now go look for canes."

Hope scampered across the store to where a counter held a variety of hard candy in jars. The more expensive varieties were wrapped or boxed, but Hope obviously was willing to bypass those for the brightly colored specimens displayed in glass. Honey turned back to the storekeeper who had watched the byplay with a smile.

"I need a few things for my sister," Honey said in a low voice. "A dress perhaps, something bright and cheerful." She scanned the shelves and spotted a likely object. "I'd like a slate and some chalk, too, sir," she told him.

With an understanding glance across the store, Mr. Sanders quickly wrapped the desired chalk and slate in brown paper, then lifted a glass case from the shelf. "I think any of these will fit your sister," he said, keeping a watchful eye out for the golden-haired child who was busily investigating his candy supply.

Honey chose a bright blue plaid, green-and-red stripes accenting its bold print. She held it up before herself quickly, careful to shield her movements lest Hope look her way, and then quickly refolded the garment. "This will be fine," she said, envisioning her sister's joy when she discovered the dress on Christmas morning.

Just in time, it was wrapped in paper and tied with string, as Hope skipped back to the counter, announcing she had found the white candy canes and a jar of ribbon candy that would certainly be appropriate for their celebration. "We can even hang the candy on our tree," the child announced, obviously pleased with her suggestion. Honey ignored the list of figures that fought to be tallied in her mind as she rashly asked Mr. Sanders to bag up a selection of each for them, the canes being of primary importance to Hope.

"They'll look just like the shepherds' staffs, won't they?" she asked. "I hope we can get a whole bunch to put on the tree."

"Well, aside from being white and the shepherds' staffs probably being brown, they'll certainly remind us of the shepherds' being in the stable," Honey said. She'd tried to implant some semblance of the meaning of Christmas in her sister's mind, bearing the weight of responsibility for her care and training during the past six months. And as if Hope read her mind, she looked up with tears in her eyes.

"I remember last year when Mama read us the story from the big Bible," she said, her mood subdued now. She leaned closer and whispered words that pierced Honey's heart with their simplicity. "If there really are guardian angels, I hope maybe Mama is mine, don't you?"

Honey's eyes closed as tears fought to be shed, and she whispered a quick response, bringing a smile to the child's lips. "I'm sure she is, sweetheart."

The candy was wrapped, the amount of their purchases counted out carefully from Honey's small leather change purse, and Mr. Sanders put everything into the sack Honey had retrieved from the pantry for just this purpose.

"Thank you," the storekeeper said with a wave. "You have a merry Christmas, you hear?"

They carried their sack to where the horse waited,

and Honey tied it behind the saddle, allowing half of the burden to hang on either side of the horse's haunches. Swinging carefully into the saddle, adjusting her skirt for modesty, she instructed Hope to stand on the sidewalk and lift her arms. It was a stretch but one she could handle, Honey decided, only to have the matter taken from her hands when a tall figure appeared from inside the newspaper office, and Zachary spoke a greeting.

"Why don't I give you a hand?" he asked, lifting Hope easily and reaching to deposit her in front of Honey.

"Thank you." With flaming cheeks, Honey faced him. "Were you waiting for us?" she asked. "Did you think I wouldn't do as your grandfather asked without your supervision?"

He bowed his head a moment and then lifted his eyes. She thought a touch of humor twisted his mouth, but his words were properly courteous. "I only thought to show you the way, in case you didn't know where his house is. I've already ridden there to let him know we're coming."

"I could have asked someone the direction," she said stiffly, embarrassed to be singled out in public. For indeed, several ladies had slowed their steps, obvious in their interest in the conversation. Honey saw more than one smile directed at her and she wanted only to ride away, unused to being the focus of attention.

"I'll get my horse and you can follow me," Zachary said nicely, and Honey was left to nod at his back as he strode across the street to where a saddled horse waited his arrival, right in front of the bank.

He turned the sleek creature toward her and smiled, his eyes crinkling just a bit as he waved his hand, motioning her to precede him. In moments he'd assumed a place beside her and spoken her name. "Honey?" At her quick glance in his direction, he shot a look at Hope and then smiled more widely.

"Is it all right if I call you by your given name?" he asked. "Or, if you like, I could make it Honoria." He seemed to be thinking, one brow rising, and then as if he'd decided something momentous, he shook his head. "No, I think Honey Belle will do. It suits you, I believe."

Again Honey felt the flush of embarrassment cover her cheeks, and she bit at her lower lip. "How far is it to your grandfather's house?" she asked, her voice strained.

"Just around the next corner," he said, apparently relenting from his teasing mood.

A woman wearing an enveloping white apron appeared at the door as they approached, and her smile was directed at Zachary. "Your grandfather is expecting you, Mr. Zachary." And then she looked intently at Honey. "And you, too, miss. And the little one," she added, including Hope in her greeting. "Won't you come on into the dining room, all three of you?"

The dining room? Honey stood by the big door, wondering at the summons, unwilling to march unannounced into the man's dining room, probably disturbing his noon meal. Beside her, Zachary nudged her forward.

"I need to close the door," he said in a low voice, and she hastily took two steps into the foyer, aware of the snow on her boots melting on the fine carpet.

"I don't want to carry snow into the house," she said in an undertone.

"You'd rather walk stocking-footed?" he asked with a cheerful grin.

She felt flustered by the turn of events and nodded, then as quickly, shook her head in confusion. He laughed aloud.

"You'll need to make up your mind, Honey Belle," he said quietly, taking her elbow once more in a grip that brooked no refusal. "Let me take your coat and hang it up on the hall tree." He looked down at Hope, and his smile was equally bright on her behalf. "And you too, sweetheart."

"That's what Honey calls me sometimes," Hope said, her fingers busy with unbuttoning her outer garment. She slid from it and gave it to Zachary, who held it before him and inspected it for a moment.

"Did you make it?" he asked Honey as he hung it on a peg.

"No, our mother did, last year," she answered, removing her own coat and giving it into his care. "She allowed enough room so Hope could get two years' wear from it.'' And wasn't that foolish, announcing their poverty to a man who probably bought a whole new wardrobe every year.

"I admire thrift," he said solemnly, filling another peg with her coat and then his own. He offered his arm and waited for her response. "Won't you come with me to see my grandfather? I believe he's waiting for us."

She had no choice, and Honey placed her fingers in the crook of his elbow, aware of the warmth of his flesh against her cold fingers. She felt them tremble and caught a glimpse of a shadowed look from his dark eyes as they traveled the foyer to where double doors stood open, inviting them into the dining room.

At the table, Mr. Bennett rose upon their entry and approached her. "I'm so pleased you could come to visit," he said. "I've asked my housekeeper to prepare a meal for us to share."

"I'm sure that wasn't necessary," Honey said quickly. "I don't want to put you to any trouble."

"You managed to make room for me in your home, Honey," the older man said quietly. "Please allow me the pleasure of making you welcome in mine."

CHAPTER THREE

THE DINING ROOM TABLE was laden with food, drawing Hope's interest from one bowl of vegetables to another, then to the platter of sliced beef sitting next to a basket of bread still warm from the oven. A tall glass of milk was beside Hope's plate, and a pillow had been provided to lift her a bit closer to table level. As if Christmas had already come, her smile sparkled as the child slanted a look at her sister.

For just a moment, envy such as she'd never known touched Honey's soul. She ached, recognizing that she would never be able to provide so elaborately for her sister. And then her conscience pricked her and she sighed. *Be thankful for what we have.* The words were her mother's, and Honey had made them her own during the past months. At least, for today, for this moment, Hope was enjoying the company of Joseph Bennett, an old man who had been kind to them both, a man she thought resembled Saint Nicholas.

"Would you like more sweet potatoes, Miss Honey?" Zachary held the bowl in one hand, offering it into her keeping, and Honey was drawn from her thoughts. "You looked for a moment like you were a million miles away," he said quietly as she accepted the serving dish.

She responded with a nod, and then, recognizing her earlier rudeness, she smiled directly at him. "I suppose I was," she admitted.

If his curiosity was aroused by her oblique response, he seemed to ignore it, not pressing her for details, but only passing the platter of beef in her direction.

"I hope you don't mind leftovers," Joseph said from the head of the table. "I didn't give Mrs. Hawkins much time to prepare our meal. She asked me to offer her apologies for the sparse assortment."

"It's lovely," Honey said with all honesty. "Much nicer than I'd have come up with at home. We appreciate your hospitality, sir."

Hope's gaze flitted over the room, lingering on pine boughs that decorated the mantel and mistletoe that dangled from a ribbon over the doorway. Her eyes dwelt at length on candles centered in fragrant circles of fir, their flame reflected in a mirror that served to magnify the effect. The child surveyed their surroundings as she ate, as if she must store in her memory each increment of festive display.

"It looks like Christmas has already come to your house," Honey said, her smile directed at Joseph. "Did you gather the branches yourself?"

He shook his head. "No, I think my handyman did. Homer does such things for me." He looked at the mantel and then at the centerpiece before him on the table. "Will you be decorating your house, too, ladies?"

Hope nodded. "Honey said we're to have a tree to decorate. We got candy canes and some shiny candy that looks like…" She curled her fingers together, and frowned. "I can't do it right."

"Are we talking about ribbon candy?" Joseph asked kindly. He glanced at the sideboard where a bowl of such delicacies sat side by side with more candles. "I like it, too," he murmured, bending closer to Hope. "Maybe we can share some after we eat." He caught Zachary's eye. "Or perhaps my grandson will spend a few moments with you and let you see the tree in the parlor that is waiting to be decorated. I'm sure he'll find more candy in there you might enjoy."

And then he looked directly at Honey, even as he spoke to her sister. "I have a few things to discuss with your sister, Hope. Perhaps when she finishes her meal, you'll excuse us for a while."

"I thought we were going to discuss this subject first, sir," Zachary said, his eyes narrowing as he looked across the table at his grandfather.

Honey ceased chewing the morsel of bread she'd just bitten off, aware of tension radiating between Joseph and his grandson. It crackled across the table, and she felt its impact as a living entity. For some reason, she'd been caught up in a conflict between the two men. As surely as she knew her own name, she was positive that Zachary did not approve of his grandfather's intentions.

The food she'd been enjoying ceased to tempt her palate, and she placed her fork on her plate. "We need to be getting home, sir," she said stiffly. "I don't mean to abuse your hospitality, but Hope and I have a lot to do before dark. I've promised her we'd go out and cut a tree to decorate, and there's baking to do if we want to hang cookies from the branches." She caught her breath as Joseph waved her to silence.

"I won't take up much of your time, my dear," he said. "I have an offer I wish to make, and you may want to consider it before you leave here."

"I'll tend to Hope." Zachary spoke the words in a terse statement of intent as he pushed his chair from the table, his eyes cold with an emotion Honey feared to explore. And yet the hand he held toward Hope was curved in welcome as he led the child from the dining room with a murmured word in his grandfather's direction. "Please don't be long. I must return to the bank, sir."

Joseph nodded agreement and set his plate aside. "Shall we talk here or would you like to come to my study?" he asked.

"This is fine," Honey said, her thoughts in turmoil as she watched Zachary leave the room with Hope in tow. The kindness he had shown during the past hour had vanished behind a stony visage, and she felt a sense of loss. And then Joseph cleared his throat and she turned to face him. His smile was kindly, his expression expectant as he leaned closer across the corner of the table, as if he ignored the taciturn behavior of his grandson.

"I told you while I stayed in your home that my housekeeper has been expressing concern over the difficulty in keeping up my home," he began, his eyes alight. "Mrs. Hawkins has two daughters who are vying for her affections, both of them trying to entice her to live with them," he explained. "And she has decided that if I can locate someone to take her place, she'd like to spend Christmas with her grandchildren, and allow her family to pamper her while she decides her future."

Honey shook her head. "I'm not sure what this has to do with me," she said, uncertain where his thoughts were heading, excitement rising within her as she began to suspect his direction. "Did you want us, Hope and me, to stay and take care of your house while Mrs. Hawkins spends time with her children?"

As soon as the words left her mouth, she felt embarrassment sweep over her. That she should be so presumptuous, so ready to leap to that conclusion was enough to have her bite her tongue in chagrin. "I'm sorry," she said quickly. "I had no right to assume such a thing."

Joseph shook his head and smiled, leaning toward her and whispering comfort. "I've always said that great minds run along the same track, my dear. I think you've been able to peer into my head and see what my plans for you are." He leaned back and folded his gnarled fingers over his waistcoat. "Do you think you'd be interested in staying here with your sister and helping me for a short while? I would pay you the going rate, and it would be doing me, and Mrs. Hawkins, a great favor."

Not to mention, Honey thought wistfully, what it would mean to Hope, and to herself, for that matter. The idea of being allowed to work in such a house was beyond her imagination. The thought of cooking Joseph Bennett's meals and making his life comfortable was bliss she could only envision. To live, even for a few short days, in a mansion such as this would make it a Christmas to remember for the rest of her life.

"When would you want us to come here?" she asked. "I have animals to consider, and I'm not sure—"

A wave of his hand, a peremptory gesture that guaranteed her silence, made her eyes widen and her words cease. In that moment, Joseph took on the persona of a man in power, a cloak he seemed to have discarded sometime in the past and now only donned when it suited him.

"I'll take care of all the small details," he said, his tone firm, his eyes gleaming with triumph. "I want you to go on home and pack your things. I'll send you in my sleigh, and Homer will drive you. I'll expect you back here in time to help prepare supper, my dear."

"Oh, I don't think—"

Again that hand lifted and waved in her direction, silencing her protests even as his smile softened the gesture. "We have no time to waste," he said, rising and stepping to her side to help her from her chair.

"I have supplies tied to my horse," she protested. "Things I'd planned to use to make cookies for Hope, and gifts I plan on giving her Christmas morning."

"We'll bring them in before you go," he said quickly. "Homer will tend to it before he harnesses my gelding. You can bake here to your heart's content, and we'll find room under the Christmas tree in the parlor for Hope's gifts."

She was stunned, unable to speak the words that raced through her mind. Broken phrases were whispered beneath her breath as he led her toward the parlor, and he chuckled as she muttered a litany of concerns. "My chickens…churning to be done… Bossy to be fed…" And then she swallowed the remainder as she beheld the huge tree standing before tall parlor windows.

It touched the ceiling, ten feet tall and at least seven feet wide at the base, and even at that it did not overpower the large room where it waited, unadorned, until loving hands should decorate it and place candles on the ends of its branches.

"Oh, my," she murmured beneath her breath, and then turned to look at the old man who had escorted her with gallant grace. "I've never seen anything so beautiful," she said humbly. "This will make Hope so happy."

"And you?" he asked, patting the hand she'd placed in the bend of his arm. "Will you be pleased to make my holiday enjoyable?"

"I'm certain she will," Zachary said sharply. "This is the opportunity of a lifetime for our Miss Morris, I'd say."

Honey's heart stuttered in her breast as dark brows gathered over equally dark eyes, eyes that bored into her with the power to banish her moment of joy and pierce her to the quick with his disdain. "I'm sure I don't know what you mean," she said quietly, unwilling to back from this confrontation.

"Be that as it may," he said, turning and striding from the parlor into the foyer where he could be seen donning his coat. "I'm sure you'll be happy to make yourself useful to my grandfather," he told her, walking back to the wide archway, hauling his gloves on as he shot her a look that chilled her.

IT SEEMED HOMER WOULD bring the cow and chickens back to town with him on a second trip, leaving them at the livery stable. Who would milk the cow and feed the hens was something Honey was not to be concerned about, according to Mrs. Hawkins, who bustled about the kitchen, showing her the various work-saving devices it contained. The lady was already packed to leave for her youngest daughter's home, her bags by the back door.

If things were moving too fast for Honey to keep up with, Hope seemed to have no such problem. She'd spent the late afternoon sitting on the parlor floor, her Saint Nicholas book in hand, inhaling the scent of the pine tree and finally curling up on a bit of expensive-looking carpet to sleep away the hours until supper should be served.

Honey looked in on her twice, and her heart seemed to melt within her as she viewed the sister who asked for so little from life and had received just about what she expected. The bonus of spending Christmas in such elegant surroundings was a gift Hope could barely understand, but she obviously intended to enjoy it to the fullest.

Supper was Honey's first attempt at cooking in Mrs. Hawkins's kitchen, and that lady nodded indulgently at Honey's queries, obviously pleased with the young woman who would be taking her place for a fortnight. A ham was delivered from the yawning oven, a pan of biscuits took its place, and potatoes were mashed to creamy perfection. The meal came together on the big wooden table that centered the large room, and then Honey carried the bowls of vegetables and the assembled main dishes to the dining room.

A pudding had been cooked according to Mrs. Hawkins's specifications, that lady announcing it was Mr. Bennett's favorite dessert. When all was ready, Honey went to the parlor door and called Hope and Joseph to supper. They'd barely crossed the foyer and reached the dining room when the big front door opened and Zachary stepped inside. The wind blew a gust of snow behind him and he quickly shut the door against the wintry blast.

"I didn't know you were coming for supper," Honey said quietly. "I'll go lay another place."

"Up until a few weeks ago, this was my home," Zachary said beneath his breath, so that the words carried no farther than Honey's hearing. "I still find a welcome here on occasion." He held his coat across his arm, his countenance cool as he took her measure.

"Come in, my boy," Joseph said from the dining room doorway, obviously unaware of the cutting remark. "Honey has outdone herself." At those words, Mrs. Hawkins peeked from the kitchen and waved a hand in farewell, and Joseph spoke to her quietly as Honey stepped closer to Zachary and took his coat, hanging it on the coat tree, an action he seemed to accept as his due.

She followed him into the dining room and found a plate and table service for him in the sideboard, holding a glass in her hand. "Would you like water?" she asked, feeling more a servant than she'd ever thought possible. The afternoon had gone so well, and Mrs. Hawkins had seemed to accept her as a part of the household so readily. Now she was out of place, wondering if she should eat in the kitchen.

"Water will be fine," Zachary said, sitting down in the designated place. Honey poured his glass full from the pitcher she'd placed on the table, then walked around to fill Joseph's glass and her own, as well. She stood for a moment behind the chair she'd assumed she would use, her hesitation obvious.

"Sit down, my dear," Joseph said kindly, his brow raising in inquiry as he shot a look at his grandson. "Is there something amiss?" he asked.

"No, I don't suppose so," Zachary answered, placing his napkin across his lap. "I didn't know we would be enjoying Miss Morris's company already. It didn't take long to have everything put into place, did it?"

"No," his grandfather said slowly, as if suddenly aware that tension ran rife between the other two adults at the table. "Homer took care of things nicely." He looked at Hope, whose hands were folded tightly in front of her chest. "Are you going to bless our food, missy?" he asked, to which Hope nodded and bent her head.

The prayer was brief and to the point, Hope obviously eager to begin her meal, and Honey reached to cut the little girl's meat and help her to vegetables and gravy for her potatoes. She buttered a biscuit and placed it on Hope's plate and then tended to her own, aware that her hunger had vanished.

Zachary seemed to have no such problem, filling his plate and eating in silence. And then he leaned back and observed her, as if he would dissect her beneath the lens of a microscope. "You've proved your talent in the kitchen, Miss Morris," he announced. "I believe I shall take my meals here while you're in residence. I haven't hired a woman to prepare meals in my home as yet, and the restaurant at the hotel across the street from the sheriff's office needs a new cook. I believe your offerings will fit my needs."

"I'm sure you'll be welcome," his grandfather said, a strange smile playing about his mouth. His glance traveled from Zachary to where Honey sat, her food almost untouched. "Aren't you hungry?" he asked, peering at the gravy that filled the hollow she'd formed in her helping of potatoes.

"I must have done too much tasting while I cooked," Honey said quickly. "I'll eat this later on." She stood and began clearing the table. "I'll bring bowls for the pudding, sir. It'll only be a minute." She walked to where Zachary sat and reached for his plate. From his body there emanated a faint scent of bay rum, an aroma of fresh air and another, more darkly intriguing, smell she could not recognize.

Lifting his plate, she became aware of his hand touching her skirt, his fingers brushing against the fabric, and she jerked from his reach. The knife and fork he'd placed across the edge of his plate slid to land in his lap and she uttered a soft gasp of horror. "I'm so sorry," she said, placing the dish on the edge of the table and reaching, without forethought, to scoop up the silverware from his lap.

Her fingertips brushed against the napkin, her hand grasped the heavy utensils and his own covered hers, lifting it from his person. "You can get in trouble that way, *my dear*," he whispered, his mockery evident as he used the term his grandfather was fond of.

"I didn't mean—" Honey closed her eyes, felt hot tears form, and in a moment had snatched up the stack of plates she'd gathered and fled to the kitchen. How had the man changed so rapidly from being a kind, considerate gentleman to a scalawag who seemed bent on causing her pain? She placed the dirty dishes on the sink board and bent her head. Behind her, the swinging door opened and even before she turned, she felt his presence there.

"Please," she whispered. "Please, just go. I'll pack our things and explain to your grandfather that this was a mistake. I'll take my sister and go back home."

He spoke from directly behind her, his footsteps silent as he crossed the room. "I don't think you will," he said harshly. "You've managed to inveigle your way into my grandfather's life very nicely, and you won't be leaving until you've served out the time you promised him. But understand that I'll be watching you every minute. He may be old, but he's sharp. You won't take advantage of him, not while I'm around."

She spun to face him, anger taking her breath. And then the words spurted forth, fury driving them. "I have no intention of harming your grandfather. He's a kind old man and I think the world of him. Where you get your ideas is beyond me, but let me tell you…''

Her index finger lifted to poke at his chest, and she wished she had the strength to push him farther from her.

''Let me tell you, I've never been so disappointed in anyone in my life as I am in you, Mr. Bennett. You have an evil mind, and you're not half the man your grandfather is. You should be ashamed of yourself, thinking nasty thoughts and accusing me of…of whatever it is you're accusing me of.'' Her words slowed as she ran out of steam, and her finger curled into her palm and then she stuffed her hands into the pockets of the apron she wore.

''Well, the lady has a sharp tongue,'' Zachary said softly, his eyes scanning her face, then dropping to settle against her breasts, their movement beneath her dress keeping time with the deep breaths she took. He touched her chin, lifted it with his cupped hand and bent close. ''If I'm to be so reviled, I'll have to give you something to be angry about.''

She leaned from him, but the sink behind her held her in place, and within a few seconds she was in his embrace, his other arm gripping her against his long body, her slender form trembling as his mouth touched hers, his lips and tongue tasting at will.

''No,'' she whimpered, pushing futilely against him. ''Don't do this to me.''

''And why not?'' he asked, his mouth covering hers, his breath blending with her own as he kissed her again, his lips softening as he lingered over her tender flesh.

She could think of no suitable reply, only the sure knowledge that her life had been forever changed in this moment. Between her own body and that of the man who held her flowed a current that baffled her with its power. His kiss gentle now, he pressed soft caresses against her lips, suckling for long seconds on her flesh, his teeth touching with care. His murmur was quiet, as if he would soothe her, yet his arms held her in an unbreakable embrace. His hands spread wide over her back, and long fingers traced the line of her spine, one palm finally holding the nape of her neck, not allowing her to escape his encompassing arms.

She'd seen her mother and father kiss, over the years had recognized that they shared a deep and abiding love, and had sometimes craved to know the depths of passion her parents shared. That such an encounter as this, with a man who she feared felt only anger toward her, could bring to life a desire that begged for the touch of his mouth against her own, was not to be believed.

Zachary was a scoundrel. Yet, his kiss melted her resistance, bringing to life within her sensations she had never suspected might be lying dormant beneath her flesh. Her breasts felt swollen, her legs trembled and she shivered as warm breath was blown against her throat. His tongue was damp, brushing against the tender skin of her jawline, his teeth were threatening the curl of her ear. And then he suckled the soft lobe and she trembled, breathing a protest against the fine fabric of his shirtfront.

Leaning back, he looked down at her from narrowed, dark eyes. "You're a tempting package, Honey Belle, but I'm serving notice on you. I won't have anyone take advantage of my grandfather."

Her eyes closed and she pushed at him. "I don't know what you mean." Her knees were weak, her lips trembling, and she could barely stand alone. His hands clasped her shoulders and he gripped her with long fingers that pressed with masculine strength into her flesh, holding her before him.

"I think I've made it clear. He's an old man and he's lonely. Don't think to make yourself a little nest here. I'll be watching you," he said quietly, looking down at her. She thought he was not totally untouched by the embrace, for his nostrils flared a bit and his eyes were dark with a smoldering emotion she could not fathom.

"What makes you think I'm out to do him harm? she cried softly. "I only want to help your grandfather for two weeks, until Mrs. Hawkins returns. I have no ulterior motives, Mr. Bennett."

"Haven't you?" he asked. And then he stepped back, releasing her from his hold. "We'll see, Honey Belle."

PERHAPS HE'D BEEN UNFAIR, Zach thought, entering his dark house an hour later. The girl had not asked for anything, only gone along with her benefactor's suggestion. And could anyone blame her? Zach pulled off his scarf and hat, then hung his coat over the banister as he passed the staircase.

In the dark, he strode through the open parlor doors, and in the moonlight sought the window, looking out on the snow-covered ground. For a moment, he wished he were still in the big house, where the two young females were bringing cheer to a lonely old man. Was he jealous? The thought pierced him and he shook his head, unwilling to consider such a petty idea.

Yet, for some reason he'd almost attacked Honey Belle, and he rued his sarcasm as he'd spoken to her, felt dismay as he recognized his harsh treatment of the young woman. Still, he couldn't find it in him to regret the kiss he'd taken—stolen, actually—from her soft lips. His own twisted as he recalled the instant recognition of a worthy opponent in her quick mind, her sharp tongue.

Perhaps he should take residence with his grandfather over the holidays, share the festivities certain to take place in the big house. Thrusting his hands into his trouser pockets, he looked toward the house, almost half a mile distant, not visible from where he stood, yet only too sharp an image in his mind.

They were probably in the parlor, the three of them. The tree was to be decorated tomorrow, and Hope had danced excitedly at the prospect. He'd even been drafted to climb to the attic to locate the decorations stored there. He shook his head in disbelief as he recalled agreeing to the plan. The noon meal would be eaten there, and then the attic expedition would take place, before he returned to the bank for the afternoon.

December 23

AN OVERLONG CONSULTATION with a customer and then papers to be signed before he could leave for his dinner made Zachary late arriving at his grandfather's home. He rapped once on the big front door, then opened it, stepping into the wide foyer. No temporary housekeeper or small child greeted him, only the silence of empty rooms.

"Grandfather? Are you here?" he called, his voice carrying to the downstairs rooms. His brow furrowed as he turned to the staircase, climbing rapidly to the second floor. Open doors lined the wide hallway, and he walked quickly past them, noting a doll against the pillows in the first room.

Hope's. He recognized the doll from the farmhouse and then noted with a quick glance the small shoes beneath the edge of the quilt, lined up neatly on the floor.

The next room was bright, draperies opened to the sunlight, the bed neatly made, a small assortment of items on the dressing table. A neatly folded bit of cotton lay tucked beneath a pillow, the edges of it in view. Probably Honey's sleeping gown—and at that thought he walked swiftly past the open doorway.

The stairway to the attic was at the very end of the upstairs hall, and that door stood open, too. From the area over his head he heard them, a child speaking, a woman's murmur, the low tone of his grandfather's laughter, and then the older man's voice, uttering instructions. Zachary climbed the stairs, feeling an intruder on the merriment taking place at the top of the narrow steps.

"Zachary! You're just in time," Joseph said, turning to greet him. Dust on the older man's sleeve proclaimed his foray into the shadowed eaves, and the smile on his face announced his pleasure with the proceedings he was in the midst of.

"We need a strong back to carry these boxes down the stairs. Honey has just given me warning that I'm not allowed to do any more climbing back and forth today."

Zachary stood at the top of the steep staircase and took in the trio before him. "I thought I was to do this chore after dinner," he said, his gaze sweeping over Honey, aiming his words in her direction.

"You were running a little late, so we decided to hold dinner until you got here, and then thought to use the time up here," Honey explained, her smile bright, her eyes shining, yet looking over his shoulder, as if she didn't fancy meeting his gaze.

"Go on downstairs, Grandfather," Zachary said quietly. "I'll tend to this." He walked forward, ducking as he allowed for the shallow height of the eaves, and then surveyed the boxes the three searchers had stacked close to the stairway. He lifted a small one from the top and handed it to Hope.

"Can you carry this one?" he asked kindly, smiling into her blue eyes.

"We've been having a treasure hunt," she told him, grinning with delight. "We found four boxes of ornaments, and Mr. Bennett sent Homer to the general store to buy all new candles for the tree." Zachary doubted if her excitement would allow for any appetite at the dinner table, her feet barely able to remain in one place as she told him of the morning's events.

"Well, if you'll carry this box and help my grandfather down the stairs, I'll help your sister bring the rest," he told the little girl, and then watched as his orders bore fruit. Joseph made his way carefully, Hope watching him descend, and she walked down the hallway beside him, her words floating upward as she amused the older man with her chatter.

"Now, Miss Morris," Zachary said, turning to Honey. "Shall we tend to the rest?"

"I think you're upset with me," Honey ventured, her eyes finally meeting his. "It wasn't my idea at all to have Mr. Bennett climb up these stairs. He was eager to get everything gathered together in the parlor for the tree trimming, and—"

"I haven't accused you of anything," Zachary said, interrupting her explanation.

She looked at him and her mouth lost its soft contours as she pressed her lips together. "Maybe not, but you seem willing to find fault with me, and I wanted to explain what happened before you decided to be angry with me again."

Zachary reached out to her, his index finger touching her lower lip, coaxing it from its firm stance. She inhaled sharply at his touch and turned her head aside.

"Please," she whispered. "Don't treat me with such disrespect."

His brow lifted as he watched her, enjoying the flash of anger she could not hide as her eyes narrowed and her chin lifted in defiance.

"I only wanted to see you smile," he said. "You were happy before I climbed the stairs. I heard you speaking, heard Hope giggling." *And heard my grandfather's laughter, a sound that's been missing from this house.* The thought of an old man's happiness being brought about by this young woman didn't sit well with him, Zachary decided. He'd rather have her smiles for himself, he thought, and then recognized again the emotion he'd set aside last evening.

He was jealous. Jealous of these few moments of joy his grandparent had gained by the addition to his household of two females. The sentiment was not becoming to him and he felt shamed by its existence. The warmth generated by the three of them, an old man, a child and this creature before him, lured him, and he felt himself caught on the hook of desire.

Not the desire for a woman, although that certainly seemed to enter into it. But the desire—the need— for family. A need never so obvious as at this time of the year. Being alone at Christmas was not a condition he relished. Yet, living in his own home, he faced that exact circumstance. His decision was made. In that instant, he recognized that he would pack a small bag and spend the next few days here.

"Here, take this one," he said, lifting the lightest of the bulky boxes and placing it in Honey's arms. "I'll get the rest." He held them securely, then motioned to the open stairway. "Go ahead. I'll be right behind you."

If Miss Honey had any objections, she could take them up with Joseph. And Zachary had a notion that his grandfather would stand behind him in this plan. For some reason the man was delighting in the course of events that had transpired over the past several days. He wouldn't deny his only grandson the opportunity to share in the holiday spirit within the walls of this household.

Dinner was served in moments, once the boxes were deposited in the parlor. Honey sent Hope in with a basket in which squares of fresh corn bread were heaped, then followed her through the doorway, carrying a soup tureen, holding the container between two heavy pads, lest the crockery burn her hands. Zachary stood and cleared a spot for it and lifted the lid. Steam escaped and with it the smell of ham and soup beans, a trace of onion and some other spice adding piquancy to the scent.

"I caught a whiff of that earlier," Joseph said, his napkin in his lap already, as if he anticipated his dinner being served. "I understand we have canned peaches for dessert. I asked Honey for something light for this meal, since tonight we'll begin our Christmas celebration with a supper more in keeping with the season."

"I think we can find enough to eat," Zachary said agreeably, unfolding his own napkin, then noticing Hope's patient look as she folded her hands, awaiting his silence.

"Hope?" Joseph prompted the child and she nodded, then solemnly bowed her head. Her words were simple, the prayer one she had obviously learned by rote, and he added his own whispered "Amen," to that of the other two adults.

Honey had outdone herself he decided, finishing his second bowl of soup a bit later. The corn bread was light yet abundant with flavor, the butter appeared fresh, with a faint imprint on top he didn't recognize. And the soup was a delight, thick with beans, carrots and onions, swimming with bits of ham from yesterday's meal.

He decided to bring forth his plan for his grandfather's opinion. Clearing his throat, he folded his napkin and leaned back in his chair. "I thought I might like to be here to help celebrate the holiday with you, sir,'' he began.

"I had expected you to join us for Christmas Eve,'' Joseph said. ''And then dinner the next day,'' he added, a slight smile nudging his lips upward.

Zachary nodded and shot a look toward Honey, who was listening intently. ''I thought I might just pack a small bag and move in for the next few days. I hate to miss anything,'' he admitted with a smile in Hope's direction.

She clapped her hands and aimed her smile at Joseph. ''Isn't that a good idea?'' she asked. And then she looked at Honey, whose face bore a look of surprise. ''Don't you think it'll be fun to have Mr. Zachary here for Christmas?'' the child asked eagerly.

Honey closed her mouth, allowing a small nod to express her silent opinion.

"Will that be too much work for you, Miss Honey?'' Zachary asked, as if he had second thoughts, knowing as he spoke that he was putting her on the spot.

"Of course not,'' she said quickly. ''I'll prepare you a room this afternoon.''

"Good.'' His voice smacked with satisfaction. ''I used to occupy the first room on the left at the top of the stairs. Will that be a problem?'' he asked. ''Or is that one yours?'' he added, knowing exactly which room she'd chosen for herself.

"No, mine is across the hall, next to Hope's,'' she said, and her look in his direction was chilly. *As if you didn't already know.* As clearly as if she had spoken the words aloud, he got the message and allowed himself a grin of satisfaction.

''Well, that's settled then,'' Joseph said, rubbing his hands together. ''Now, let's talk about decorating the tree tonight.''

CHAPTER FOUR

A LADDER WAS REQUIRED to reach the topmost branches, Zachary designated as the tree trimmer for those high areas. But first he'd lifted Hope high above his head, his hands gripping her firmly as she balanced amid the tallest branches, settling the star over the pinnacle. Candles surrounded it, tipping each branch, so that when they were lit they would reflect from the tin surface of the star.

They'd taken turns handing him the smaller ornaments, Hope tilting her head first one way, then the other, as he patiently placed each sparkling ball, every glittering spun-glass icicle, until the last shimmering globe was exactly where she ordered it to be hung. And then he stepped from the ladder and folded it, laying it aside as they moved on to the trimming of the lower branches.

It seemed that the candles must be placed just so, Joseph supervising their attachment to the ends of each branch. Boxes were opened, one after another, Honey finally surrendering to the wonder that filled her to overflowing as the shimmering bits of Christmas came to light. She touched them with reverence, aware that Joseph cherished each memento of his past. He spoke of other years, other times, and Honey listened to the undertones that gripped her heart as he spoke of his wife and their single offspring, Zachary's father.

"I remember the last Christmas before they went east to New York," he said. "It was while you were in school, Zack." His pause was long, and Honey thought he subdued tears. "They haven't been back since," Joseph said quietly. "Life in the city was more to your mother's liking, I fear."

"She came from there originally," Zachary reminded his grandfather. "Her family is there, and my father lives to please her."

"Well," Joseph told him with a brilliant smile, "I can only say that their loss has been my gain. I'll always be grateful that you decided to take my offer."

Zachary looked around at the parlor, his gaze filled with pride as he viewed the portraits of his forefathers on the walls, going back two generations and more. He was surrounded by the bits and pieces that made up his family's history. Honey thought him most fortunate to be so immersed in the keepsakes that told a story he'd probably heard from his earliest years.

"I'm happy to be here, sir," Zachary said, his arm reaching out to clasp the old man's shoulders. "I wouldn't have missed this for the world." His eyes sought out Honey where she stood in the shadows, a box of decorations in her hands, her heart in her throat. He was limned in the light of the fireplace, his eyes reflecting the glow of lamplight overhead, his mouth softening with a smile as he caught her eye.

"Have you more ornaments there for us to hang?" he asked, crossing to where she stood. "Here, why don't I hold the box and you do some of the work for a change?" he murmured, teasing her gently.

"I'll help, too," Hope offered, approaching with an eagerness that warmed Honey's heart. If they never again celebrated this wondrous holiday in such a way, Hope would forever have this memory to cherish.

"Why don't we decide where they should be hung, and you put them in place?" she said to Hope, glancing up at Zachary for approval.

"That sounds like a good plan to me," he said agreeably. "Why don't I hold you up for the ones you can't reach?" And so saying, he lifted Hope into his arms and motioned to Honey to step closer. A gleaming ball, with tinsel captured inside the clear glass sphere, was hung at Zachary's eye level, and then a sparkling, glitter-covered icicle was put in place a bit lower.

They worked together, laughing, following Joseph's instructions as he directed the proceedings, hanging box after box of family treasures, until finally they were left with only the lead tinsel to untangle and drape over the branches. Again Zachary put up the ladder and carried a handful to the top of the tree, Honey watching anxiously from below, lest he lose his balance as he reached to place each strand carefully in place.

He climbed down after decorating the highest branches, and together they finished the lengthy task, taking care to distribute them evenly over the fragrant boughs. Hope clapped her hands with glee. "I was afraid we wouldn't have enough to go around," she said, standing back, the better to take in the majestic beauty before her.

"Shall we light the candles?" Hope asked, and Joseph shook his head.

"No, tonight we only decorate. Tomorrow night we go to church and then light the candles afterward for the first time."

"We'll go to church at night?" the child asked, turning to her sister. "I don't think we ever went to church at night, did we?"

Honey shook her head. "No, we always spent Christmas Eve at home. It was too far to drive into town, and Mama always—"

"I know. I remember," Hope said, finishing her sister's litany of events. "She always read the Christmas story from the Bible, and then we had special treats before we went to bed." Her eyes filled with tears and she turned to Joseph, as if for comfort. "My mama gave me my favorite book on Christmas Eve last time."

"The Saint Nicholas story?" he asked, holding out his hand to her, inviting her to come to him. He lifted her onto his lap and she curled in his embrace, clutching the book to her chest. His gnarled fingers brushed her golden curls as he spoke. "I'm not your father, Hope, and I certainly can't be your mother, but I'd be happy to read the book with you tonight, if you like."

She straightened on his lap and looked up into the kindly face. "I think you're my guardian angel, Mr. Joseph." Honey turned aside, unable to hide the tears that gathered in her eyes, unwilling to spoil Hope's moment of pleasure with the grief that welled up within her own aching heart. Beside her, a tall figure shielded her from the child's sight, and Zachary's murmur was low, directed only to her hearing.

"Your sister has made Grandfather happy, you know. This is the most enjoyment he's had in several years."

"You have no idea how much he's given us," Honey whispered, and then looked up at him quickly. "Not in money or anything tangible," she amended, "but the memories Hope will always hold dear because of our being here for Christmas."

"I owe you an apology," he said quietly, turning to glance aside as Hope's laughter caught their attention. She was turning a page in the book, and Joseph waited until she prodded him into reading the next words. And then Zachary finished his thought.

"I thought you might have motives that were not totally…" As though he could not phrase his thoughts, he allowed the sentence to remain unfinished, and Honey took it up, repeating his words.

"Motives that were not totally pure?" she asked. "You thought I would take advantage of an old man who only wanted to help us?"

"Put that way, I seem to be a real doubting Thomas, don't I?"

"I suppose I can't blame you," Honey said. "I might have thought the same, had the shoe been on the other foot." She looked back at the tree, where the lamplight reflected from over a hundred precious ornaments. "I won't take advantage of your grandfather, Zachary. I'm standing here counting my blessings, acknowledging that they are as numerous as the stars in the sky or maybe, to be more realistic, as beautiful as the stars and candles and icicles we've hung on the tree tonight.

"And when the time comes for us to leave, I'll go with memories I might never have had if Joseph hadn't come to our door three nights ago. I'll always be thankful he got lost that night." She looked aside at Hope, her head tucked against Joseph's waistcoat while he read the story aloud for probably the third time in the past days.

"Hope is convinced he's her own special angel, you know."

"I heard her say that," Zachary said. "I didn't know what she meant."

"Up until three nights ago, Hope had lost much of her innocence. She declared that Saint Nicholas was just a story and that angels didn't exist. I fear she grew up in a hurry when our parents lost their lives last July.

"Joseph coming to us was like a miracle for Hope. He did something for her that I can't begin to describe. She really loves him."

Zachary nodded. "I can see that. And he loves her. He's gone to the orphanage every year, not only at Christmastime, but throughout the year at various times, carrying treats to the children. I think he wishes he'd had more grandchildren." His laughter was low as if he feared to disturb the book reading.

"He's told me for the past year that I must find a wife. He wants great-grandchildren born into this house, he says. He wants to leave his legacy to his family, and it seems I'm all he has left here."

"Have you been looking for a bride?" Honey asked, even as the words caused a pang of sorrow to touch her. If only she were of his class, a more sophisticated woman, fit for a man such as Zachary Bennett.

"A bit," he admitted. "But there's been no one that met my grandfather's standards. I've kept company a bit with one young woman. Perhaps you know Ellen Phillips?" And at the quick shake of Honey's head, he continued.

"I doubt you'd have met her. In any event, I don't think I'll be seeing her again. She's set her sights on marrying a man with a tidy bank account, and her motives leave something to be desired. Or so my grandfather tells me. I fear he's not enamored of her.''

Honey laughed aloud. ''You can't be telling me that your candidates must come up to his qualifications.''

Zachary's smile was rueful. ''He's pretty fussy about women, you know.'' His gaze touched Hope again, and his words were filled with good humor. ''Perhaps I'll wait for your sister to grow up.''

Honey's heart raced as she heard his teasing, recognizing it as being just that. Zachary would find his bride one day. For surely, in a town like Fort Collins, there were numerous women fit to be his wife. No doubt, if the call were to be sounded, the line would stretch from one end of the city to the other. He was handsome, his manners were those of a gentleman, and even given his bent for touching her and the day in the kitchen when he'd kissed her, she respected him. He was a man any woman would be happy to see waiting before the altar on her wedding day.

Indeed, she thought wistfully, she would give much to be at the head of that line of contenders for the honor of being Mrs. Zachary Bennett. Her honest heart knew better, even as it ached for what would never be, and she turned away from him, leaving behind the hope she'd harbored for those few moments.

''I think it's time for bed,'' she said, standing beside the chair where Hope was snuggled in comfort. Joseph looked up, his finger holding the place in the book they'd shared. His white hair and beard shone in the lamplight and his eyes twinkled as if he knew a secret that was bursting to be divulged. And then he simply smiled.

"One last page to go, Miss Honey. Then Hope and I will both be ready to climb those stairs. We've had a long day." His tilted head begged her permission, and Hope looked up expectantly.

"All right," Honey said, stopping beside the chair to place her hand on Joseph's shoulder. "I'll just close up the kitchen and be sure the door is locked."

She left the parlor and walked down the passageway, aware of Joseph's voice as he spoke the words that ended the long poem, drawing them out slowly. "'Happy Christmas to all...'" he said, his hesitation long, and she smiled as she opened the kitchen door.

Entering the dark room without hesitation, she left the door open behind her. The moonlight shone through the windowpanes, and she pushed the lace curtains aside to peer upward to where the sky was clear, the snow clouds blown to the east. The back door was cold to the touch, and she shivered as she slid the bolt into place with a click.

Lifting the stove lid, she peered inside where coals glowed beneath a layer of ash, then turned to leave the comfort of the warm kitchen. In two short days she'd come to love this place, she thought wistfully, come to be at home here. Her sigh whispered in the shadows of the big room and she turned toward the passageway door.

A tall form leaned against the jamb, bringing her to a halt. "It's only me," Zachary said quietly. He straightened and approached her, blocking the lamplight from the foyer beyond. "Are you all right?" he asked. "Your sigh sounded a bit sad, Honey."

"I'm fine," she said. "Just checking the stove before I go upstairs." He blocked the doorway and she hesitated, uncertainty slowing her steps. "Did you want something?" she asked, and looked up, seeking to peer into his eyes. They were shadowed, heavy lidded, and he was silent for a moment, then reached out a hand to her.

"I think I do," he said, his voice a low murmur. "But I fear I'll frighten you, and that would be the last thing I'd want to do."

"I don't frighten easily," she said, and knew her words were akin to a lie. Her attraction to Zachary bewildered her. She felt a warmth radiate from him, beckoning her to move closer to its source. Here in this kitchen, just two days past, he'd kissed her and she'd begged him to desist.

Tonight she would welcome his kiss, would allow him to hold her close, should he so choose. Because he'd been kind to her and to Hope? Or perhaps because he'd melted her resistance to his appeal with teasing words and the offer of a joyous Christmas beneath his grandfather's roof. She watched as his hand lifted to her cheek and with a sigh, she leaned into its warmth.

"I was not kind to you the last time I did this," he said quietly. "I'd like to make up for it, Honey."

She tilted her head back, her eyes closing as his head bent to accept the gift she offered. It was but a whisper of lips meeting, brushing a welcome, his moving a bit as if he murmured beneath his breath. His palm cradled her cheek, his other hand rising to clasp her face between long fingers, and she was held immobile by the tenderness of his caress. Her hands circled his wrists, fingers curling to grasp his strength, and she pressed her lips to his, then parted them to catch a breath.

"Honey." He spoke her name and it warmed her mouth with its sound. She tasted his flavor, inhaled his scent, and then held her breath as his tongue edged carefully, gently, past the soft, tender flesh of her parted lips, circling the inner surface. Trembling, she knew a moment of shivering delight, and then he retreated, brushing once more with a gentle pressure of firm lips against her own.

"I've taken advantage of you," he whispered. "You're not angry with me?" She thought amusement tinged the query, and she stiffened. She could not bear it if he should ridicule her, if he thought her gauche and childish.

"No. I'm not angry."

"Nor frightened?" His hands released her, reluctantly she thought, and he stepped to one side of the doorway, as if he allowed her room to escape the kitchen. She yearned for the touch of those long fingers, those wide palms, and her fists clenched at her waist lest they betray her by lifting to his chest.

"No, you don't frighten me," she said. "You did, the other time. But you were angry then. At first, anyway."

"I'm not angry with you now," he told her. "Puzzled, perhaps, is a better word. I don't understand what it is about you that I find so hard to resist, sweetheart. You're too young for me, too innocent and far too dangerous. I'm afraid I've found something I wasn't expecting, something I wasn't looking for."

She shook her head. "I'm young, and perhaps innocent, but I'm just an ordinary woman, Zachary. There isn't anything dangerous about me."

"No? I'd have to disagree with you, my dear. As for being ordinary, you're far from bearing that dubious distinction," he said, and she thought his voice developed an edge, as if he withdrew from her, an invisible barrier forming between them. "I think we'd better go upstairs. Your sister will be waiting."

"Yes, all right." She walked past him and then turned back, at an advantage now with the lamplight behind her, his face no longer in shadow. His mouth twitched and his gaze narrowed.

"What is it, Honey?"

He was once more the aloof gentleman. Gone was the teasing, tempting glimpse of heaven she'd had within her grasp for those few short moments. She'd surrendered to temptation, welcomed his kiss, and

he'd no doubt already regretted his lapse of gentle-
manly behavior. "I only want to know what time you
need to eat breakfast in order to be at the bank on
time," she said quietly.

"When I'm at home, I usually eat at the restaurant
around eight," he said. "Since I'll probably be walking from here—seven-thirty will do. If you don't
want to be up so early, I can—"

"No," she said, interrupting quickly. "I don't
mind fixing your breakfast. I'll be up long before
that, anyway."

He followed her to the broad staircase. "I've
checked the front door, and my grandfather and Hope
have long since gone up," he said. He paused in the
dimly lit foyer, then reached up to lift the globe,
blowing out the faint flame before he offered her his
arm. She placed her fingertips in the bend of his elbow and climbed the stairs beside him. In the hallway a table held a lamp, its flame subdued beneath
a dark shade.

"My grandfather must have lit it for us," Zachary
said, blowing gently within the chimney, leaving
them in quiet darkness, save for the soft glow from
Hope's room. The child was perched on the bed, a
candle burning at her bedside.

"I was waiting for you," she said, spying her sister. "Are you gonna help me get undressed?"

Honey went to her, crossing the room quickly.
"Of course I am," she said, sitting next to her, smiling as a yawn caught Hope unaware and she lifted

her hand to cover her mouth. Zachary stood unmoving in the doorway, and Honey remembered her manners.

"Thank you," she said quietly, and noted his lifted eyebrow as if he wondered at her polite words. Not for the kiss, for those moments of intimacy in the kitchen, she wanted to say. But for the evening as a whole. And perhaps he knew what she meant, for he nodded then, and smiled.

"You're most welcome, Miss Honey. I spent an enjoyable evening."

She felt a flush touch her cheeks, knew the heat of yearning as his eyes touched her with male appreciation, with a warmth she was only beginning to understand. And then Hope slid from the bed and ran to Zachary, reaching up to him with the certainty of a child who knows she will be welcomed.

"If you bend down, I'll kiss you good-night," she offered. "Everybody needs a good-night kiss. My sister says so."

"Does she?" Zachary looked over Hope's head toward Honey. "And who kisses your sister good-night?" he asked, bending for the promised caress.

"Me, silly," Hope told him, giggling as she stood on tiptoe and placed a kiss on his cheek. "I always kiss her before I go to sleep. First she helps me say my prayers and then she tucks me in, and then I kiss her good-night."

"That sounds like a good plan to me," Zachary said.

Honey's heart beat like a tom-tom in her chest as he smiled, his eyes warmed with a dark fire. Danger lurked in the shadows of this house, she decided, most of the peril she faced coming from within her own soul, where a yearning to be near Zachary Bennett had been born on this night. He'd seduced her with his kindness, throwing her off guard, then had tempted her with the warmth of his kiss, luring her into the circle of his embrace. And in all of that had managed to totally confuse her.

He was beyond her, and though he might desire her, he would look elsewhere for a wife to share his life. Honey Belle Morris was not born and bred to be the bride of a man like Zachary. She'd might as well realize she was facing a broken heart if she allowed herself to wish for that which she could never have.

She held out her arms to Hope and lifted her to her lap, her fingers running through the curls, removing the ribbon from the child's hair. And when she looked up again, the doorway was empty.

December 24

''WE DON'T HAVE PRESENTS for Mr. Joseph and Mr. Zachary,'' Hope whispered, tugging at Honey's apron to speak more closely to her sister's ear. ''What will we do, Honey? I just saw a present under the tree with my name on it, and it has a red ribbon all the way around it.'' She cupped her hand and murmured the secret with excitement filling each syllable. "It's a really big box, Honey. What do you suppose it is?"

Honey's breath caught as the message became clear. If they were to spend Christmas Day in this house, they must somehow do as Hope expected. It would mean a walk to the general store, where they could only aspire to find the sort of gifts suitable for two such gentlemen as Joseph and Zachary.

Breakfast was over, Joseph settled for the morning in his study with his books at hand, and she had a free hour or two before it would be time to begin the noon meal. They would eat lightly again today, on Joseph's orders, since Christmas Eve supper would be a festive occasion.

Honey again felt the tug of Hope's eager fingers on her apron and she looked down at the child, aware she hadn't paid proper attention to her sister's query.

"I can't imagine what's in the box, Hope. But I agree that we must do something about gifts for the two of them." She lifted her hands from the dishwater and wrung out the cloth she'd been using. "As soon as I wipe off the table and hang up my apron, we'll get our coats and go for a walk."

Hope skipped from the kitchen, calling back over her shoulder. "I'll get my hat and gloves from upstairs and put on my boots, Honey."

"And I'll try to scour up some cash," Honey murmured under her breath. She thought of the money set aside for the mortgage payment, the amount insufficient to cover the total due by a long shot, and her mind was made up. One way or another, she'd make this the best Christmas Hope had ever had, probably the most wonderful holiday season either of them could wish for.

She walked with purpose, up the stairs and into her room, kneeling on the floor in front of the small valise she'd brought from the farmhouse for their visit. The money was there, tucked into an envelope beneath her few items of clothing. She held it in her hand, then took two gold coins from its contents and slipped them into her pocket. It was akin to sealing her fate, she thought. Using this money effectively put to rest the notion of meeting the mortgage in two weeks.

The valise was closed quickly, before she could change her mind, and in moments she'd left the house, Hope's hand in hers as they walked toward the general store.

Mr. Sanders left them to sort through a bin of fine Irish linen handkerchiefs, and Honey chose half a dozen, deciding that three for each gentleman would be an appropriate gift from Hope. They were the best he carried, Mr. Sanders had said, and only thirty-five cents each. For that price they came, three to a box and Hope was delighted with the thin tissue that lined the cardboard and then folded nicely over its contents.

A container of driving gloves caught her eye, and Honey picked up one pair after another, holding them against her own slender hand as she considered the sizes she would need. Mr. Sanders returned to watch her dithering and approved her choice. At ninety-five cents a pair, they were a bargain he told her. She watched as he wrapped each pair in tissue and searched beneath the counter for boxes that would fit.

"Will that be all, ladies?" he asked, his curiosity obvious. "Your gentlemen friends will approve of your gifts, I'm certain," he told Honey.

"I'd like some pipe tobacco, also," she said, thinking of the scent Joseph's clothes held within their fibers. He sat in his study during the afternoon and enjoyed his pipe, and it seemed fitting she should include that small luxury for him. A two-ounce bag was thirty cents and with a smile, Mr. Sanders wrapped a pipe and included it with the purchase.

"Is this for the elder Mr. Bennett?' he asked, and at her smile, he nodded his head. "It's his usual choice, young lady. He'll like it."

It seemed that the fact of their presence in the Bennett household was common knowledge, Honey decided, and she sought to clarify the situation. "We're staying there to lend a hand while Mrs. Hawkins goes to visit her daughter for Christmas," she said quietly.

"That's what I heard by way of the grapevine," Mr. Sanders replied. "You two young ladies lost your ma and pa some time back, didn't you?"

"Last July," Honey told him, glancing down at

Hope, fearful lest she catch the drift of the conversation.

"Maybe old Mr. Bennett will keep you on at the house," Mr. Sanders suggested, reaching for a scrap of paper to scribble down the prices of Honey's purchases. "Mrs. Hawkins has been talking for a while now about taking it easy and moving in with some of her young'uns."

A vision of heaven couldn't have been clearer in Honey's mind than the thought of living in the big white house with Joseph Bennett, tending to his welfare and keeping his house spick-and-span. "I don't know about that," she said quickly. "I think this is just to be for two weeks, sir."

"Well, he could do a whole lot worse than to have a nice capable young lady like you there to look after things," Mr. Sanders said, wrapping the boxes in brown paper and tying them with a length of string. "That'll be four dollars and thirty cents, young lady," he said, accepting the five-dollar gold piece she offered.

He counted her change back with care and then smiled down at Hope, whose attention had been on the comings and goings of several customers. "Why don't you go choose yourself a candy stick?" he said, turning Hope in the direction of the candy display across the store.

Her smile was bright as she whispered her thanks and skipped across the wooden floor. "Thank you,

Mr. Sanders,'' Honey said, repeating the words and gathering up the package. "I appreciate your help."

"No problem there," he said. "You have a nice Christmas, you hear? I suppose you're going to church tonight."

Honey nodded, keeping a close eye on Hope as she edged from the counter. "Yes, we're going with Mr. Bennett."

Another customer caught his attention, a young woman who cast a derisive glance in Honey's direction before she turned her gaze onto the storekeeper. Honey's cheeks flamed as she wondered at the spiteful look she'd received, and then she hurried to where Hope stood before tall glass jars of candy sticks.

"I don't know which one I want," the child said, turning to grin up at her sister. "I think the green one will be good, don't you?"

"It's probably wintergreen flavor," Honey told her, reaching to open the jar and lift a long specimen from its depths. With the candy clutched firmly in one hand, Hope offered the other into Honey's keeping and together they left the store, Honey feeling a chill run the length of her spine as she looked back at the young woman.

"What can we wrap our presents with?" Hope asked, her eyes wide as horses filled the street and buggies and wagons vied for space before the stores.

"I saw a box of tissue paper in the attic when we brought down the decorations," Honey said. "I don't think Joseph will care if we use a bit of it for wrapping.'' She'd seen an assortment of colors there, and recalled extra bits of ribbon tucked into the box with the tissue. As soon as the potatoes were peeled and the vegetables put on to simmer, she'd climb the stairs and seek out the box beneath the eaves.

Supper was a festive affair, a roasted chicken centered on a large platter, surrounded by whole carrots and potatoes, with carmelized onions glistening in the lamplight. Applesauce from a mason jar in the pantry accompanied the meal, along with fresh bread and the last round of butter Honey had brought with her from the farm. She'd have to find fresh cream somewhere in the next few days. There must be a churn in the pantry; and even though there weren't any cows in any of the yards she'd noted during her walk to the store, there must be somewhere to buy the makings of butter.

Maybe she could walk to the livery, where her own cow had been taken. She frowned as she stirred the gravy, wondering how folks in town handled such things. Perhaps they all bought eggs and milk from the general store, where her own butter had been sold.

At any rate, there were only half a dozen eggs left in the crock and a quart of milk in the icebox. The icebox—another marvel she'd found to wonder at. The iceman came to the back door twice a week, and carried in a chunk of the stuff, sawdust clinging to it as it swung from huge tongs, depositing it in an upright, well-insulated wooden box, where food could be kept cool for days on end.

Living in the city was a far cry from the farmhouse where she'd spent her life. The water came into the house, a pipe bringing it in from the backyard, and she had only to turn the handle on the spigot to have a ready stream of water at her disposal. Carrying hot water from the reservoir on the side of the stove, she dumped in a bit of soap and then watched as the spigot released cool water into the pan, splashing into the sink with enough pressure to make suds in the dishpan. Such luxury was unheard-of so far as she was concerned, having carried water from a pump in the yard for all of her life, until just a year ago when her father had installed a length of pipe, extending it to the kitchen, where a red pitcher pump had seemed the epitome of labor-saving devices.

She sighed, looking around her at the brightly lit room, then plunged her hands into the dishwater, making short work of the plates and silverware. The men would be ready to leave for church soon, and she must change her own dress and Hope's and then use a hairbrush on Hope's curls. The temptation to allow her sister to open the new dress was urgent, but Honey resisted. They would be wearing their coats anyway, and it would spoil the surprise if she gave the dress to her now.

"I've had the sleigh brought around," Zachary said from the kitchen doorway. "How much longer will you be?"

Honey turned quickly, his words catching her unaware. "Just a minute more," she said, dumping the dishpan and wringing out the cloth. She dried her hands on the towel and took off her apron. "There. I'm finished," she told him, unwilling to look directly into his face, her memory of last night's encounter within these walls still fresh in her mind. But Zachary seemed only too aware of her reticence, and he closed the kitchen door, then blocked the entryway, leaning with casual ease against the doorjamb.

"Are you upset with me?" he asked. "Did I make you angry last night?"

She shook her head. "No, of course not."

"Then look at me, Honey." The words gave her no room to quibble. He stood in the path of escape and ordered her attention to be directed at him, and she shrugged, giving in to the inevitable.

"I'm looking," she said, tilting her chin, her lips thinning as she faced him. She felt a tress of hair against her cheek just seconds before he reached to tuck it behind her ear. "I need to brush my hair and get Hope ready for the church service," she told him, hoping he would take the hint and move from her path.

"I won't keep you," Zachary said quietly. "I just wanted to tell you that I appreciate you being here. My grandfather is grateful for your help, and I haven't eaten so well in months. Mrs. Hawkins is a passable cook, but you put her in the shade, Honey. You've made this Christmas very special for an old man.'' And then he bent to brush his lips across her forehead.

''And for a younger man, too,'' he said. ''I don't know when I've enjoyed myself so well. Thank you for staying on and lending a hand.''

Honey nodded, unable to speak. Zachary was being kind, and that was all. His kiss was warm but free of passion. Just a simple salute from a man to a woman he appreciated. And yet, her forehead felt as if it held a brand, as if his lips were imprinted there, and she felt her cheeks burn as she sought a reply.

''You're welcome,'' she said, swallowing the lump in her throat. ''But you'd better let me past, Zachary. Hope is waiting for me to get her ready.''

He stood aside and she pushed the door open, aware of his warmth, inhaling the scent that clung to his skin and clothing, a clean smell she'd come to associate with him over the past days. Brimming with excitement, she carried Zachary's fresh, teasing aroma with her, and hastened up the stairs to where her sister waited.

CHAPTER FIVE

Christmas Eve

THE CHURCH BELLS TOLLED majestically, blending their sounds in the silence of this most blessed of nights. From all over town families walked, rode in sleighs or buggies toward candlelit buildings where they entered, preparing for the joy of Christmas. And then, after carols had been sung, the ancient story had been told and children had performed in pageants, they returned to their homes.

Somehow, Honey had found herself tucked into the front of the sleigh beside Zachary, with Hope and Joseph occupying the back seat. The air was crisp, the stars bright overhead and snowflakes formed patterns on the woolen lap robe that warmed her. She watched the man whose capable hands held the reins, recalling their touch against her face, their strength against her waist, and wished with all her heart that this night might never end.

She'd savored every minute, stored up memories enough to last for the lonely months ahead when she would once more have only herself to rely on. Deep inside her heart she found the courage to admit, if only to herself, that she felt more than friendship, more than gratitude toward Zachary for his kindness. A love she had never before known bloomed within her, nourished by his gentle touch, his kiss, the moments they'd shared in the dark.

She felt the nudge of his arm against hers, and her gaze skidded from his hands on the reins to the smile he bent in her direction. "You're looking solemn," he said quietly. "This is a night for joy, Honey."

"I know," she said. "And I'm all wrapped up in being thankful for every minute of it. I've never had so wonderful a Christmas."

"It's barely begun," he reminded her. "We have the tree lighting and gifts to open when we reach home."

"You don't open presents on Christmas morning?" she asked. "Hope will be delighted, you know. She's been on tiptoes all day, waiting to see what's in that big box under the tree."

"I hope she likes it," Zachary said. "I chose it myself."

"She's easy to please." *And so am I.* One kiss, the warmth of his arms around her, private moments, all things he could so easily bestow on a willing female should he so desire. And she was willing, Honey admitted. Far too willing, if the truth be known. Her mother would be appalled by her daughter's thoughts, if she could know how Honey's hungry heart yearned for pleasure at the hands of Zachary Bennett.

"Out you go," Zachary said, climbing down from the sleigh and turning over the reins to Homer. He lifted Honey from the seat and turned to offer a hand to Joseph. Hope clambered out last, her laughter sounding like music on the air, her eyes brilliant with anticipation as they walked up to the front porch. Zachary held the door open and they trooped into the foyer, coats being shed, boots loosened and deposited on a mat beneath a bench.

"I'll get the wassail," Honey offered. "Will we have it in the parlor?"

"Yes," Joseph told her. "Hope and I will get the pole and begin lighting the candles. Zachary can lend a hand in the kitchen."

Lamps were lit already, Homer having prepared for their arrival, and in minutes Honey had the tray ready, cups and plates stacked, napkins and an assortment of cookies arranged. Zachary offered to carry the wassail bowl, and together they set off for the parlor. The tree was huge in the shadows, and already almost half the candles were ablaze. A long pole carried the flame and Joseph held it upright, lending the fire to the white tapers.

"I'll finish, if you like," Zachary said, depositing the punch on the library table. Joseph gave up the task and retreated to his chair, holding out a hand to Hope as he sat down. She stood beside him, her small hand almost lost in his palm, her eyes fastened on the multitude of lights that reflected in the glass and crystal ornaments.

Zachary reached for the topmost branches, completing the circuit of the magnificent tree, and then blew out the flame. Honey watched him, noting the firm line of his jaw, the strength of his broad forehead and the blade of his nose. His eyes were dark, aglitter from the candles, yet they shone with a glow of their own as he turned them in her direction. His hand reached to her and he drew her next to him, then pointed at the treetop.

"The angel looks like you," he said quietly. "The golden hair, the pure lines of profile and the clear vision to see beyond this night to what is to come in the future. I think even the Bethlehem angels knew what would come to pass, as they sang to the shepherds. Don't you?"

"I don't suppose I ever thought about it that way," Honey told him. "And I'm not at all sure I look anything like that angel. Aren't angels supposed to be males, anyway?"

"Mine isn't," Zachary said, his eyes conveying a message that made her heart swell in her breast.

A hand tugging on her skirt broke the spell he wove, and Honey looked down into Hope's blue eyes, their corners crinkled as a smile brought dimples to life in her cheeks. "Mr. Joseph says we can open our presents tonight, Honey. Is it all right?"

"Of course," Honey said, brushing a stray curl from her sister's cheek. "Why don't you pass them out?"

It was a long process, each opening a gift, holding

it up for approval, and then thanking the one who had chosen and offered it in love. The linen handkerchiefs were praised, the leather gloves tried on and the pipe tobacco set aside for the morrow. Hope held a warm, bright red woolen coat in her lap, a fur collar giving it a touch of elegance that awed the child and brought quick tears to Honey's eyes.

Her own gift was a new dress, one that would fit, that would require no mending for months to come, that would make her Christmas a festive time, garbing her in a blue plaid that almost matched that of Hope's new dress. Joseph smiled as Honey held it up to herself, and nodded at Zachary, giving approval of his grandson's choice.

"It's beautiful," Honey whispered. "I can't wait till morning so I can put it on."

"Honey hasn't had a new dress in a lo-o-o-ng time," Hope said, drawing out the word dramatically. "She's patched the old ones and cut up Mama's old dresses to make things for me."

Telling family secrets was inexcusable, Honey thought, but could not work up any aggravation, given Hope's propensity for honesty. "We all do what we have to," she said quietly. "Wearing mended dresses was small potatoes compared to what some folks have to do to survive."

"You'll never have to wear patches again," Joseph said, his words a solemn promise. "I'll see to it."

Honey turned her head, catching the full warmth

of his expression head-on. "I'm not sure what you mean," she said haltingly. "You can't expect to provide for us, Joseph."

"I don't know why not," he told her bluntly. "I need you here, Honey. I've only just found you and Hope, and I'm not ready to give you up." His jaw was firm and his eyes shone with determination. "I want you to stay on here with me."

"I may have to argue with you on that score," Zachary said, drawing Honey's attention back to him. He stood behind her, and she turned to face him. His hands reached for hers and he drew her closer. "If you agree to my grandfather's plan, I'll have to change my whole lifestyle," he said, amusement tilting his lips into a smile.

"I don't know what you're talking about," Honey said, her heart in her throat as the two men discussed her future as though she had no say in the matter. "We can't just stay on here, you know. We have a farm to work, animals to tend. And besides, your Mrs. Hawkins will be back in a little better than a week. I'd only be in the way."

"Why don't you and Hope have your cookies and share some wassail?" Zachary suggested, shooting a look at his grandfather. "Honey and I need to discuss something." He took her hand and led her from the room, across the hall and into the dining room doorway. The scent of pine boughs drew them toward the arrangement on the mantel and it was there Zachary took her. "Look up," he told Honey and waited till she tilted her head back, finally noticing the mistletoe branch hanging from the ceiling.

"I didn't put that there," she said. "Joseph had me hang a bit from the parlor lamp, and in the foyer, but—"

"I hung this piece," Zachary told her. "I brought you in here for two reasons, Honey. One involved the mistletoe, the other this package." He lifted a small, wrapped box from the mantel and placed it in her palm. "Would you open it?"

"You already gave me a dress, Zachary. And even that was not entirely proper, you know."

"Joseph had me choose it for him," he told her, dismissing her protest. "This gift is from me." He watched her patiently as she turned it in her hand, her fingertips touching the silver ribbon, tracing its path around the square box. "Shall I help you?" he asked after a moment, his smile tender.

"No, I'll do it," she said, her breath catching in her throat. It was a dream, this whole scene. Her with her best dress on, the only one she owned fit to wear in public, Zachary garbed as a gentleman, the gold chain across his waistcoat proclaiming the presence of a watch in his pocket, his collar and cuffs pristine and starched within an inch of their lives. And now he offered her a gift that might be the answer to any woman's dearest desire. A gift she could not accept, unless it was given with love.

The box opened readily and a pearl gleamed in the light from the fireplace before them. It centered a ring, two sparkling stones cradling it, showing off the depths of simple perfection in the lustrous treasure he offered her. "Oh, Zachary." She could say no more, could not express the overflowing love she felt for the man before her.

"Will you wear it for me?" he asked, lifting the ring and seeking out her left hand. It fit, a bit loose, but nearly the perfect size. "I can have it made a little smaller," he told her. "Mr. McHenry, at the jewelers, said it would only take a day to change the size if we needed to do so."

"Zachary…" She looked up at him, her eyes brimming. "I can't accept such a thing from you. This should be given to a woman worthy to be your wife, not someone like me."

"You're the woman I want," he said, his voice gruff, as if he concealed deep emotion. And indeed it seemed to be so, for his mouth trembled just a bit as he whispered words she'd thought never to hear from his lips. "I fell in love with you the moment you poked your finger in my chest, Honey, and scolded me that day in the kitchen." His smile faltered, and he made an admission she hadn't expected.

"I'd wanted you before that, and was ashamed of myself for taking advantage of you. In fact, I wanted you last July when you left my office in a huff, and I almost chased you down then." He looked up at the mistletoe overhead and smiled ruefully. "I wish now I had. I've wasted a lot of time, it seems."

"How…" Honey shook her head in disbelief. "I don't know what to say."

"Just say you'll wear my ring. Say you'll trust me with your future," Zachary said quietly, his words intense with a depth of feeling that almost convinced Honey of his sincerity. Almost.

"Are you doing this for your grandfather's benefit? Because he wants it to happen, because he thinks he needs me here?"

Zachary laughed, a sound she had not expected to hear. "I love my grandfather, more than you can imagine, but if you think for one minute I'd ask any woman to marry me, just to make him happy, you're dead wrong, sweetheart. I'm asking you because I love you and I want to share my life with you."

"I won't know how to be the wife of a man like you," she countered, her chin firm as she listed her lack of qualifications. "I'm not from your background, and I don't have pretty manners or much education. I'm a farmer, Zachary, not a city girl who's been raised to fit into a life like yours."

"You're exactly the wife I want," he said firmly. "I love your stubborn determination to do what's right for you and your sister. I respect the way you take on a job and do it well. I admire the way you've taken hold in my grandfather's house, the way you look after those you love." He tilted his head to one side and measured her with a long look. "Is that enough to begin with, Honey? Can we start from here and make a life together?"

And then he paused and his eyes narrowed. "Or perhaps you can't find it in your heart to return my love. Maybe I've misunderstood your feelings."

"You make my heart ache, Zachary," she confessed. "I feel so full, as if something in my chest is running over with feelings I can't describe."

"Try." He spoke the single syllable softly and waited expectantly.

"I want to touch you, I want your arms around me, and I need something from you that I can't find words for. My body aches when you hold me, as if there is more you can give me. I don't know what it is, but I need to find out."

He smiled, his mouth softening as he bent to touch his lips to hers. "This is because of the mistletoe," he whispered as he took her mouth in a kiss that brought her up against him, standing on her toes as if she must get closer to him, pressing against his body as though she craved the warmth of his flesh through the layers of clothing they wore. He held her there, lifted her from the floor and turned her in a slow circle, there in the light of the fire, beneath the mistletoe that offered its blessing on the kiss they shared.

"That was because of the mistletoe," he reminded her, lowering her to the floor, where she attempted to force her legs to hold her erect. They trembled beneath her and she clung to his arms. "This…" he said softly, "This is because I love you and I want you to be my bride. Please say yes," he murmured as his lips touched hers again, and she was lost in the heat of a kiss that brought her to the edge of desire, then pushed her over the brink into a vibrant excitement that filled each part of her.

"Yes. Yes," she whispered, caught up in the bliss of arms that held her fast, strength that promised shelter, and a love that would last for all the years to come.

Christmas Day

AGAIN, THE CHURCH BELLS RANG out the joyous sound of Christmas, and again, Honey was bundled into the sleigh for the journey to the small white church. She wore her new dress, feeling resplendent in the taffeta plaid, her ears ringing with sounds of Christmas morning.

The congregation sang with gusto. "Joy To The World," and "God Rest Ye Merry Gentlemen," and an assortment of other carols played on the small organ, sung by the sixty or so members who'd journeyed out to celebrate the coming of the Christ child. Hope wiggled on the seat beside Honey, her excitement barely contained as various children of the congregation rose and solemnly recited verses they'd learned for this occasion.

"Maybe next year I can do that, too," she whispered, tugging Honey's sleeve to get her attention.

"Maybe so," her sister agreed, and then lifted her face to look up at Zachary.

He was filled with the holiday spirit, his plan coming to fruition, his grandfather delighted with the news that Honey wore the pearl ring. And he was to be given the greatest gift of all, the woman he'd come to love wholeheartedly over the past days. His doubts were gone, his mind set on an early wedding, his desire at fever pitch as he looked into blue eyes that promised pleasure beyond his wildest dreams.

They left the church and were approached by several members of the congregation, one of them Ellen Phillips, the young woman he'd spoken of to Honey, and his heart sank as he recognized the light of battle in his erstwhile companion's eyes. She was pretty enough, he supposed, but once he'd spent time with Honey—indeed, after their first encounter over five months ago—the other women in town had paled in the memory of the golden-haired woman beside him.

Now Ellen spoke to Honey, and her words were tinged with bitterness. "I saw you one day in the general store. Mr. Sanders told me you're living in the house with these two gentlemen," she said, lifting a brow, awaiting a reply.

"Yes, I'm working for Mr. Bennett," Honey answered, sending a quick look toward Zachary. "My name is Honey Morris. This is my little sister, Hope."

"Oh, I've heard of you, *Honey,*" Ellen said. "I don't wonder that the Bennett men preferred you to Mrs. Hawkins. You're much easier to look at."

"I don't think I understand what you're saying,"

Honey answered, and Zachary felt his blood boil, stepping closer to Honey's side as Ellen Phillips sank in her claws of jealousy a bit deeper.

"It didn't take you long to move in and make yourself at home, did it? Most young women would want to be wearing a ring before they made their home with a gentleman. Let alone two of them." Her laughter was enough to send a chill down Zachary's back, and he gripped Honey's arm, facing her accuser with fury almost choking him.

"That's enough, Miss Phillips," he said curtly. "Your accusations are totally unfounded."

"*My* accusations?" she chirped. "Surely you know the whole town is talking about your little refugee."

"The town has no basis for thinking anything is wrong with the situation in my grandfather's home," Zachary said harshly. "To begin with, Honey is wearing my ring. We are betrothed, and will soon be married." He turned Honey aside with a hand at her waist and led her to the sleigh where Joseph and Hope were waiting.

"What's wrong?" Joseph asked, his eyes clouded with concern as he met Zachary's dark look. "What did that young woman say to Honey?"

"All the wrong things," Zachary answered. "She's a filthy-minded—"

"That's enough," Honey said sharply. "I don't think Hope needs to hear this."

Zachary nodded his agreement. "We'll speak

later,'' he told his grandfather, and lifted the reins, setting the team in motion as he turned the sleigh and headed back to the big house.

The noon meal was eaten in silence, Hope smothering a yawn as she finished her last bite, Honey barely eating at all. With a smile, she sent the little girl into the parlor. ''Why don't you go in and enjoy the Christmas tree, sweetheart,'' she told the child. ''I'll clean up the kitchen and join you in a while.''

''All right,'' Hope said agreeably. Honey watched as her sister left the dining room, then rose and began clearing the table.

''We need to talk,'' Zachary said at her elbow. ''You've been deeply hurt by that woman's stupid accusations, Honey, and I won't have it.''

''I don't think you can say much to make it better, Zachary,'' she told him quietly. ''I've been labeled unfairly, but I've learned that we can't change what people think of us.''

''She's only one person,'' he reminded her. ''And you've lived a life above reproach.''

''I'm in a situation that won't hold up under close scrutiny,'' she told him. ''The woman was right. I'm living in a household with two men, and I'm a young, single woman. I should have known better. I only wanted to help Joseph, and instead, I've probably damaged his reputation.''

''It was my fault for coming here to stay for Christmas,'' Zachary said. ''I'd have done better to come back and forth and not be here at night. I should have known better.''

''It's too late now to have second thoughts,'' Honey told him resolutely. ''The damage has been done.''

''Can we set it aside?'' Zachary asked. ''We'll set a date for our wedding for next week, and stop her in her tracks.''

''Did you give her reason to think she was important to you?'' Honey's eyes were dull with sorrow as she spoke the question she'd harbored for the past hour.

''No. She flirted with me at several picnics last summer, asked me to accompany her to church and then to a party, and, very frankly, offered herself to me. I told you I'd kept company with her a bit, but that was as far as it went.''

''You turned her down?''

If a touch of skepticism rang in her query, she could be forgiven, he supposed. Most men would have been pleased to be given the chance to taste Ellen Phillips's charms. She was a popular young woman, set on making a good marriage. And had he not already had a ten-minute exposure to Honey Morris, he might have, very possibly, been tempted to at least consider the idea.

But it hadn't even increased his pulse rate, Zachary recalled. The pressure of his work and the knowledge that his grandfather was watching him closely had been enough to keep his nose to the grindstone during those summer months. And the memory of a golden-haired girl who had walked away from him, her dignity intact, clung to his mind like a burr, collected during a walk through the fields, against his skin. Always there, a reminder of that day.

"I turned her down," he said, looking Honey fully in the face, willing her to believe his words. "She's jealous of you, sweetheart, and with good reason. You're pretty and smart, and you've won the heart of a man she wanted for her own."

Honey turned from him, carrying a tray filled with dishes, pushing the kitchen door open with her hip, then allowing it to swing shut behind her. Zachary watched her retreat from his presence and silently cursed the woman who had dropped a bomb in the midst of this day.

December 26

"I'LL STAY TILL THE END of the week," Honey said, her lips firm as she spoke her decision aloud.

Joseph sat in his study, pipe in hand, a frown wrinkling his brow. "I can't say anything to change your mind, my dear?" he asked quietly. "You won't reconsider?"

"I can't," she whispered, her eyes filling with tears even as she fought them. "I won't do anything to shame you, Mr. Joseph. I love you too much to allow people to say nasty things about me being in your house."

"Even though Zachary has gone home?" he asked. "This will blow over, you know. Folks will know better than to listen to a troublemaker like Ellen Phillips."

"Folks are always willing to listen to gossip," Honey said, correcting him firmly. "Zachary moving back home only will make people think there was something going on here. I have to go back to the farm, sir. I don't want to leave you in the lurch, but I can't stay here." She took the ring from her left hand and held it out to him.

"Please give this back to Zachary for me, will you? I knew I wasn't the right woman for him. I've only brought trouble to both of you."

"He won't accept it," Joseph told her, allowing her to drop the golden circle in his hand. The pearl was lustrous, gleaming in the afternoon sunlight from the window. "You'll break his heart, my dear."

"I should have known better than to reach beyond my boundaries," she said. "I know I said I'd stay longer, but if I go now, people will forget all this within weeks, and Zachary will be just fine."

"You underestimate my grandson's love for you," Joseph told her, then sat in silence as she turned and left the room.

The farmhouse was cold when the big wagon pulled up to the back door. A cage with six hens sat at the rear of the vehicle. Both a horse and a cow were tied behind, placidly following at a slow pace. The livery stable owner helped Honey down from the high seat, then turned to lend a hand to Hope as she climbed from the rear. Tears stained the child's cheeks, and she trudged silently toward the house.

"I'll just get your things carried to the porch," the man said nicely, the silence of the trip no doubt making him aware that this journey had been undertaken in sadness. Honey untied the cow and led her to the barn, then returned for her horse.

"If you'll help me with the chickens, I'd appreciate it," she told him quietly, and then, at the wave of his hand, allowed him to handle the bulky load. Her bundles were on the porch, Hope already inside the cold kitchen, and Honey followed her. In less than ten minutes she'd started a fire in the stove, waved her thanks at the helpful gentleman who had followed Joseph's instructions to the letter. Without hesitation, she sat down at the kitchen table and lowered her head, her tears falling like bitter rain.

It took only a day or so to be back in the routine of the life she'd left just two short weeks ago. The New Year had begun and yet, her life was the same—unending work from morning to night. Feeding animals, milking the cow, churning butter and baking bread. She'd at least found a source of income on a regular basis. Mr. Sanders at the general store had agreed to take all the eggs she could bring him to sell over his counter, in addition to the rounds of butter he'd taken off her hands in the past.

She thought of Joseph and the house she'd left behind—the wide staircase, the fragrant tree in the parlor, the festive decorations of Christmas in the dining room. But most of her memories were of Zachary, of dark hair and eyes, of hands that touched her, of lips that offered pleasure. And her pillow was damp at night from the silent tears she shed.

That Hope wandered the rooms of the farmhouse like a lost soul lent more pain to Honey's heart. The child didn't understand the reasons for their leaving the big house. And Honey didn't have it in her to disillusion the young girl by explaining the pain that could be dealt by a jealous human being. If life could get back to normal for Zachary and Joseph, if the talk around town would die out, if folks could only forget that once a young woman had been installed in the house that two bachelors called home, then her leaving would bear fruit.

She tried her best to coax Hope into smiling for her, fixing treats from the storehouse of food Zachary had sent with them on the back of the wagon. She thought of paying him, of leaving an envelope for him at the bank on her next trip to town, and then recognized she would only offer an insult. He'd already been deeply hurt by her refusal to stay, had turned from her and walked away once he recognized that she would not budge from the stand she'd taken.

"When will the snow ever melt?" Hope asked wistfully, drawing Honey from her pondering as she kneaded the bread dough. She looked up at the window where flakes drifted lazily to blend in with the foot or so of snow that covered the ground.

"Not for a long time," she said. "But we can go out and make angels after a while if you want to." Somehow the sport of making a row of the heavenly beings appear in a bank of pristine snow had lost its appeal to both of them over the past days. And Hope only shrugged her narrow shoulders and turned back to look out the window.

"Can we go to town and visit with Mr. Joseph?" Hope asked, sending a silent appeal from blue eyes that tore at Honey's resolution. "He said he wants to see us."

"I know he told us that," Honey answered. "But we need to stay away from his house for a while."

"I don't understand," the child said sadly. "We had such a good time there."

"I know," Honey agreed. "We did, but sometimes things happen that we don't expect. We'll visit him again before spring, I promise."

"That's a long time away," Hope said, turning back to the window.

"Yes." Honey could only agree, aware of an empty place in her breast where once a love had blossomed and bloomed for a tall man with dark eyes and a tender smile. Now she forbade herself to revisit that place, that memory of happiness she had grasped for so short a time.

The days passed slowly, and soon they marked the third week since their arrival back at the farm. Two trips to town had allowed Mr. Sanders to apply credit to Honey's account at the general store, and brought her a few smiles from ladies who were there to shop during her visit with the storekeeper. She'd noted their interest in her, put it down to a final bit of gossip left over from the Christmas debacle, and nodded politely.

Mr. Sanders had gladly accepted her supply of eggs, and the rounds of butter she'd formed with care, imprinting her small mark on each as a sign that it had come from her kitchen. Perhaps some of it found its way into Joseph's kitchen, she thought, her hands busy wielding the flat paddle that formed the butter in her wooden bowl. Six loaves of bread cooled on the table, and she'd already decided to take five of them along to town on this trip. She could bake more in a day or so, and people were happy to get fresh bread, the storekeeper had told her.

"Are we gonna go to church again?" Hope asked, kicking her heels against the chair rung, her chalkboard before her as she practiced her letters.

"Maybe this Sunday," Honey told her. Surely enough time had passed to allow them to slip into a morning service without calling too much attention to themselves. She missed the hymns, the sound of the organ, the minister's encouraging words, and as Hope's request hung in the air she made up her mind.

"Yes, we'll go this week." Let folks lift their eyebrows if they liked. She had nothing to be ashamed of, and she'd go and hold her head high.

CHAPTER SIX

January 16, 1898

SMILES GREETED THE SISTERS as they approached the door of the church on Sunday morning. Hope made a valiant attempt to be sedate but failed miserably when she caught sight of Joseph standing on the stoop. Her hand lifted, her fingers wiggling in a wave that brought a smile to his lips, and Honey grasped her firmly by the other hand, lest she take it into her head to plunge past the group gathered by the door. Getting to where Joseph stood was definitely on the child's mind.

Honey slowed her pace, turning to answer a greeting from Mrs. Sanders, the storekeeper's wife, and found herself the recipient of a genuine smile of welcome.

"It's so good to see you again, Honey," the lady said warmly. "We've missed you since you moved back to the farm. I don't believe I've laid eyes on you more than twice in the past three weeks. But no matter," she murmured, leaning a bit closer. "It won't be long before you're a regular visitor to the store."

Honey's smile wavered as she heard the prediction, her thoughts in direct opposition to the lady's suggestion. She'd be busier than ever come spring, what with planting and such. Of course, all of that hinged on whether or not the bank made arrangements to foreclose on the mortgage in the meantime. She'd heard nothing from Zachary and held her breath each time she ventured to town, fearing he would one day soon be the bearer of bad news.

"Honey," Hope whispered, the sound rising in protest as Honey gripped her hand. "I only want to go see Mr. Joseph." Her mouth drooped at the corners, and Honey bent to whisper a warning.

"Behave, Hope. We'll see him later."

Joseph had, thankfully, gone inside the sanctuary by the time the sisters passed the threshold. The congregation had conveniently left the back pew empty, and Honey, with an eye to being inconspicuous, settled there. Even slouching a bit in the seat didn't help, for several ladies turned and sent surreptitious waves in her direction, then bent to whisper to their neighbors. Before long she was the object of overt attention and her face flamed, embarrassed at being on public display.

And then, the one man she'd hoped not to face this morning entered the church door and made his way to the family pew, seating himself next to Joseph. His dark head bent closer to Joseph's snowy hair, and as she watched, Zachary stiffened, then turned just a bit, angling his head, the better to look toward the corner where she sat. His eyes lit with a look of surprise, and then glowed with an emotion she recognized.

Don't come back here. She sent the message in his direction, then bowed her head as if deep in thought or perhaps praying before the worship service should commence. She'd never been much of a believer in mind reading, and Zachary's appearance by her side just moments later only served to strengthen her skepticism of that particular gift.

"May I sit with you?" he asked in an undertone, and Honey looked up beseechingly, shaking her head just a bit. And then, recognizing that they were being watched by at least half of the congregation, not to mention the pastor, who had entered the pulpit and was looking in their direction, she slid over.

He sat down beside her, seeming to take up more than his share of the pew, she thought. What a fool she'd been, putting herself in this predicament. Anywhere else in the world would be a preferable spot to the one she found herself in right now. Any other church in town would have done as well. She wasn't Catholic, but surely God visited Saint Mary's church on Sunday morning as well as the Methodist chapel.

Beside her, Hope wiggled in the pew, leaning forward to grin her widest at Zachary, and whispered a greeting that was clearly audible to at least half of the pews.

"Hi, Mr. Zachary. We came to church," she said,

her feet swinging, her eyes sparkling as she looked around at the smiles that met her own.

Beside Honey, Zachary's thigh was pressed tightly against hers and she shifted over a few inches, only to find he had made the adjustment even as she moved, placing him as close to her as possible. He reached for her clenched fists, lifted them and enclosed them both in one palm.

"Your hands are cold," he whispered against her ear.

She shivered, her eyes brimming with tears, her throat aching. And then she looked up at him and knew that three weeks had made no difference. She would never cease loving this man, no matter how many miles she put between them, no matter how many days passed before she saw his beloved face again.

From the pulpit she heard the pastor's deep voice speak a name and she inhaled sharply, uncertain of her hearing. *Zachary Tobias Bennett.* He'd spoken Zachary's name, and now he was speaking hers. *Honoria Belle Morris.* Confusion filled her and she looked up to see a smile causing Zachary's eyes to crinkle, bringing a dimple alive in one cheek.

"He's speaking our banns," Zachary whispered. "This is the third week, Honey."

"Our banns?" Banns were only spoken in preparation for a wedding. And she had left town specifically because she could not become Zachary's bride.

"Our wedding will be next Saturday," Zachary said quietly, and she shivered at his words.

"It's not possible," she returned, her voice trembling, her words barely audible.

"On the contrary," he said. "If I have to carry you to the church, I'll do it, Honey. One way or another, you'll be marrying me, Saturday next."

She made an effort to rise, panic striking at his ultimatum, and he placed his hand on her thigh, his fingers squeezing gently. Her bottom hit the pew and she pried at his hand. *"Zachary!"* The whisper was louder than she'd intended, and once more the ladies sitting in front of them turned to see what was going on.

"*Behave* yourself," he told her, the words muttered beneath his breath, even as he nodded at Mrs. Blivens, who'd craned her neck, the better to observe his conduct.

Honey cringed, hunching her shoulders and bending her head to look down at her dress. The final words of the pastor's announcement rang in her ears, and she felt the urge to punch Zachary on the arm, or perhaps scream at the top of her lungs, protesting the unfairness of his conduct.

"...on Saturday next, at two o'clock in the afternoon. A reception for friends will be held at the home of the elder Mr. Bennett immediately following." The minister then set aside the paper he'd read from and cleared his throat, announcing a hymn, and inviting the congregation to stand. The organ emitted a majestic chord, and enthusiastic voices were raised in song.

Honey stood beside Zachary, her knees barely holding her erect, her heart pounding a mile a minute. He couldn't force her to marry him, could he? And yet, why cause a fuss over the dearest wish of her heart? If Zachary Bennett was willing to face the rumors and gossip such a union might bring about, who was Honey Morris to quibble?

The music eased her mind, the minister's sermon gave her food for thought as he preached about the lilies of the field, his words assuring her that she was being looked after by a God who loved her. And when the final prayer was given and the kindly pastor passed their pew on his way to the church door, she breathed a sigh of release, silently giving over her fears to the heavenly Father she trusted above all else.

"Feel better?" Zachary asked, his mouth almost touching her ear. "Are we still going to fight about this?" He stood beside her, his big body shielding her from those who would have paused in the aisle to speak congratulations to the couple.

And Honey could only look up into his dark eyes, eyes that held a depth of love she could not deny. "No matter what happens this week, no matter who has anything cruel or unjust to say about me, if you really want me, I'll marry you. I love you, Zachary," she whispered.

His hands framed her face in a gesture she recalled

from another time, and he looked deeply into her eyes. "I'll hold you to it, sweetheart." And then they were surrounded by the congregation, those fickle folks who were apparently willing to set aside gossip and innuendos for the sake of a love match between a rich man and his bride of choice.

January 22

THE BRIDE WORE WHITE, as was her privilege. Until the last day before the wedding she'd planned on wearing a dress from the general store, a nice gown, to be sure, but not befitting his bride, Zachary had obviously decided. Instead she was the very picture of a bride, garbed in a dress delivered to the elder Mr. Bennett's home early this morning, sent directly from Denver, a gift from her groom.

Hope, her flower girl, carried a basket of roses and carnations, imported on that same morning train, fresh from a hothouse that specialized in such things. Mrs. Sanders, resplendent in blue satin, paced sedately ahead of the young woman.

Honey walked on Joseph's arm, down the aisle to Zachary's side. With whispered words, the elderly man bent to the couple, as if he gave them his own personal blessing, and then crossed to stand beside his grandson. Enjoying his task as best man, Joseph looked with satisfaction upon the proceedings, his white hair and beard gleaming in the lamplight, his smile a wreath of pure delight. The flower girl moved to stand next to the elderly gentleman once the wedding was in progress, and he reached for her, then placed his palms on her shoulders, as if claiming her as his own kin.

The bride was radiant, her golden hair caught up in a coronet, topped by a veil that surrounded her. It was an elegant veil, sent from Denver, wrapped in tissue, along with the dress that lent her a look of purity. A look she could claim with all honesty. To the eyes of the townsfolk whose presence threatened to burst the walls of the small church, she might have been an angel in disguise, so perfect was her appearance in the pristine gown she wore.

The groom wore his triumph well, his dark hair smooth and shiny, his shoulders wide beneath a new suit that fit him like a glove. He spoke his vows in a clear, ringing voice, his eyes unwilling to be swayed from the beauty of his bride.

Half the town appeared at the Bennett mansion, Mrs. Hawkins reappearing in time to put together a groaning table of food that surpassed even Zachary's standards. She'd agreed to come back to work, so long as she didn't have to climb the stairs, and Honey had consented quickly to tend to the bedrooms herself, even though the elder Mr. Bennett vowed to find an upstairs maid by the time the honeymoon was over.

A For Rent sign appeared in front of Zachary's new house, and all of his personal belongings were to be moved back to his grandfather's home immediately following the wedding. It seemed that the two young ladies would not be separated from the old man who had come to their rescue, and Zachary was agreeable, so long as Honey shared *his* part of the Bennett home place.

And then it was time for the newlyweds to leave. Amid a shower of rice, they ran down the front walk to where a sleigh awaited them. The evening train to Denver pulled into the station as they stepped from the sleigh, and in moments they were on board, settled nicely in a Pullman car reserved for this occasion.

Honey was flushed and breathless, a combination Zachary thought delightful. He held her close as they stood in the middle of the railway car, enjoying her wide-eyed expression of wonder. "Do you like it?" he asked.

"Oh, yes. You knew I would," she answered, taking in the lush upholstery, the velvet hangings and the heavily draped bed at the far end of the long car. The train rolled into motion, jerking just enough to deposit her against him, and he scooped her up in his arms, cashmere coat, fur muff and all, only to place her in the middle of the wide bed.

"Zachary, I still have my shoes on," she exclaimed. "I don't want to soil the covers."

"By all means," he said cheerfully. "I'll just help you get rid of all your excess baggage." His fingers were deft as she eased her shoes from her feet, and then he took the muff from her hands and set to work on the buttons of her coat.

"I can do this," she protested, covering his hands with her own. "I'm a big girl. You don't need to take care of me."

"Oh, but you're wrong there, sweetheart. I'm planning on taking care of you for the rest of your life. I decided that a long time ago. It just took me a while to pull this thing together." Even as he spoke, his hands were stripping her from the beautiful new coat he'd produced for her approval only yesterday, and then he sat her upright and faced her across the wide expanse of the mattress.

"Please let me do this," he asked, his smile gentle, his eyes pleading as he touched the hem of her dress and inched his fingers past her narrow feet to circle her ankles.

"You really want to undress me?" she asked.

"Yes." It was a simple reply, and he awaited her permission, his hands warm against her skin, venturing no further until she should acquiesce to his request.

"I love you, Zachary," she whispered. "I'll do whatever you want." She bit at her lip and her face grew rosy with anticipation or embarrassment, either of which he was prepared to handle.

His sigh was a murmur of thanksgiving as he drew her to himself, his arms around her, his hands busy with the buttons that made her a captive of the fine white silken gown. Layer after layer of lace and fine fabric was placed to one side as he unwrapped the gift of purity she brought to him. He bent his head to press warm kisses against curves and hollows, and she breathed her delight, whispering broken phrases that only served to increase his need for what was to come.

He stripped off her stockings, hung her garters on the bedpost, to her delight, and then eased her from the last of her undergarments, thankful for the light shed by a parlor lamp at the other end of the Pullman car.

His own clothing was set aside quickly. And as the train rolled into the twilight, he joined her on the bed, his embrace gentle, his hands careful against her skin, his mouth visiting each soft, tempting place he'd yearned to discover for himself.

"Can I touch you, too?" she asked, and he could only nod his approval. "You won't mind?" she asked, moving her hands to his shoulders, and then down his body to where his waist narrowed.

"Oh, no, I won't mind," he muttered, his body aching to join with hers, his control stretched almost to the limit as she whispered soft words of praise for the width of his chest, the solid firmness of his muscles and the scent of his skin. Her mouth opened against his flesh and her tongue flicked out to taste his throat. Slender hands stroked his chest and then moved to unknowingly tease him with the brief, tantalizing brush of fingertips against his back.

He groaned, shifting to place himself directly over

her, his hands gentle as he nudged her legs apart to accommodate his presence between them. She inhaled quickly, her body trembling beneath him. She'd felt the urgency of his arousal against her woman's flesh and he was still, lest she be frightened.

And then blue eyes opened and he met her gaze. "I'll try very hard not to hurt you," he said, his voice ragged as he sought to reassure her. His reward was a look of trust from soft eyes that spoke in a language he had become familiar with over the past month.

"I know, Zachary." She frowned then and amended her words. "I don't suppose I really know, but..." She paused, searching, it seemed, for words to better explain her meaning. "But I trust you."

He groaned and bent to kiss her, fearful of causing pain yet yearning to breach her innocence and make her truly his wife. Her hands clutched his back as she lifted her body against his, and then her fingers swept with featherlike touches across the line of his hips, then lower to explore the taut lines of his thighs.

"I love you, Zachary," she whispered, and then her breath caught and quivered as he lowered his head to her breasts. He nuzzled there, his mouth opening to suckle, leaving a residue of moisture on her skin. She shivered, and the dark crests crinkled as he watched. His palms cupped her soft, swollen weight and he took the puckered bits of flesh in his mouth, first one then the other, waiting patiently for her response, smiling with delight when her hips lifted against his manhood, tempting him beyond measure.

With gentle care, he coaxed her, his hands tender as he sought her pleasure, arousing her with lips and tongue, with palms that caressed and fingers that explored. Heedful of her innocence, with a control he fought to maintain, he entered her, piercing her maidenhead with a slow thrust that brought a single, soft cry from her lips.

A primitive sense of triumph gripped him, and he bent to take her lips in a kiss that swallowed her pain, his whispered apology spoken between brief touches of lips and tongue against her mouth. "I'm sorry, sweetheart. I know it hurts."

She shook her head, a small movement he might have missed had he not been so aware of each whisper she uttered, every shiver of delight that trembled against his flesh. "Only for a second," she said. "Now..." She lifted her hips against his and he felt his penetration deepen, heard her small gasp as she shifted to better contain him.

"Now it's as if you've become a part of me, Zachary." Her words were soft, a trembling whisper, as though she could not speak aloud the wonder of this moment.

He could barely breathe, his body clenching with the need to deliver his seed to her most secret place. And yet, he could not leave her wanting, could not bring himself to take his pleasure at the expense of hers. And so he prayed for patience, wooing her afresh, coaxing her response with the rhythm of dancing fingers, the tempting touches of mouth and teeth against her flesh.

Only when she moaned his name, writhing beneath him, her inner muscles clenching him, did he begin to move once more, his patience faltering as she wrapped her legs around him, submitting herself to his will. And then she clung, weeping aloud his name as shivers of delight possessed her.

He took her fully then, allowed himself those final moments of passion, his seed flooding her willing, virgin flesh. He spoke quietly, praising her beauty, murmuring his love, promising his devotion. And then he closed his eyes and gave silent thanks for the gift he had been given.

EPILOGUE

June, 1898

THE SMALL CEMETERY was quiet, except for the songbirds that were wont to nest there in the peaceful surroundings. Rows of headstones told stories of family history, small markers gave notice of children who slept beneath the sod, and in one shaded corner four people stood beside a new gravestone.

The ground was damp where they had walked, and the sky was shrouded with clouds from a recent rainfall. Before them the grass was still gently mounded over the two graves they visited, and even though sorrow dwelt here, those who came bore bright symbols of life. Flowers, overflowing the pails the men carried, bloomed as if determined to spread their message of cheer to all who glimpsed their beauty, even in the wake of summer rain.

With a small spade, Zachary dug holes and Honey placed the blossoming plants within the earth's embrace. Joseph visited a nearby pump and carried back a watering can, tilting it, allowing the water to fall gently upon the newly planted blooms, to insure they would live in the days to come. Hope watched, crouching beside the graves, brushing her small hand over the new, bright green grass that covered them, her eyes damp, her usual exuberance stilled by the solemnity of this visit.

"I'm glad I have my own angel," she said after a moment, rising and brushing her skirts into place.

"Do you?" Zachary asked, his smile amused as he watched the little girl's absorbed expression.

She looked up at him, the surety of her knowledge making her appear solemn and old for her years. "Oh, yes. Grandpa's my own angel. My guardian angel, you know."

Zachary looked puzzled. "Is he? And here I thought you had him confused with Saint Nicholas."

Hope considered the idea, and then shook her head. "No, I'm not sure I really believe in Saint Nicholas. I think he's just a man in a storybook. But I know angels are real. They're as real as can be. Aren't they, Honey?" Her trusting eyes rested on Honey's face as she awaited confirmation of her theory.

"Yes, they are. Some things we may not know about, but angels are always with us," her sister answered, her own faith as sure and certain as the knowledge that she was loved by each of those surrounding her—those who'd gone on before and those who formed the new family she claimed as her own.

Joseph, whose generosity had given them a new beginning and the happiness they'd found in the home he shared with them.

Hope, a child who gave joy to all around her, each day she lived.

But most of all, Zachary, the man who loved her, who had given her the gift of himself and the precious child she carried within her womb.

They turned to leave the grave site, walking down the hill to where a new surrey awaited their return, a vehicle large enough for all to ride in comfort. Honey waited till Zachary helped Hope climb into the back seat, watched as he lent a hand to Joseph and then turned to lift her onto the wide front seat.

As his hands touched her waist, she looked back up the hill and caught her breath in awe. Zachary's quick eye noted her rapt look and turned to follow the direction of her gaze. He reached for her hand, and she clasped it tightly against her breast as they watched an almost unearthly happening.

A shaft of sunlight speared through the rain clouds, touching the hilltop with a brilliance that seemed to be an answer to all the questions they might ever ask concerning their past, present and future combined. For reflected high above it, far beyond its beginnings, there shone a rainbow, a promise of renewal, of eternal hope—and love.

Dear Reader,

Christmastime in Canada, where I live, is always snowy and beautiful. Despite the weather, it's sharing the holidays with people we care about that makes this time extra special.

Like many of you, I love traditions. In my house we often open presents on Christmas Eve and go for a walk at midnight in the snow. Have you ever wondered where our Christmas traditions originated? How did people celebrate the holidays more than a hundred years ago? Much of my research for *The Long Journey Home* began with these two questions.

Logan and Melodie's love story came to me on one of my early-morning walks, while listening to my Walkman filled with my favorite Christmas carols. The couple's separation two years previous had been particularly harsh and cruel, but Logan's homecoming and their tumultuous reunion affirms the power of love. And what could be more in the spirit of Christmas than that?

This is my first story line about a member of the North West Mounted Police, and I hope you find it entertaining. Formed in 1873, the Mounties were the heroes who tamed the Canadian West. If you enjoy this story about Logan, you may be interested in my December novel next month, *The Surgeon*, about another tough and honorable Mountie, Dr. John Calloway.

From my home to yours, have a beautiful Christmas season, and all the best for a healthy and prosperous New Year.

Kate Bridges

THE LONG JOURNEY HOME
Kate Bridges

Dedicated with much love and admiration
to Samantha and Courtney,
who always brighten my Christmas.

CHAPTER ONE

Alberta, December 15, 1888

HE HAD TO FIND HER. In the rising wind and squalling snow, Logan Sutcliffe, an officer and veterinary surgeon of the North-West Mounted Police, unstrapped the snowshoes from his weary feet. He slung them over the heavy fur pelts of his overcoat, then peered down the early evening streets of Calgary, wondering where to begin. He moaned with fear and anticipation, the kind a man felt when he'd been gone for two suffering years. Logan wasn't even sure Melodie still lived in this town.

Gripping his leather sack, he trudged along the boardwalk of Macleod Trail toward Fort Calgary, assuming it was still there. If it were daytime and clearer, if he looked above his shoulder to the west he'd see the jagged wintry peaks of the Rocky Mountains that marked the prairies' end.

He nodded to passersby, none of whom he recognized.

"Howdy." His warm breath formed a cloud in the icy air, adding more crystals to the icicles in his mustache and beard. Street lighting from the oil lamps flickered off his shoveled path and the sparkling snowbanks piled high along the road.

Would Melodie know him? He was a man in his mid-twenties now, bundled up in animal skins, with dark blond hair trailing down his shoulders and a long, unkempt beard he hadn't had the opportunity, nor desire, to shave.

The town had grown. The dozen stores he remembered had multiplied to three dozen. Some had leaded tinsel streaming down their square-paned windows, some had red bows tied to their pine doors. One had a painted wooden picture of Saint Nicholas. In the horse-plowed street, a crowd of youngsters and their folks surrounded one enterprising fellow who'd strapped jingle bells to his donkey and was giving rides. Disregarding the twenty-below temperature, children took turns as mothers and fathers chuckled. It brought a smile to Logan's lips. He hadn't seen a child in two years.

When he looked up again, he saw *her* store.

The sight knocked the breath out of him. Halting in his tracks, he leaned against the corner post to steady his trembling hand. It had to be hers. The sign above it read Melodie's Bath and Barber House.

So she hadn't left. And she'd finally opened her shop.

Did she live her life alone? Had she found another man? What man wouldn't cross a desert to be with her?

Her shop was decorated with strings of dried berries and holly branches, the most colorful on the block. It was just like her to do it up special. She'd always loved everything about Christmas.

Well...his heavy feet wouldn't move. How long had Melodie and the others searched for him?

How long had it taken before they'd presumed him dead?

What if she no longer loved him? What if she couldn't tolerate the way his looks had changed, or simply told him...to go away?

With a wave of resolution, he stepped off the curb into the squeaky white snow, heading for her door. To feel her warm embrace again had driven him this far. He'd take her reaction however it came.

The bell above the door tinkled as he entered. A wet newsletter clung to the door window, but its headline was clear: Christmas Social At Fort Calgary, Saturday December 15. That was tonight at eight, in roughly two and a half hours.

"Evenin'." The dark-haired young woman at the counter glanced up at Logan while she took change from another man who was leaving.

With heart leaping, Logan peered over her shoulder into a room dimly lit by lanterns and candles. Four men shuffled in their seats, two with towels wrapped around their faces, heating up for shaving. No Melodie.

Logan swiveled to the stone fireplace, taking in the Scotch pine Christmas tree decorated with fruits and nuts. The fragrance of pine needles and dried fruit was comforting. A speckled sheepdog lay curled on a mat by the burning fire, one Logan didn't recognize. He let the heat warm his frigid gloved fingers, waiting until the other man left before he spoke to the woman.

"Is Melodie here?"

"You're one of her customers, are ya? I'll get you set up in the back with your bath, then you can take one of the far seats and she'll get to your cut and shave after the others. Melodie's in the back room gettin' fresh towels."

He'd found her! His legs almost buckled beneath him.

"Have you been on the road for long?"

Forever. "Four weeks." Logan stared at the woman's black braided hair and rosy cheeks. She seemed familiar but he couldn't place her.

"What's your name?"

"Smith," he mumbled, not wanting to tip his hand before he got a chance to explain to Melodie. It wasn't true, but he'd gone by that name for most of the months he'd been gone, named by the old man who'd found him facedown in the snow with a bullet wound to his face, with no remembrance of who or what he was.

"I'll go tell Melodie you're here."

"Thank you."

"And I'll ask Boris to haul another tubful of hot water."

She obviously thought Logan was a customer and he didn't see the need to tell her otherwise.

She disappeared through the hallway of the large log building as a baby cried. Baffled by the sudden wail, Logan peered behind the counter. In a wooden cradle, bundled in a blue wool blanket with a head of black hair, the infant looked to be around two months old. Whose child was he?

Please, not Melodie's. He did a frantic calculation. Two months plus nine for carrying him equaled eleven months. Logan had been gone for twenty-four.

Before he could let the shock of that sink in, Melodie brushed by him, arms full of linen towels. His joy knotted with his sorrow in one trembling lump.

She smiled up at him, as beautiful as the day he'd met her.

"Good evening, Mr. Smith." She set down her pile of huge towels on the side counter beside his leg and frowned at him.

His heart stopped pulsing.

Deep, coffee-brown eyes assessed him. Straight black brows framed her eyes and the tip of the pert nose he used to kiss every night was dotted with soap. Pretty peach lips turned up at him. The same lips that had first whispered "I love you" to him on a beaten-up old rocking chair one sultry autumn evening.

She flicked a handful of her silky black hair back

over her shoulder from where it had fallen. A dimple caught in her cheek as she held his gaze.

It came to him like a powerful explosion. *Melodie didn't recognize him.*

His throat tightened with unspoken words.

The baby cried again.

"Timmy, what's the matter?"

Logan swallowed past the dryness in his mouth as he watched her with the infant. Every time she smiled at the baby, Logan's heart turned over in response.

He didn't recall her clothes. Although they were a bit worn-out, they were new to him.

She wore a light rose-colored blouse, buttoned to the top of her high collar, with a soft gray skirt swirling about her feet. Her sleeves were rolled up well past her elbows, revealing smooth creamy arms. She was plumper now, thickly padded around the middle. She used to be so skinny. The extra pounds filled her out in luscious places.

She was happy. He could see it in her energetic walk and the way she turned to stare lovingly at the baby.

When she gathered the infant in her arms, the ring on her left hand glistened in the firelight. The ring had a stone, so it *wasn't* the one Logan had given her.

He staggered back at the horrific implication. Was it a wedding ring?

"Momma's going to feed you soon," she whispered. She kissed the chubby face.

Who was Momma? Melodie or the other woman?

Logan remembered the tender kisses Melodie used to place on his temples, the spot she liked to kiss him most. *You're the sweetest right here,* she used to say.

"Will it hurt?" she asked Logan, setting down the baby. She cupped a hand to her face, indicating the scarring down Logan's left cheek. "Can you take the heat of the warm cloth on your face, or should we skip that part?"

He tried to clear his throat of all the pain he felt at having been ripped out of her life, beyond his control and hers. Self-conscious of his injury and his left droopy eyelid, he rubbed his face with a gloved hand. "It doesn't hurt."

"Have you been here before?"

He shook his head, no. Not technically in this shop. It was new. Then his eyes watered with the ache of maybe having lost her forever. He nodded yes. He'd been with *her* before.

She seemed flustered by his response. "*I've* never cut your hair before though, have I?"

"Actually," he said softly, "you have."

She opened her moist lips as if to protest, but changed her mind. "Well then, sir...you can hang your coat by the fire and go on to the back. We'll try to finish up with these four gentlemen by the time you've finished your bath. I think you'll be my last customer of the day."

When she gracefully walked away from him, he stared after her, exalting in the sheer simple beauty of her walk. Her hips flared from the waistband of her long dark skirt, hinting at the provocative legs beneath.

How could he tell her who he was in the most compassionate way possible?

If he took a bath and cut, it would buy him time to regroup, to find out where he stood. He could pry information out of the hired hand in the back room—Boris, Logan had heard the other woman call him.

And if Melodie were already spoken for, if the baby were hers, what would Logan do then? Walk away?

While he watched her lean over a customer, Logan felt like crying out for joy. He'd found her.

And then he felt like weeping with misery.

A new shop. A new dog. Different clothes. A different ring. A small baby. Everything had changed.

But...Melodie couldn't have remarried.

Please, no.

She couldn't have remarried because Melodie Sutcliffe was still *his* wife.

CHAPTER TWO

"WHEN DID I LAST CUT your hair?"

Melodie felt Mr. Smith's intense gaze on her shoulder as she rearranged combs in the wicker basket an hour later. He'd just emerged from his bath and was standing behind her, staring at the charcoal sketches on the wall. It was six-fifteen, fifteen minutes from closing.

"It's been a very long time."

Something in the catch of his voice made her glance up. It seemed a bit...raspy. From being out in the cold too long, maybe. His hair was wet and straggly from his bath, but the grime that had creased the hollows of his cheeks was gone. It seemed to her that the stranger was dying for conversation. He'd asked twice about Boris, but after Boris had filled the tub, she'd sent him to chop logs for their three fireplaces.

Now Mr. Smith's eyes followed *her* everywhere as she tidied for the day. He'd probably been traveling for quite some time, judging by the neglected look of him. He was a tall, lean man, muscular and tanned from the wind, not an ounce of extra flesh on him. His brown flannel shirt hung loose over torn baggy trousers—a fresh change of clothing from his sack, but ragged nonetheless.

As she worked at the counter, a burning candle fluttered with her movements. The other four chairs farther down the room were empty save for two. The older gentleman, Mr. Dodd, was sliding on his spectacles preparing to leave, and Mr. Johansen was waiting for his shave with his face wrapped in a warm, wet towel. She hadn't gotten to Mr. Johansen as quickly as she'd thought, due to everyone's desire to chat longer than usual, exchanging wishes for the season.

The dog was still snoozing in his favorite place by the fire and Timmy, the little angel, had been fed and was sleeping in his cradle.

Slapping her razor blade back and forth on the leather strop to sharpen it, Melodie looked back to Mr. Smith. "I'm surprised I don't remember cutting your hair. But then, we do get an awful lot of customers."

Trying to be discreet, she noted his winding jagged scar, partially hidden beneath an overgrown blond beard. Sadly, she would have remembered him for his injuries.

His face clouded with unease. Penetrating blue eyes looked away from her toward the wall and its sketches. "I didn't have this the last time you cut my hair."

That explained it then, why the man seemed sort

of familiar but…totally unfamiliar. "I'm awfully sorry…has it affected your vision?"

"No," he said gently, turning back to her.

She sensed he didn't mind talking. "What happened?"

"I was chased by a gang of outlaws. One of them shot before I ducked."

She shuddered, certain she'd never get accustomed to the violent nature of some men. "My Lord. I hope… I hope they caught the men responsible."

His gaze held hers and her stomach tingled.

"Not yet, but we will." Turning slowly, he raised his hand to the sketch of the town's crowded marketplace. "*You* drew these, didn't you?"

She smiled at his astute observation. "Yes, I did." Most customers overlooked her small initials displayed in the bottom right corner, rarely asking about the passion that consumed her evenings.

"I remember."

Her throat tightened for some inexplicable reason. "*Pardon?*"

"They're good."

Heat rose to her cheeks at the lovely compliment. "I'll be a minute longer. If you have a seat, I'll take the customer at the door, then I'll finish up with you and Mr. Johansen here beside you."

But Mr. Smith didn't take his seat. His powerful, clear eyes followed her to the door. Deliberate, searching eyes. She *felt* them on her back, and this time her spine tensed. Something about those eyes seemed almost recognizable, but the droopy eyelid threw her off balance. She *had* met him before.

She made change for Mr. Dodd, admiring the judge's three-piece worsted-wool suit. They remarked on the wild weather.

"Since I won't see you again till next month," he said, "here's something for you, darling, from my wife and I."

Digging into his breast pocket, he removed a square envelope. It was addressed "To Melodie and Donald" in a lovely swirl handwriting. On top of it sat a white candy cane.

She gasped and slid out the Christmas card. "It's beautiful. No one has ever given me one of these."

Her fingertips raced along the satin green bow, then the red silk tassel dangling from the folded edge. In the beautiful oval painting on the front of the card, a deer was sniffing the snowman Santa and two youngsters were building beside his sleigh. She couldn't take her eyes off the pretty scene.

Although born and raised in Canada, Mr. Dodd was proud of his German heritage, often telling them the story of when Queen Victoria had first met Prince Albert in Germany, and how she'd been delighted by their Christmas customs. After they married, it was Prince Albert himself who'd raised their first Christmas tree in Windsor Castle in 1848. Although Christmas trees had been popular at *Kensington* Palace for years, when the *Illustrated London News* had featured Prince Albert's at Windsor Castle, the Christmas tree became fashionable. All of England had followed suit, then the colonies.

Greeting cards were a Victorian creation and the tradition was just catching hold in North America. Glass-blown ornaments and Christmas carols sprouted from Germany, too, and white candy canes shaped to symbolize a shepherd's staff. The origin of the traditions had something to do with Martin Luther in sixteenth-century Germany lighting the first Christmas tree with candles, to symbolize peace on earth.

Spinning around to show the card to the others, Melodie eagerly read the inside. "'To Melodie and Donald, May this festive season be the start of a lifetime of happiness.'"

She glanced up briefly to see heavyset Mr. Johansen peeking out from beneath his towel smiling with interest, but even from this distance, she saw Mr. Smith withdraw. He grew pale.

His reaction took her aback. Perhaps it was selfish of her to show off her card. It must have cost a fortune and most folks couldn't afford such luxuries. But she was thrilled and had only wanted to share its beauty.

When Mr. Dodd left, he fought to open the door against the snowstorm whipping down the street. Cool air bristled on her skin.

Francis came racing down the hallway. "I've got time to help you with one more customer before I leave. I'll cut Mr. Smith's hair while you shave the other one, then that'll just leave you with Mr. Smith's shave.''

Melodie laughed. Francis made the men sound like potatoes who needed to be peeled as quickly as possible for supper. ''That's fine. Then I'll have time to do my own hair before the social.''

Walking to the fireplace, Melodie threw on another spruce log. The sound of the sizzle brought about a rush of…remembrance. Of the first December she'd spent here on the prairies, with her first husband.

The one regret she had was that they'd never made love.

Maybe if she'd had Logan's child, the pain of his absence would be duller.

Two years ago on the evening of December twenty-fourth, it had also been the celebration of their wedding. During the lively reception, Logan and his Mountie detachment had been unexpectedly called to duty. No one had suspected the rustlers would strike during Christmas Eve, let alone a wedding reception. Logan had kissed her lightly on the lips and promised he'd come back to her within three hours.

He'd promised.

''I'll be back in enough time to lift you off your feet and carry you to our bed, my love. Enough time to unbutton the beads of your wedding gown and slip it off your shoulders.…''

Poking the fire with a shaky hand, Melodie tore her thoughts away from melancholy history.

She thought of Donald instead. Although he wasn't Logan, he was a widower, too, and he'd shown her kindness and support in those agonizing months when she hadn't wanted to go on.

And Donald wasn't a police officer. Donald would never be called away to duty. Donald would never disappear on her.

Sighing, she turned back to her work. Francis was lifting her scissors to Mr. Smith's shoulder-length hair. His booted feet were propped on a footstool, yet he looked uncomfortable. Some men weren't used to the fuss of good hygiene. "Lean back and relax," Francis urged. "Most of our customers enjoy their time here."

"No need to worry." Middle-aged Mr. Johansen, the town's best gardener and recent importer of Dutch tulips, mumbled from beneath his towel five feet away. "These women are good at their work. And speakin' of Christmas, I've got a little gift for you both. Let me get them from my bag before you start my shave."

Melodie exchanged a giggle with Francis.

The man returned and gave each woman a round object wrapped in tinfoil. It felt heavy in Melodie's hands.

"Is it a ball?" asked Francis.

"It's a fruit. An orange."

"Oh!" Melodie unwrapped the precious gift. "I've heard of these. They grow in the American South."

"My son sent them from San Francisco."

"They're like the lemons I sometimes have with my tea," said Francis with delight. "It's perfect, thank you kindly."

Melodie thanked him, too. "How do you eat it?"

"You peel the outer skin then eat the inside, like a melon. It's more sour though. You best eat it within a day or two. They tend to dry out."

Francis tugged on Mr. Smith's shoulder to lean him back, then continued cutting his hair. "I'm not sure I can eat something sour while I'm still nursin' Timmy."

He started in his chair. His brows flexed with surprise. His gaze, almost desperate, flew to Melodie's, but he spoke to Francis. "He's your child?"

"My first. Almost three months old. Bend your head down a little, sir, so I can trim the back."

Francis was done with his haircut two minutes before Melodie was finished with her customer. When the older man got up to pay, she helped him at the counter.

"Good night!" Francis barreled around behind her, bundled up in a beaver coat and strapped leather boots. "Boris is in the back cleanin' up if you need him. He won't leave until you leave, Melodie." Francis was talking to her but looking pointedly at the stranger.

Melodie smiled self-consciously but couldn't bring herself to gauge Mr. Smith's reaction. Francis was protective, but two women running a shop this late in the evening had to be.

"Good night, Francis."

Francis picked up her little boy, placed the wriggling bundle inside her bulky fur coat, then left.

Stepping to the door window, Melodie peered over the lace curtain and saw Francis's husband, Eli, leaning on his cane standing by the door across the street and around the corner, waiting. Melodie turned the door sign to Closed, then locked the latch. Turning back to the cozy, golden room, she rubbed her arms. It was finally heating up again.

Mr. Smith removed the warm towel Francis had laid on his face before she'd left. "Does Francis live nearby? Will she be safe in this weather?"

Melodie nodded, touched by his thoughtfulness. "Right across the street. My brother-in-law is waiting for her."

"Brother-in-law? Is Francis your sister?"

She nodded.

He smiled gently, for the first time since entering her shop. She would have guessed that his smile would be lopsided from his injury, but it wasn't.

"You two look alike," he said. "She must be the sister from Vancouver."

Melodie frowned. How had he known that? It was another indicator that she'd obviously cut his hair before. "I told Francis she didn't have to come back to work so soon after Timmy was born, but she insisted on helping with the busy holiday season.

We've been partners for a year and a half, and she's stubborn about doing her fair share. Would you like to hold the hand mirror while I trim your beard? So you can follow what I'm doing?''

"No," he said quickly. Then more softly, almost apologetic, ''No, thanks.''

The poor man didn't want to look at his face. She stepped awkwardly to the jar of combs, pulled out one and picked up her scissors. She shouldn't have suggested it. What a terrible shame. He'd probably been a very handsome fellow at one time.

"How much do you want me to trim?"

He pondered the question for a moment. "Shave it all off."

"The beard, the mustache, everything?"

He nodded, watching her reaction.

"Sure thing."

She had to trim his beard with scissors first to make it easier for the straight blade, and worked without speaking, ever so conscious of the contact she made against his shoulder. He bristled with every accidental brush of her hand. His thighs shifted as he rearranged his feet on the footstool. And she felt suddenly shy.

For heaven's sake, she'd been alone with a customer before. She'd touched a hundred men, and their faces and their skin. She'd rubbed lotion into their necks. She'd been so close she could detect what soap they used. But this man…she gulped and glanced to the empty hallway. Where was Boris? She'd feel more comfortable with her hired man here.

Rufus got up from his mat and sauntered across the pine floor. His paws clicked as he walked to their side, the sound mingling with the wind's howl that was slapping against the windowpanes.

Mr. Smith must have felt the fur beside his hand, for he reached out and patted the dog between the ears. Rufus closed his eyes, savoring the touch.

"Is he yours?"

"Yeah."

"Good dog." He spoke quietly. "Your *husband* will be wondering why you're so late this evening."

Melodie glanced down at the ring he was studying. Why was she so conscious of this man?

Because he was close to her own age?

Because he was bulkier and more intense than the other men she'd served today?

"Donald Dawson is not my husband yet."

He brightened at her words. His blue eyes lit up and his shoulders straightened.

"The wedding's taking place on New Year's Day."

She watched a play of emotions on the stranger's face. "*Dawson* you said?"

"Mmm-hmm."

"But he's—" He cut his words short.

She stopped working, her scissors perched in mid-air, her focus on his wide brow. "He's what?"

He didn't finish his sentence. "Is he still living

beside your aunt's boardinghouse? The place you used to stay?''

''That he is.'' She rolled down the collar at the back of his neck to gain access to his throat. Her cool fingertips brushed against his smooth hot skin. Her touch seemed to disturb him. It was part of her job to touch a man's neck and face, yet…the contact had never felt this personal.

''Do you know Donald?''

''Not that well.'' Mr. Smith shifted on the chair. ''What made you pick that day for your wedding?''

''Another new year, a fresh new start.'' She meant to say it in a cheerful tone, but it came out subdued. The sadness wasn't as frequent as it had been in the beginning and she no longer had as many sleepless nights, but when the sadness came, it settled with a louder, more resounding thump.

''How long have you been engaged?''

For some unfathomable reason, the topic didn't suit her. She rebalanced her weight from foot to foot. ''A month.''

He blinked.

She tried to change the subject. ''Are you back in town for Christmas to see family?''

''I'm not sure I've got family to return to.''

That, more than anything, affected her. She didn't want to pry further, but she swallowed at the man's obvious sorrow. Living in the West was hard. Many settlers lost their lives just traveling across the drought-ridden, fly-infested prairies. She and Francis had arrived two summers ago themselves when their folks had passed away, both of them still in their teen years and aiming to help their only remaining relative, elderly Aunt Alice, with her boardinghouse.

Francis had met Eli almost immediately and they'd moved to Vancouver two weeks before Melodie had met Logan. After Eli's mining accident, Mclodie had convinced her sister and brother-in-law to return to Calgary, where Francis could help provide for the family.

Melodie placed a comforting hand on his shoulder, over the towel wrapped around him, and squeezed. "I know what losing family is like."

He turned his head to her hand, gently acknowledging the gesture. "Melodie." His voice caught.

The intimate way he said her name made her nerves tingle. It was getting *too* intimate between them.

Stepping back, she whisked up a lather in her tin cup, thankful to break the touch between them.

Taking out her straight razor, she leaned back from Mr. Smith as far as possible without seeming obvious, then scraped the hair above his lip then alongside the scar. "I'm not hurting you, am I?"

"No," he murmured.

She wondered who he was in the scheme of things, and where he had come from, and what he thought about the important things in life.

She finished with his cheeks and made her way toward his jaw. As her elbow fanned by his face, he closed his eyes. She scraped the white lather off one side, then reached above and over him to scrape the final patch from his good cheek.

His clear blue eyes tugged open and he looked directly up at her. They froze, faces six inches apart. In one sweep, she took in the clean-shaven jaw and the short blond hair and a bolt of panic seized her. It couldn't be!

Dear Lord...!

She dropped her razor blade to the floor and screamed.

CHAPTER THREE

"YOU'RE A GHOST!" Shaking from her fingertips to
the roots of her scalp, Melodie barely felt the pine
counter digging into her backside.

He leaped up from his chair, arms outstretched but,
luckily for him, keeping his distance. "I'm not a
ghost. It's me, Logan."

Her muscles clenched, ready for battle. "Logan
died!"

"I didn't die, Melodie." His blue eyes grew moist.
The scar on his cheek tugged as he spoke. "It's me."
He stepped toward her, brown flannel collar still
folded under at his neck, tight shoulders bearing
down on her like a moving mountain.

She screamed again.

Boris, heavy and out of breath, thundered into the
room with unlaced boots pounding the hollow floor.
He bellowed at the stranger. "What is it?"

The stranger took a step back, planting both palms
in the air in a gesture of surrender. The dog sniffed
his boots as his towel dangled from his shoulders.

As Boris eyed him with suspicion, the stranger
ripped the towel from around his neck and wiped off
the remaining streaks of shaving lather.

"Ma'am, has he hurt you?"

Dazed, she looked into Boris's round pale face, swallowing rapidly and shaking her head. Then she turned back to the audacious man who claimed to be her long-lost husband. *"How?"* Her voice crackled. "Whoever you are, how can you explain this?"

The stranger's gaze didn't waver. His voice was firm. "They took me with them. They'd planned it all along. The Grayveson gang knew I was a veterinarian. They knew I had a skill with horses and cattle. They put a gun to my head and they made me ride with them."

Boris spanned the room to stand protectively in front of Melodie, shielding her vision. "Listen, stranger, you best get out of here."

In the year and a half she'd been in business, this was the first time she'd ever physically needed protection.

A muscle flinched in the stranger's cheek. "I'm not here to harm anyone."

Melodie remained silent, grappling with the possibility of his claim. She clutched at her apron.

His voice did sound like...*Logan's.* Sagging under the weight of her shock, her body dipped forward against the countertop and her heart squeezed inside her ribs.

Boris crept forward. "Are you dim-witted, mister? I said take your things and get out of here."

The stranger looked past Boris's threatening stance to her again, waiting for her response.

She couldn't give one. It couldn't be. They'd searched for Logan for a full year. The superintendent of the Mounties had telegraphed every town between here and the U.S. border, hoping to receive even the tiniest scrap of information.

He was dead.

Boris made another move toward him. Seeming to come to a conclusion of his own, the stranger blinked and lowered his haunted eyes to the floor. Weakened by her lack of response, he staggered his way toward the fireplace, then pulled his fur coat off the peg and picked up his sack.

Laying one open hand on the wall beside the door, he held the knob with the other.

In a burst of new surprise, she sucked in some air.

Lord, his hand looked familiar. The long, smooth fingers, the splay of his knuckles, the way he placed his thumb…his wavy blond hair, his full lips…the pointy chin. And his blue, blue eyes.

"Melodie, do you remember the last promise I made to you?"

She gasped.

"I kissed you on the lips. I promised I'd return to you in three hours' time…to help you with…" He glanced down to her blouse. He couldn't finish the words.

To help her with her gown.

She watched his eyes brim with sentiment while she agonized.

The door latch clicked. He pulled it open. A slice

of the weather filtered in, snow gusting around his dejected face. "I'm sorry, Melodie... I'm so sorry."

"Wait," she whispered, almost unable to bear the pain. "Logan...please don't go."

She reacted with instinct, without thinking. Racing into his arms, she collided with his muscled chest. She buried her face in his shirt, wrapped herself in his arms, let her heart thrum against his, didn't exhale until she'd filled her lungs with him...not realizing what was happening until he tugged her arm to separate their bodies to kiss her.

Stumbling back, she couldn't see his face for her blur of tears. "No." Maybe she was dreaming. Her trembling hand shot to her collar. "No, I can't...*never again.*"

DEVASTATION ROCKED Logan. For one hallowed moment, he'd believed the chasm of space and time that had separated him and Melodie hadn't mattered. But as he followed behind her and Boris down the cold hallway, a knot quivered in his gut.

He feared he was two years too late.

Boris led them into her private parlor. A roaring fire blazed from the fireplace of one log wall, a horse-hair sofa and leather wing chair filled another, and Melodie's charcoal sketch paper lay open on the pine desk.

The room obviously doubled as her bedroom. A single bed in the corner sat covered with a white down tick.

It was a new house, built since his absence. Logan recognized nothing in it—not the photographs on the wall of Melodie and her sister, not the pewter vase on her desk, not the feather quill pen.

With an urgent fever, his gaze raced around the room. Hadn't she kept anything of *theirs?* Even a small trinket, a symbol of something of his from the past? He'd been by no means a wealthy man, but he'd owned a few personal items.

He saw *nothing.*

Boris stood with a menacing hand on the open door, assessing Logan but speaking to Melodie. "Are you sure you'll be all right, ma'am?"

Logan knew he shouldn't be offended; Boris didn't know him. He should be comforted by the fact that Melodie had such good protection. And he was. *He was.* But right now blood pumped through his biceps and the heat of fury primed his fists, ready to pounce in defense. He was Melodie's *husband!*

Sid Grayveson was responsible. He'd fractured their marriage and he would bloody well pay for everything he and his vicious gang had done.

Melodie nodded at Boris with obvious discomfort. Her voice shook as she removed her apron. "I can't believe it's you," she said to Logan. Then she answered Boris. "I'll be fine. And please, don't mention this to anyone until I...until I speak with you in the morning."

With a slight hesitation, Boris shuffled out the door. "Yes, ma'am, but I'll make myself useful in the back room for a while longer. I won't leave till I check with you one more time.''

Logan's lips tightened with frustration.

Stepping back so Melodie could pass by to light the desk lamp, he noticed she hadn't stopped shaking. The brush of her bouncing sleeve against his sent prickles up his arm. Her feminine scent caused another wave of hungering need.

This was the woman he'd pledged to spend his life with. He'd fallen in love with her warm nature, her keen ability for an intelligent conversation, her eagerness to be kind to a stranger, her love of animals and her love of the Christmas season and all things festive. He still saw all of these things in her, and longed to reach out to weave his callused fingers through her glossy hair. Instinct held him in check.

When the lamp illuminated, it washed her face with a gilded glow. He hadn't had a photograph with him on his journey to remind him of the details of her face. Now he stood galvanized by the upturn of her ivory cheek and the satiny contrast of her throat against her silky black hair.

Melodie, he wanted to shout. *Melodie, don't treat me like a stranger.*

Logan set down his coat and bag. His rough-clad figure stiffened. Suddenly aware of his empty hands and how displaced he felt in her room, he jammed a hand into his pant pocket. ''I guess it's wise to keep my reappearance in town quiet until we sort this out.''

There were others involved here. Donald Dawson, for one.

The rosy hue in her cheeks heightened. "Boris doesn't know much about you. I don't think I've ever mentioned your name to him. He's only been with me for six months, almost to the day he arrived in town. But he's trustworthy and he'll do as I ask."

The coolness in her voice wedged in Logan's heart. *I don't think I've ever mentioned your name.* Why not? The hurt of rejection burned deep within him. "God, you look so good."

They stared at each other for a long time. Her eyes widened, the pulsing at her throat beat wildly and he was barely able to hold himself together.

"How did the other men fare?" He asked the question that had hounded him. "The other Mounties who rode out to duty that night. Did any of them come back alive?"

"Haven't you seen them yet?"

"I came to you first."

Her chin quivered. "They all came back," she said softly, "alive and well...." And then, almost inaudibly, she added, "Except for you."

His eyes stung with tears. "Thank God," he muttered, breaking away from her stare. He couldn't face the painful depths of her brown eyes knowing the tragedy they bore. How long had she stood by the window in her gown, waiting for him to return? And how thankful had the other wives and mothers been when their men had returned safely?

"Logan, where have you been for two years?"

"I wasn't well. I was injured and didn't recall my own name."

She wavered on her feet, then gripped the back of a chair for support. He knew it must be difficult for her to hear the details. Again he vowed to repay the Grayvesons.

"Five minutes ago," he whispered, changing the subject, "you hugged me so tight I thought you'd never release me."

She closed her eyes. "I thought I was dreaming. I thought I was reliving the nightmare again." She walked around the desk. "But this time it had a different ending. You've come back alive." There was joy in her voice. "Why didn't you tell me who you were before I gave you a shave?"

"I was going to...then when I came into your shop, I saw the baby and the new ring on your finger."

"You thought the baby was mine?"

He nodded and she inclined her head in sympathy. "This is difficult to understand. I don't... I just can't believe it's you."

He'd had some time to think about the impact of his return while traveling from Montana to Calgary, but it must have been a staggering surprise for her. Was that all she needed? A bit of time?

Unfortunately, he had his doubts. "They took me to Montana Territory."

"Why?"

"They were stealing cattle and horses. They'd rustle them off the ranches in Calgary, then smuggle them across the U.S. border and sell them in Montana, where the brands weren't recognized and they could easily skirt the law. Several months later, they'd reverse the order. Steal down there and resell up here. They'd use me to groom and treat any unhealthy animals so they could maximize their profits. They had the best equipment—stolen from somewhere—but no expert to use it. They knew what they were doing when they took me hostage. They planned it."

He stepped away to the fire, fuming with rage and humiliation at what they'd done to him, but trying to speak calmly for Melodie's sake. He didn't want to frighten her by falling apart.

"I didn't want to do it," he said. "To help them in any way...but a sick horse or steer, I couldn't let a sick..." A lump welled in his throat and he couldn't finish. Maybe he *was* going to fall apart.

He heard her soft footsteps beside him. "You were right to help the animals. You've got a gift with healing, and you were meant to use it. It wouldn't be like you to walk away from a suffering beast. Horses and cattle don't know who they belong to. They just want to feel the wind on their manes and the grass beneath their hooves."

Melodie had always understood him. A little of the shame he felt at having helped the outlaws vanished.

"I think the Mounties are still after that gang," she added.

"The Mounties here and the sheriffs down there. There are a number of gangs that have been busted over the years, but no ring this big. There must be at least two dozen men involved."

Cross-border gangs were one of the main reasons the Mounties had been formed fifteen years ago. The policemen were federal agents commissioned by the government in 1873 to bring law and order to the West, to make peace with and contain the Indians— which they had before any settlers had moved in— and to dismantle the illegal whiskey trade and cross-border gangs.

"The bigger the ring, the easier it should be to find the men."

"I agree," he said, turning toward her. "You'd think with more culprits involved, it'd be harder to hide and harder to keep a secret when they spend their money in a strange town." But he shook his head. Even without speaking to the Mounties back at the fort, he knew no men had been captured yet because Melodie would have heard about it and would be telling him now.

"Two years is a long time to be forced to ride."

"Most of it was spent in the foothills of Montana after I escaped."

"Oh, Logan. How did you escape?"

"I waited every night until they went to bed. Most of the time they locked me up in shackles, both my wrists and ankles. About six months after they took me, they got drunk one night and shackled my wrists, but forgot about my ankles. I hit one over the head and stole his gun. I managed…to get to their horses. When I did, Sid Grayveson gave chase. He shot me in the face, but I got away. I…I don't remember much after that, except that an old man found me. A mountain man and fur trader, Tex was his name. He took me for dead until he got closer. He tells me I damn near blew his head off with the gun I still had between my hands. I didn't remember anything, not my name, nothing."

She swallowed hard. "They shot you in the face."

"Yeah."

"They locked you up in shackles while I slept in the comfort of my bed."

His heart melted. "You couldn't have had it easy."

She turned away, but he saw her wipe her cheek. "You didn't remember *me?*"

"No," he said as gently as he knew how. He was conscious of the cold space between them. They weren't touching and all he wanted was to touch her.

Her gray skirt rippled around her hips as she took the poker from the hearth and played with the fire. "But you remember now. How did it come back to you?"

"About a month ago, there was a traveling sales caravan that came through the area by our shack, where we lived. Tex told me he was keeping me around because I showed him how to nurse his cow back to health. I guess he figured he wanted to nurse me back so we'd be even.'' Logan smiled.

Melodie rubbed her cheek as she listened. ''You've got a nice smile, Logan.''

He was caught off guard and stumbled for a moment. It was a kind thing for her to say, but made him more self-conscious of his scars. What did she see when she looked at him?

He pressed on. ''I didn't remember that I'd been trained as a veterinarian in Toronto, but somehow I did recall many of the practical things I'd been taught in my college classes.''

''That's remarkable.''

''Our nearest neighbors ten miles away came to tell us about the caravan. Tex needed to buy new rope and I needed a new pair of gloves, but the salesman took out this little music box. When I opened the lid, it played a Christmas song. You know that one from Austria that they played at…at our wedding reception?''

'''Silent Night,''' she whispered.

He nodded in agreement.

''In the end,'' she added, ''it was the most silent night of my life.''

Struggling with his sorrow, he was quiet for a moment. ''The images came rushing back to me then. You in your wedding gown was the first one. And then saying our vows and then…being called away. We rushed back to the fort to get our guns and change out of our dress uniforms. Normally, I wouldn't have gone with the troops, but we were short-staffed due to the recent transfer of several constables to Edmonton. The outlaws later told me they knew that, and that we were preoccupied with the wedding.''

Although Logan had been schooled as a veterinarian, he'd also been trained as a commissioned police officer when he'd enrolled for duty. At the time, he'd been the youngest commissioned officer at the fort.

Melodie swayed on her feet, almost as if she couldn't bear to hear more, then gently fell onto the sofa. Placing her face in her hands, she moaned. ''How horrible it all was.''

He sank onto the sofa beside her, wanting to reach an arm around her, but something held him back.

''I thought… I thought you'd been killed.'' Her voice sounded raw and uneven. ''But your life was spared. I'm so thankful for that.'' And then something else dawned on her. Her face twisted. ''Your mother. Oh Lord, and your brother and sisters back East.''

Logan's pulse raced, thinking again of the agony his mother must have gone through. ''I plan on sending a telegram in the morning.''

She drew herself up higher. ''You've got to tell the other Mounties, too. They roamed the countryside for a year, hoping to find a trace of you. They telegraphed every jurisdiction for a thousand miles. They'll be thrilled to know you're alive. The surgeon, John Calloway, was especially hard hit when you disappeared. He ignored his own grief to help me cope. Well, as best as he could.''

Logan smiled, eager to return to his friends as well. He'd only been with the force for eight months before his disappearance, but he knew they were good men. Sturdy, honest and hardworking, mostly of Irish or Scottish descent, or English like himself.

Logan shoved his fingers through his newly cropped hair, feeling slightly off balance due to its short length. He rose and went to the desk, then ran his hand along the sketch paper Melodie had been working on. It was a dashing silhouette of a horse and rider, lightly outlined but no details of the rider's face and hands drawn in yet.

He fingered the smooth corner absently but pressed on with his urgent questions. ''What happened to the wedding ring I gave you?''

Behind him, she nervously cleared her throat. ''The Mounties collected some money on my behalf after your disappearance. I used it to open this shop, but it wasn't enough. I had to sell your private horse and buggy. Your private gun. And the ring.''

Spinning his wide shoulders around so he could look into her eyes, he stared without blinking. ''That was wise of you.''

She was tougher and more independent than when he'd first met her, serving him the occasional Sunday dinner at her aunt's boardinghouse. On the surface, Melodie seemed the same, but he could no longer dig beneath that surface as he had in the past. One of the things he'd most loved about her and the reason he'd believed she'd make a great policeman's wife was her ability to put troubles behind her and plow ahead, despite grueling, challenging circumstances.

He flinched at the irony. Had this ability helped her to put *him* in the past, and to plow ahead?

''Time has passed and things have changed,'' she added numbly. ''What do we do now?''

He wobbled at the possibility of losing her. He couldn't have come this far only to lose her. His gaze raced along the wall behind her, searching for any remnant of their past. If he could find one small thing, one token…it meant there was hope.

A shelf of books sat in one corner. He'd never seen them before. Dickens and Austen. A map of the new Dominion of Canada.

Nothing of his.

Lowering his gaze to the umbrella stand, he spotted a brown paper parcel tied with white string. ''What's that?''

Ill at ease, she rubbed her neck. ''I'm ashamed to tell you.''

He frowned at the parcel.

''It's something I've kept for a long time. I thought they might get more use out of it at the fort, seeing how they always seem to be in short supply when the new recruits come in. I'd told the superintendent I'd return it this week. It seemed like the proper time, what with…New Year's Day coming.''

He paused. ''What is it?''

"Your dress uniform."

The muscles in his face grew taut. Considering she was about to marry another man, Melodie wanted to get rid of the last bit of *him*.

She stepped forward, trying to explain. "A lot has happened since you've been gone."

His jaw pulsed. "I can see that."

"I've opened my shop."

"I can see that, too."

"Donald Dawson befriended me at time when I needed it most. I suppose he gave me a diversion and encouraged me to stay in Calgary when what I wanted to do was to return to where I'd grown up on Prince Edward Island, to where things were familiar. Instead, he convinced me to write to Francis. Eli's leg wasn't getting any better, and Francis could help me open my shop. Mr. Daw—*Donald*—" she corrected herself "—Donald helped me."

"He's two and a half times your age."

"It doesn't matter."

Logan jarred with the realization that she cared about the man.

"What is it that I'm supposed to tell Donald now? How do I break the news that my first husband is back?"

"You just say the words."

"What's going to happen, Logan?"

"Whatever you want to happen."

She rubbed her arms, uncertainty flickering across her features.

"Do you love him more than you love...
loved me?"

Her lips parted open.

When she didn't say, he drew himself taller and turned around to leave.

"Where are you going?"

"To speak to Donald."

She let out a small gasp. "You *are* right. He has to be the next person who's told about your return. It affects him more than anyone else."

Logan bit back the sharp reply that threatened to burst from his lips. He and Melodie were the ones affected more than anyone else. Donald Dawson be damned! "Where is he? At his store or at his home?"

"You know it has to be me who tells him."

He exhaled, long and heavy. Should he give her the dignity of privacy with Dawson? How much longer could Logan wait for this two-year ordeal to end?

"Donald's at the store. We were supposed to meet at the Christmas social tonight, but I don't know..."

Logan's demeanor hardened.

She rambled on, perhaps because she wanted to avoid talking about the significant things between them. "A shipment of Dutch china and English cutlery that was supposed to have arrived last month arrived yesterday instead. He's there, unpacking the pieces. Or repacking them for the women who'd already preordered their holiday place settings."

"Melodie," Logan began, walking closer.

She moved away from him, as a stranger might.

The shock of that made him reel. His usual air of authority and confidence when dealing with people escaped him. Melodie's reaction battered him more than anything the outlaws had physically done to him.

Pressing a hand on the desk in front of him to steady himself, his eye caught the bottom tip of a rocking chair peeking out from behind the door of the next room. It looked like a cramped supply room, stuffed with mops and buckets, and a spring overcoat and two bonnets. And…a beaten-up old rocking chair.

Yes! She'd kept the chair! She'd kept that big, ratty chair they used to sit on together. Their bodies had barely fit and she had to climb onto his lap to make it possible, but they used to sit and talk for hours at the boardinghouse in front of the fire when everyone else had gone to bed.

So he'd found something of theirs. There was hope!

"Where will you be staying?" she asked.

He felt the tense lines in his face ease. "Is the boardinghouse at the end of the street open?"

Melodie nodded. "So is Aunt Alice's."

"I'll try to find a room at the end of the street first. If it's full, I'll try your aunt's." He didn't want to because it was next to Dawson's place. Peering out of the windows at the house of the man who was to wed his bride would certainly chafe any goodwill Logan had.

"I'd let you stay here, but it wouldn't be proper."

Wouldn't be proper? They were married!

"I'm being ridiculous," she said in a flutter. "Of course you can stay here. After all you've been through, I *want* you to stay here. I'll…I'll take my bedclothes and knock on my sister's door—"

"I'll get a room at the boardinghouse," he interrupted, trying to end her embarrassment and his agony.

Her chin caught the light. Orange flames flickered across her creamy skin.

"I'll give you two hours lead to speak with Dawson."

Her hand shot to her throat. "What?"

"Two hours. Then I'm going to talk to him." Logan would tell the man that a grave mistake had been made, that Dawson had to find himself a new wife. As long as there was hope—and there was—Logan would do what was necessary.

He'd court his own wife, and win her back. Not because they were still legally married. He prayed it'd be because she might still love him.

She seemed too startled to argue.

Slowly making his way out the parlor, he stopped as he passed the bookshelf. Peering down at the brown paper parcel, he tried to conceal his anguish. "Would you mind if I took back my uniform?"

CHAPTER FOUR

MELODIE HAD THIRTY MINUTES left of her two-hour lead.

"Donald, I don't know how to tell you this." Alone in the covered buggy behind half a dozen others heading down the freshly ploughed road toward the fort, Melodie practiced what she'd say. None of the words seemed right.

She wrapped her cloak tighter around her neck to drive away the icy air. The wind had subsided; the falling snow came in milder gusts. Cedar trees lining the road shook as she rolled by. The brilliant white snow, and the hanging lanterns swinging from each buggy were the only things lighting their pathway.

She hadn't been able to find Donald. By the time she'd dashed down the two streets to his store, it was already locked. She'd come back to her home, had Boris hitch her horse and buggy, then raced for Donald's house. He wasn't there, either. That meant he was already heading to the social. Yesterday, she'd promised to meet him there. She knew he was arriving earlier because he'd kindly volunteered the cutlery and dishes he normally rented out for these formal events.

"Donald, there's been a development." No, that didn't sound right either. "My first husband, you remember Logan? Well, thank God, he's come home alive."

Melodie urged her mare into a faster trot.

He was alive!

No matter what else happened, Logan was alive!

"Thank you for this miracle," she said beneath her breath.

The turmoil of the past two hours tightened around her. The news both thrilled and frightened her. What would happen now?

The buggy slid on a patch of ice, the horse neighed and Melodie gasped. With heart careening, she tugged back on the reins to slow their pace. Lord have mercy, she wouldn't create an accident in her haste to arrive.

Hot sweat trickled down her cold forehead. She ran a mitted hand along her face and told herself to calm down.

The problem was that her joy at Logan's safe arrival was tangled up with the heartache of the past two years, and her blossoming feelings for Donald.

She wasn't sure she could *ever* be a Mountie's wife again.

Having the man she'd loved with all her heart disappear on their wedding night never to return again was indescribable. Wondering what had happened to him, how long he may have suffered, where his remains had been buried—*or not*—were questions that had tormented her.

May Logan find the grace to forgive her, but she couldn't do it again. She lacked the courage.

She had to find Donald. He was always calm and rational. They'd discuss it, and he'd help her decide what to do.

They passed through the palisade gate into the fort, to the newly built community hall. Policemen dressed in scarlet uniforms helped the ladies disembark while taking the horses from the gentlemen. It was the first Christmas social of the season, the Police Ball, each year marking the herald of parties and festivities. Since the terrible raid two years previously on Christmas Eve, however, the Mounties made sure they were never ill prepared again.

"Good evening, Mrs. Sutcliffe," said a young constable as she entered the bright hall.

"Good evening."

"May I take your cloak?"

"Yes, please." Passing it to him, she slipped her rough woolen mittens into one side pocket.

"You look lovely," he said, then went on to help the lady behind her.

Self-conscious of her dowdy appearance, Melodie brushed at her gray skirt and rose-colored blouse. She hadn't had time to think about her clothes. The new homespun gown she'd intended to wear tonight was still lying on her bed, spread out as she'd laid it there this morning after she'd ironed it. Her hair wasn't done up in the ringlets she'd intended either, and sagged across her shoulders from the wet snow. The lovely pearl necklace Donald had surprised her with on their engagement was still sitting in its velvet pouch at home.

Straining her neck above the crowd, she searched for Donald, figuring when she found him, they'd head home to talk.

When she passed a group of boisterous Mounties, the dark-haired and handsome chief surgeon, Dr. Calloway, slipped to her side with the friendly auctioneer's daughter beside him.

"Merry Christmas, Mrs. Sutcliffe."

"Thank you, and the same to you."

They looked as if they wanted to engage her in conversation, but Melodie pressed on.

She couldn't tell any of them about Logan's reappearance until she spoke with Donald. They'd all be as shocked as she was, especially the doctor. Logan had once told her that Dr. Calloway was a no-nonsense type of man and downright critical at times, but after what she'd witnessed in these two years, she reckoned that's how a man had to be to practice medicine in the harsh frontier. Fresh supplies were hard to come by, and the doctor coped with outrageous wounds. He dealt with mountain fever, vigilantes, and rustlers like the Grayveson gang who slit throats and broke legs.

The Mounties made this country safe. Each and every one of them was a hero.

And she didn't belong with heroes. She was a coward.

Above the crowd in the far corner, she spotted Donald's top hat and wove her way toward it.

"Donald," she said, breaking through to stand in front of the table laden with fresh-baked scones and raisin pies and hot tea simmering in the silver tea service Donald had brought. Speaking with the mayor and his wife, Donald stood tall and elegant in his black waistcoat and Caribbean cotton shirt. His angular face, lined with wrinkles of age that Melodie barely noticed, glowed with warmth and good humor.

"Melodie, so good—" He glanced down at her dress. "Darling, I thought you were going to wear that pretty new gown. And the pearls."

"Sorry, there's been an emergency," she whispered. "I've come to take you home."

Donald's cheery smile withered into a grimace. "What's happened? Is someone hurt? Your sister?"

"No, no. I believe Francis and Eli are already here. The baby's fine with his sitter. I—I need to talk with you. We have to leave."

"It's not *my* sister, is it? Good God, not a telegram saying her heart ailment has worscncd—"

"No, she's fine." Melodie took his hand and led him into the throng.

"I'm coming."

One of the things she appreciated about Donald was that he didn't quarrel with her. He listened in a compassionate manner, a charming characteristic that evaded many men. Despite his years, he was as energetic as those half his age, with a mind sharper than most.

Was he sharper than Logan? Was he more energetic?

''You've been looking forward to this social for over two months,'' Donald said, weaving behind her. ''It's the first dance you've gone to since...''

Since her mourning over Logan's disappearance.

''What's the emergency? Please tell me.''

A commotion started at the back door. People screamed, others shouted. But they were happy sounds, laughter mingled with shrieks of surprise.

Trying to decipher what was happening, Melodie spun toward the back. The crowd whooshed ahead of her, racing to the door. When the group parted slightly, Melodie stared at the man standing calmly in the center of the disruption, dressed in the full red tunic and tight black trousers she'd given him two hours earlier.

She gasped and turned to Donald. His lips parted in shock and his face drained of color. For the first time in two years, she felt their difference in age.

Turning back to the man at the center of everyone's attention, Melodie felt her chest constrict with the same awe and nervousness as when she'd spoken with him earlier.

Logan Sutcliffe had arrived.

BURIED IN THE CROWD, Logan reacted with laughter and elation. Hands grabbed at him for proof it was him in the flesh; men clapped him on the back, openly conveying good cheer; older women cried with disbelief. And Logan had never felt this good in all his life.

When the shouting was over, murmurs began at the far end. The shuffling crowd parted to clear the space between Logan, Melodie and Donald.

It took a moment for Logan to recapture his breath. He felt sharp eyes boring into him.

So they were both here, Melodie still in the same clothes he'd left her in, Donald looking every bit as dapper as he always had.

Logan had an urge to step forward to make Melodie feel at ease, but no one seemed to know what to say. In the background, the band stopped playing, people stopped talking, and everyone stood nailed to their spots. Ceiling lanterns lit their faces. Streamers of colored paper clung to log walls. On the tables, hand-painted ornaments sat nestled against pine-cones. To Logan, it all looked and smelled wonderfully like Christmas.

Donald nodded hello to Logan, then turned to Melodie. "You knew about this?"

Melodie fidgeted with her skirt pockets. "Logan came to see me earlier in the day. It's what I needed to speak to you about."

Voices whispered around them, as if they were on a theatrical stage for everyone's viewing.

The older man made the first move, extending his hand to Logan. "It's good to see you back."

Logan gripped the hand and shook. He wanted to dislike Donald, but knew the sole reason would be because he'd proposed to Melodie.

Judging by his cool expression, Donald definitely knew that Logan's arrival meant his own wedding on New Year's Day was in jeopardy.

Three hundred heads turned toward Melodie, expecting something from her. What could she say? Logan wondered. What could any of them say with an audience this large?

Then he noticed Francis slowly make her way to her sister's side. Francis spread her arm around Melodie's shoulders and she leaned against the support.

Logan's good friend Dr. Calloway jumped forward, as if to bridge the gap of silence. "It's bloody well good to lay eyes on you again. What happened?"

As Logan explained, some of his unease melted. Friends he hadn't seen forever asked questions and he answered. Donald and Melodie stood apart from everyone else, shoulders brushing quietly as they watched him.

There were loud murmurs of getting even with the Grayveson gang, plans Logan agreed with, but now was not the time to display his fury. He'd lived with it for the first six months of his kidnapping, and the last month of hell getting here.

Now was the time to win back his lovely wife.

Finally the accordion started up again. People filtered away, promising to return to speak to him before the evening was over, promising to help him move his things from the boardinghouse back into the barracks. Melodie's sister left to rejoin her husband.

Logan clenched his jaw to kill the sob in his throat due to everyone's kind offers to help him resettle back into his life.

Everyone's offers except the person who mattered most.

The doctor examined Logan's scarred cheek. Both of them were muscular men. "You know, the scars can be reduced if we trim the jagged skin to make a tighter close." He pulled at Logan's droopy eyelid. "Looks like I might be able to fix the eyelid, too, if I stitch here and here."

Logan's confidence evaporated. Just how awful did he look? He turned to his wife. "Should I do it, Melodie?"

Donald raised his hand to stop her from answering, obviously offended at the significance of the question. "It's your decision," he told Logan. "Yours alone."

Logan bristled at the harsh reply, as did the doctor and Melodie. Unnerved, Logan's first response was to tell Dawson to go to hell.

But not here. And could he truly blame Dawson for outlining the boundaries of their battle? He'd been caught in the middle of this, too. As much as

Logan despised the thought of their engagement, they hadn't done it behind his back. They'd done it because they'd thought he was gone for good.

Nevertheless, he was alive and well!

When the doctor left, the three of them were alone. Dawson toyed with the brim of his top hat, which he held in nimble hands. "It's a damn bit of good luck that you've come back alive. But you know…you know you should let Melodie go on with her life."

Logan winced. Was that all the man thought there'd be to it? That he only had to ask, and Logan would retreat?

He decided to ignore the statement in case he lost his temper. He turned to Melodie instead, determined to try again for her opinion. There was a soft color in her lips.

"What do you think of the doctor's suggestion? Should I let him have a go?"

She clasped her hands and studied them for a moment. Ignoring Donald's scoff, she looked to Logan with grace and assurance.

"Yes, you should. He's a brilliant surgeon."

Logan felt his shoulders straighten beneath his tunic. Although a bit surprised at her direct response, he took her comment as a huge step in the right direction. She cared enough about him to venture her opinion.

Donald, however, loosened his tie. Anger flashed across his thin face. "Melodie has explained certain things to me about your marriage,'' he insisted. ''It's only right you let her move on.''

Logan tensed. ''What things did she explain?''

''About that night…under those circumstances.''

''What circumstances?'' Logan grimaced, uncertain he wanted to hear this. Melodie frowned as well. ''If you've got something to say, speak your mind.''

Dawson had the gall to say it aloud. ''We all know why your marriage can be easily annulled.''

Logan didn't appreciate the man's tone, nor his insinuations. *''Why?''*

''Because your marriage was never consummated.''

Melodie took a quick, sharp breath as Logan stared, momentarily speechless.

He'd thought that the intimacies of their marriage were sacred. How could she have revealed them to Donald Dawson?

Her embarrassment was painful to watch.

How in hell could Dawson hurl the accusation into Logan's face? It was true, but none of Dawson's business! Logan itched to punch the man but somehow found the strength to restrain himself. He turned to Melodie again. ''Do *you* want an annulment, Melodie?''

Her face clouded with apprehension. ''Logan, I don't know.…''

He faltered in her silence.

A look of satisfaction flitted across Dawson's face.

Logan's despair increased as she tried to find the right words to say but couldn't seem to find any.

Closing his eyes, he felt his composure slipping, the pain of separation taking root again. Unable to take it, he walked away and didn't look back, stalking out of the building into the black wintry night. He didn't stop until miles later, when he was enveloped by the dismal solitude from which he'd come.

CHAPTER FIVE

STANDING ALONGSIDE his young assistant and warmed by the fire in the far corner of the police fort stable, Logan looked at the hind leg of a two-year-old mustang. He hadn't approached Melodie for three days, hoping something would change in their situation, or that she might ease her way back into his life. Everyone in town knew her wedding to Dawson was on hold. But *annulment?*

For the first time in his life, Logan wondered if he'd taken too much for granted before his kidnapping. Everything had come to him easily, from veterinary college when he was only seventeen, to signing up with the force, to finding a beautiful wife. Whatever he'd wanted, he'd gotten. Not anymore, it seemed. How could he win back Melodie?

"Have ya figured out the mare's problem?" Twelve-year-old Shamus, who was apprenticing as a veterinary assistant, squinted in concentration.

"She's got a capped hock," said Logan.

"What's that?"

"An injury most likely caused by the mare striking her hock against the boards of this stall. It's because there's not enough bedding in here. And why are we using barley straw? Shamus, replace this stuff with wheat straw from the loft. Most horses would rather *eat* barley straw than bed down on it, and it contains bristles that irritate their eyes. Make sure you bank it up real high against the boards.''

"Okay," said the boy, looking eager to start.

Logan called across the boards to a constable watering a horse in the next stall. "We'll need to apply cold water to reduce the swelling.''

"I'll get it for you. It's good to have you back, Sir.''

Logan nodded and smiled gently, then turned to watch the boy pick up his pitchfork. An unexpected twinge of loss settled around Logan. He and Melodie had often joked that they wanted many children so they could fill their own stables.

"Shamus, when you're done, we'll go over that list of wild poisonous plants once more. The ones you have to insure horses don't eat. You can draw me the shape of the leaves again.''

Shamus began reciting. "They have to stay away from buttercup, ragwort, foxglove, hemlock, horsetails and rhodo…rhododendron because it can cause failure of the resp…respera…respiratory systems.''

The boy was a quick study. When Logan was finished bandaging the hock, he walked to the far corner of another stall to *his* horse. Technically, it belonged to the Mounties, but he'd broken in the bay two years ago. "Hi, boy." Sighing with pleasure, Logan picked up a grooming brush.

No sooner had he started combing than shadows flickered on the straw floor. He looked up to see five of his friends peering at him. The Mounties were dressed in their work clothes in billowing white shirts, dark pants and suspenders.

"What's this, Sir?" Logan asked of Dr. Calloway.

John was close to forty and a good fifteen years older than Logan. Logan was still the youngest commissioned officer at the fort and he outranked all the men in this group except for the doctor and the assistant surgeon.

"We've got something for you. I thought—*we* thought—it might cheer you up." John thrust out a book.

Logan took it. "My old work journal. How'd you get it?"

John looked uncomfortable. "We feel bad that you've returned only to find all of your possessions have been given away."

Logan shrugged, knowing life had gone on without him. Even the buildings themselves were changing. They'd had a fire last year at the fort, and new barracks were under construction.

"A year after you disappeared, Melodie had to make some difficult decisions. She sent a few of your personal things back to your family, but thought your friends should each take an item as a token of our friendship. I took your work journal in honor of the hard work you did around here."

Logan fingered the worn black leather spine of the journal, touched by its return. "Thank you."

Wesley Quinn stepped forward. "I took your quill and inkwell for good luck that some of that intelligence might rub off on me. You might have to fill it up though... I think it's almost dry."

Logan removed the cap and tipped the blackened jar, expecting it to be empty. It was full and he accidentally dripped ink onto his work pants. *"What!"*

"Got ya," said Wesley, the troop's most notable joker. "I just refilled it."

When the men laughed, Logan was engulfed by their warm camaraderie. He supposed he needed a jolt like this to pull him out of his sour mood.

"Next," said the corporal, who was smaller and more limber than the rest of them. "Here's your bed quilt. I took it because it reminded me of that spring afternoon when you won it."

Logan set down the journal and inkwell so he could take the quilt, with its patches of red and white and gold. He'd won it by buying a ticket at the ladies' church raffle one quiet Easter Sunday. He and the corporal had spent the morning riding, pleasantly surprised at the warm chinook wind that had come out of nowhere to melt the snow.

"All right," said the old cook. He had his hands behind his back. "I ain't got much to show for what I took, but you're welcome to have 'em back." He pulled out a pair of red long johns that were tattered at the elbows and worn plum through on the buttoned seat. "I took 'em 'cuz I figured they'd keep me warm, simple as that."

Logan laughed. "I'm not touching those. You can have them!"

More laughter ensued, with Logan in the middle of it. Then one of the stable hands made his way around the stall.

"Are you limping?" John asked him.

"My foot's sore. It's a boil or somethin'."

"Take it out. Let me see."

When the man revealed his foot, it was wrapped in a checkered blue flannel cloth.

"Why didn't you come to me with this?"

"It only happened last week. And I still had this checkered shirt of Logan's. I thought… I thought if I wrapped it around my foot, it'd be like Logan was takin' care of me. Like he did the time I got kicked by the mule. This is the shirt he was wearing when it happened."

The men grew serious. Logan sobered, touched by the items each man had taken in his memory but thunderstruck by the thought that these men had declared him dead. *Dead.* He knew they were trying to cheer him up, but the moment only underscored all the time he'd lost with his friends and with his wife. Was he too late to recover Melodie?

John replaced the boot. "Swing by my office later."

The feeling of lost hope amplified in Logan. He was bonded to these men. They shared a similar dream of a civilized country, men living in peace among each other, loving their wives and raising their children, in a society unencumbered by the wars and perils of the past. But he'd lost two prime years. They'd been hacked out of his life, leaving nothing but a big gaping hole and a lot of fury. And an injured face that would never be the same. Melodie could barely look at him.

Despite the new information they had about the Grayveson gang, and a sighting in the area two months ago, Logan felt no closer to resolution.

John patted the stallion. "That's all we've got to return, Logan. There wasn't much," he said gently. "It seems you've got more friends to go around than things. I hope I fare as well when I'm dead and gone."

Dead and gone.

"John," Logan called as they were leaving, his emotions barely held in check. "I need you to help me with something."

John swung back. "Sure."

"Promise you won't breathe a word to anyone. Could you set up a couple of dinners? I want you to invite me…and invite Melodie. Do you think there's any way we could omit Donald, but that Melodie would still come?"

THE NEXT TIME Melodie saw Logan, it happened by surprise at the superintendent's house on December twentieth. Her dinner invitation had come unexpectedly while she was closing the barbershop the day before. Working late, she felt it was her obligation to finish the week's appointments with the folks counting on her to trim their hair, or arrange their fancy dos for various holiday functions.

She'd purposely kept her distance from both men for several days. Besides which, she would have throttled Donald if she had five minutes alone with him. Instead of waiting for her so they could speak to Father Walsh together, Donald had gone without her to inquire about annulment. They must write to the Vatican for permission, the Father had said. He made it clear he meant only Melodie and Logan. Three days ago, Donald had stopped by during his brief lunch hour to tell her this, knowing she had to quietly turn around and serve three customers. What's more, he'd brought expensive stationery with him, expecting her to do it on the spot.

"Logan had to wait twenty-four months to return home," Melodie had replied, much to Donald's dismay. "The least I can do is take two weeks to think about our future."

Now, finished for the evening and gripping her gift basket beneath her arm, Melodie knocked on Superintendent Ridgeway's door. She would deliver her gifts to their children, then set out to the fort to speak with Logan. She wasn't quite sure what she'd say, but it was time she said it.

Superintendent Ridgeway was the Mountie's top commander, with a large private house overlooking the junction of the Elbow and Bow Rivers. Gazing out across the quilt of whiteness, she took note that the rivers were frozen solid. Drifting snow blew in her direction, dusting her with white powder. While she waited, she wove her gloved fingers together.

Keeping busy with customers all day—and listening to their unsolicited opinions about which man she should choose—had only postponed her desperation. Many thought she should reunite with Logan, but Donald's close friends supported him. Francis had been her best confidante, doing more listening than talking.

The door opened. Annabelle Ridgeway, the commander's wife, beamed from the hallway, her face as round as a frying pan, her short, plump figure reeling with delight. "How nice to see you."

Melodie stepped inside and hugged her friend. "Thank you for the invitation. I've brought some things for the children."

"They'll be tickled."

Peeking above Annabelle's shoulder across to the dining room, Melodie noticed the group of Mounties dressed in formal civilian clothing sitting at the table. Those who were married had brought their wives, and there, smack in the middle facing the door, sat Logan. He was leaning back in his chair, loose and lean, cognac snifter in his large fist.

She was hit with a pang of surprise. Her hand flew to the cameo pendant at her throat, then her wind-blown hair. "I didn't know you had company."

"But…that's why you got the invitation. It's a dinner party, my dear."

"But had I known… I would have insisted more strongly to Donald that he should close the store to accompany me." How had the mix-up occurred? The way the note was written, Melodie could have sworn it was an informal note requesting her to drop by to share dinner with only Annabelle and the children.

Melodie wasn't dressed properly. She was wearing her gray work skirt again, and her old white blouse that had been washed so frequently the threads were fraying. After showing up in her work clothes at the social, these people would think she was a pauper.

Annabelle looked nervously to the basket. "We'll see Donald again soon. I'm glad you could make it." She hollered up the wide stairwell. "Children!"

Logan turned his head at the sound of thudding footsteps tripping down the stairs. When he spotted Melodie, he instantly sprang from his chair.

Again she was taken aback by the severity of his injured face. But his eyes were warm and true.

Unsure of how to respond, Melodie nodded cordially. She was hoping to speak with him in private, but here they were in the center of watchful eyes again.

The two children reached her side the same time Logan did.

"You look wonderful, Melodie—" he began.

"Howdy," interrupted the children. The younger girl, Henrietta, squeezed Melodie around the middle while the adolescent one, Charlotte, smiled from a few steps away.

"Hello everyone," Melodie responded, first to the girls, then looking up to Logan's smiling face. For peace of mind, she had to deal with the children first. Logan's broad shoulders and the care he'd obviously taken to slick back his hair and press his shirt made her heart hammer uncontrollably. "I've brought you each a Christmas present."

Henrietta's eyes opened wide as she tried to contain her giggle.

"Charlotte, you're becoming a young woman right before my eyes. Your mother has told me how much you like to sew." Melodie reached under the cloth of her basket and pulled out a brand-new Butterick pattern. "I ordered this from the catalog."

Charlotte gasped as she took it. "A store-bought pattern."

"It's much too extravagant," declared her mother.

"I insist," said Melodie. "It's for a formal gown. I know there are many occasions where she'll be able to use one." The commander and his wife entertained dozens of foreign dignitaries and government officials from Ottawa. "And for you, little one, something very special that I ordered from the blacksmith. Ice skates that you strap over your boots. You'll be able to join the bigger children and learn how to skate this year."

Their hugs and kisses came spontaneously and

Melodie savored each one. When she looked up again, Logan and Annabelle were watching her.

"It's nice to see you again, Logan."

Nodding silently, he took her cloak and hung it in the armoire with the others. It was a tender thing to do, and reminded her of the times he used to do it before they were married.

She rubbed the outdoor chill from her arms as Annabelle led them to the table.

After their hellos, one of the men moved his chair so that Logan and Melodie could sit side by side.

She was beginning to think this arrangement had been planned. When she turned to Annabelle to ask, the other woman conveniently rose to leave, saying she had to check with her housekeeper on dinner.

"Would you like some wine?" Logan held the decanter of Beaujolais above her glass.

"It would take the chill out of my bones." When she sipped, it also eased her nervousness.

Growing thoughtful, he outlined the rim of his glass with long, lean fingers, in the same slow manner he used to stroke her shoulder blades. The memory lingered around the edges of her mind and made her legs go warm.

On the day she'd met him, while serving lunch at her aunt's boardinghouse, he'd stroked the rim of his coffee mug with a similar swirl. She'd always been fascinated by the way his hands moved, like a sculptor's. And unbeknownst to anyone, she had once craved for Logan to use those warm heavy hands to explore her body like a sculptor might.

But they hadn't gotten that blissful opportunity.

And she couldn't turn back the clock, no matter how much she wished it.

As the meal of ham and roast potatoes was served, they chatted with the others. Melodie knew them well and felt surprisingly at ease. All of them here had attended their wedding reception, except for the newest wife to join the Force, one of the rancher's daughters.

It was almost like old times.

Almost.

In comparison, her wedding reception with Donald was supposed to be a tiny one. Still, the postponement had hurt when she had to explain it to their handful of relatives. On her side she'd told Francis and Eli and Aunt Alice, and on Donald's side, he'd wired his two daughters, both of whom lived outside the district.

Lifting a forkful of ham to her mouth, Melodie suddenly felt more like an observer than participant at the dinner table.

If she decided to stay with Donald, would she live out the rest of her days feeling guilty for deserting Logan? If she and Logan both continued living in this town, how would she react to seeing his injured face on a continual basis, knowing how the smooth skin of his jaw and throat had once felt beneath her lips? Knowing how much passion and desire had coursed through her veins on their wedding night in anticipation of their lovemaking?

Sweet, pounding love that was supposed to weave their bodies together in exquisite harmony.

But he'd never kissed her naked breast, and she'd never kissed the inside of his thigh.

Tonight, their bodies accidentally brushed beneath the table, his firm leg against hers, making her senses come alive, but she was well aware Logan hadn't purposefully touched her once. It felt unnatural to be sitting beside him without pressing her hand over his or nudging his leg beneath the tablecloth at some small amusement in the conversation.

"I missed this most," Logan whispered against her temple. "Even when I'd lost my memory and couldn't recall anyone specifically, there was a weakness in my heart and I knew there was someone special I'd left behind."

His voice was strained and he pulled away as quickly as he'd come. She was shocked by the impact of his words, and his warm breath against her face. It left her with a feeling of regret. She sat in lonely silence.

The superintendent rose from his leather upholstered chair. "Shall we retire to the library? Us older men can occupy ourselves with billiards. The rest of you folks are welcome to join us or use the domino tables."

The group rose, but Melodie declined.

"I have to go," she said to Logan. "It's another day of work tomorrow."

She used the shop as an excuse but knew there were other reasons to leave. How could she sit this close to Logan when every breath reminded her of what they'd lost?

How could they have an honest discussion in the middle of a crowd?

"I'll walk you home."

"I can manage."

"Please."

Perhaps he should. They'd be alone and they could talk.

"All right." When she got up, he followed her to the door. All eyes were upon them, even though they'd been very good not to stare till now.

Outside in the clear night, Logan carried her empty basket as she buttoned her wool cloak. The wind snatched her hair and threatened to loosen the knotted bun at her nape.

Looking awkward, Logan shoved his hands into his coat pockets. "John will wait till the spring to do my surgery. He says healing's always faster and better when the weather is warm. He's right. It's the same for animals."

She felt such sympathy for Logan but was uncertain how to express it. "I'm glad that he can do this for you."

"When I pick up the mirror, it…does it look as frightful to you as it does to me?"

Removing her glove, she reached out and ran her warm hand along the scarring. His skin felt nice. Not perfect, but touching *him* felt nice.

"It doesn't look terrible at all. It's you, Logan, and you look wonderful."

His muscles hardened at her touch. "I wish I looked better for you."

"It's your spirit of kindness that attracted me. That still shines through for *every* woman to see."

He smiled and she blinked away her unshed tears. She was through crying; it didn't help either one of them. They began up the road again. Bright stars twinkled above his shoulders.

"How are you getting on at the fort?"

"As far as my daily work routine goes, it's almost like I didn't miss a day."

"How about as far as everything else goes?"

He nodded. "You know the questions to ask, don't you? You always did."

"Then tell me how it goes."

"It's awful," he confessed. "I look at those men and see how much they've accomplished in two years. Between them, five new children have been born since I've been gone. Four men have gotten promotions. Three were transferred to the southern border. Two finished their term and are now ranchers. One became a grandfather. And me...I haven't...nothing's changed."

"You've come back from the dead. Everything important has changed."

A smile flickered sadly across his face.

"Have you notified your family back East?" Melodie had never met them, but Logan had often told her stories, full of pride about his older brother and two younger sisters.

His smile deepened. "I received a reply telegram this morning."

"What did it say?"

"They can't believe it. Said if I can't get my leave this summer to visit, they're coming here to visit me."

A burst of happiness rushed from her throat, but it came it out as a quiet sob. "Do you think you'll get the leave?"

"I'm not going to request one. I've been gone too long from here already. There's no place I'd rather be."

To the exclusion of his family. His work always came before his family.

"Because of you, Melodie."

The statement took her by surprise.

As they stepped onto the boardwalk of Macleod Trail, the gap between them got warmer and narrower. "Has there been any word about the Grayvesons? The people who did this to you?"

"There's been some, but…" He looked apologetic. "I can't talk about it."

She felt a snap at the unexpected insult. "Of course. Official business of the North-West Mounted Police. I'm only allowed to know about it when my husband disappears. Otherwise, it doesn't concern me. I should learn to keep my mouth shut.''

"I'm sorry. The nature of my work is the one thing that I can't change."

"And it's the hardest thing about being your wife. You and your men not only battle criminals, you fight forest fires. You disarm mobs of angry cattle ranchers when they argue over land claims with grain farmers. You toss out threatening drifters from saloons. Last year, the superintendent himself was knifed in the stomach by a drunken man accused of rape."

"So I was told. Fortunately, he has healed."

"But has his wife? What about Annabelle's invisible wounds?"

"Maybe you could talk to her and it might help you. She's been married to the superintendent for twenty years. Maybe she could help you through this."

"I *have* talked to Annabelle. When you disappeared, I stayed with her in that very house for two months. When I wasn't able to rise from bed, she brought the soup to *me* and forced me to eat. In the end, when I saw what had become of me, I was ashamed of my weakness…especially in front of their children. If they had been *my* children—*our* children—and I'd been unable to cope, God only knows who would have helped them."

His voice lowered. "Annabelle would have helped. Your sister would have helped. Just as you would help them." He swallowed with difficulty. "I had no idea... I'm sorry you went through that. I *can* guarantee you that no one in that room tonight thinks less of you for how you reacted, but I can't keep apologizing for what I do to earn a living."

"And I wouldn't want you to." She sped up as they reached her door. "Don't you see? That's why it could never work out between us."

CHAPTER SIX

"BUT YOU'VE GOT TO GO." Alone in the shop two evenings later, Francis brushed Melodie's hair.

Melodie twisted in her chair, trying to deny the stirring deep in her soul whenever she thought of Logan's sad smile. "But I suspect it's another false invitation. The timing seems to have been calculated so that Donald can't attend. I'm sure the doctor knows that tonight Donald's store is open late. And Logan is bound to be at the private party. It's being given by Dr. Calloway, this time in the officers' dining room at the fort."

Rufus sat at her feet while Francis fussed over her, and Melodie remembered how often the two of them had sat like this together back home, when their folks had been around to share their Christmases. Family is what matters most, they'd often said. *Devote your time to the people who matter to you.*

"But you enjoy the company of those men and women. It would be an insult to ignore the doctor's invitation."

"I didn't go last year."

"There, you see. He throws a party every year, so it isn't calculated."

"But last year it was smaller and given in his home."

"And you couldn't go because you were still in mourning. You've got no reasonable excuse this time."

Melodie didn't answer. It had been pleasant to enjoy dinner with Logan the other night, to sit beside him and pretend she fitted in, but several times she'd felt like a stranger who'd been invited in from the cold simply because no one knew what else to do with her. And their difference of opinion on how much Logan should confide in her about his work hadn't changed.

Francis yanked a handful of hair as she pinned. "Last year at this time, do you remember what you were doing?"

Melodie winced from the hair-pulling. "No."

"I remember it well. You'd passed on the surgeon's invitation, and you'd passed on my invitation to spend the evening with Eli and me. Instead you went to church, then for that long walk to the river's edge where you and Logan used to sit for hours, you later told me. The next day you were stricken with that stuffy nose and fever. Well, Logan's back and you don't have to sit at the river's edge to respect his memory. You can sit across the table from him tonight and talk."

"I wouldn't know what to say. We…argued the last time we were together."

"Tell him how much you missed him when he was gone."

"He knows already."

"How can he know if you haven't told him?" Francis braided the strands at Melodie's temples before pulling them back.

"When Eli got hurt in that mining accident, it wasn't easy for me, either. When they dug him out and told me he'd survive with nothing more than a broken leg, I got down on my knees there in the mud and thanked the Lord. Turns out, Eli has a permanent injury just like Logan does, but it'll get easier for you both, I promise."

"It's not the injury I fear. I appreciate what you're saying, but there's one difference between your position and mine. Eli left the mines. Logan hasn't left the Mounties."

There, she'd said it. She'd told her worst fear to her sister. Of all people, Francis would understand.

Francis was stumped for a moment. Then she waved a brisk hand in the air. "Poppycock. Now, I'm going to do up your hair nice and pretty, and you're going to talk to that man if I have to bundle you up and deliver you myself."

"GIVE ME A FEW SPRIGS of that." Corporal Travis Reid grinned as he grabbed at Wesley Quinn's cluster of mistletoe. Logan looked on in amusement from where they stood at the bar of the officers' dining hall.

The guitarist and pianist played softly from the corner, capturing the high spirits and lively mood of the crowd. The champagne was helping.

"Now boys, there's enough mistletoe to arm everyone," said Wesley.

"But we aim to please *all* the ladies."

"I know what I want for Christmas," joked the corporal as he looked in the direction of two unattached young women standing by the fireplace holding punch glasses. "A kiss from the mayor's daughter."

"He's a little touchy about his daughters."

The corporal pinched a strand of mistletoe as he left in her direction. "I don't see him here tonight."

Logan leaned back in his tall brown boots and raised his glass in salute. One thing hadn't changed in two years. Women were still as scarce as they ever were on the prairies.

With a population of three thousand, Calgary had only been settled for thirteen years. The Mounties had been present for fifteen, ordered by the government to tame the land and its people before any settlers moved in.

Single men outnumbered women by the hundreds. English women in particular were difficult to find. As far as wives went, some of the Indians working for the government in trading post positions had daughters who were married to policemen. Other policemen sent away for mail-order brides. Some went east on leave and came back married. Logan had been lucky to meet Melodie when he had; otherwise, she would have been snatched up like sweet strawberry pie herself.

He quivered with the thought. She might still be snatched away from him. Would she come tonight?

He scoured the huge dining area, which was rapidly filling with Mounties and their companions. There was no sign of Melodie. He tried not to let his disappointment show.

One of the men asked Wesley, "Has anyone responded to your ad for the mail-order bride?"

"Several," he said, much to everyone's laughter.

"Perhaps you should send the extras our way."

"Perhaps we should order one for the chief surgeon," came Wesley's reply. He lifted the champagne to his lips and sipped.

Logan scoffed. "For John Calloway? Without his knowledge?" Wesley had definitely had too much to drink.

"He's much too straitlaced," said another.

"Maybe that's the reason I should do it."

Logan shook his head and joined in the laughter. As the assistant surgeon, Wesley was closer to John than anyone, but the man must be joking.

Brimming with sudden good cheer, Logan felt a tap on his broad shoulder. He wheeled around.

"Hello," said Melodie. "I thought I'd find you here."

Logan took in the warm scent of her, the fragrance of her light perfume and the high color in her cheeks.

Her hair was braided up, showing a vast expanse of creamy white skin at her throat and along the deep neckline of her calico gown. This was how he'd envisioned her the months he'd been gone. A bit of red ribbon tied in her hair, wearing the gown from the first dance he'd taken her to on Thanksgiving Day.

"I wasn't sure you'd come after our last discussion."

"I'm trying to understand how this might work…how I might fit in…but it's rather difficult." She fumbled with her reticule.

"Come join me for dinner with the others." He was careful not to touch her, not to pressure her in any way. She either had feelings for him, or she didn't. Her arrival alone proved she did.

He couldn't imagine what it must have been like for her the night he'd left. They'd exchanged their vows as husband and wife, he yearning to make love to her rather than go to duty, she expecting to be a wife in every sense of the word. And here they were, two years later and desperately unfulfilled, barely a physical brush between them, more awkward with each other than the first time they'd gone for an evening stroll.

But some inner sense told him to be patient, that things would get better, that she would find her way back into his arms and into his heart and into his bed.

He was committed to her and it would always be that way. Those years he'd spent moving from one place to another had made him want to share his life with the one special woman once he'd found her. He wanted to give her everything, to build a family on their strong foundation of mutual respect and love.

She'd once told him she'd felt the same way.

Trying to concentrate on their present situation rather than torture himself with the past, Logan seated her at the table beside Annabelle and Superintendent Ridgeway.

To strangers who may have witnessed the dinner, he knew he and Melodie spoke of lighthearted topics, things one might not expect from a man and wife separated for twenty-four months. She asked about the champagne and the new barracks being built, he asked about the hours she kept at the shop and where she'd gotten her dog. They were not deep, insightful topics, but they were necessary for a man and woman robbed of time.

When the meal was over and plates cleared, the musicians began again. If Logan could dance with her, embrace her in his arms, perhaps this stiffness would disappear.

"I feel like a fraud," she whispered.

"Why?"

"I didn't let Mr. Dawson know I was coming here this evening. I should be getting back."

She'd called Dawson by his formal name again and hadn't seemed to realize it. How curious.

"Don't leave," Logan drawled. Standing up beside her, he reached out and snagged her fingers with his own. The heat of her touch felt exhilarating. He walked beside her toward the door, lost together in a sea of bodies. "What is it you want to say to me? I can see it in your eyes. What are those unspoken questions?"

Her lashes flashed. "Why did you marry me, Logan?"

"Don't you know?"

"I want you to tell me."

"Because before I met you, I was living my life half-asleep. You awoke me from my slumber."

She moaned tenderly. "I missed you when you were gone."

"Let's leave this place. Let's go home now."

"I wish it were that simple."

"It can be."

"It can *never* be."

He stroked her cheek. "Do you know what I see when I look at you?"

"What?"

"I see how safe your life has become since I've been gone."

She withdrew. "*Safe?* How can you say that?"

He wanted to be honest. Nothing could be solved between them until they were. "You're engaged to a man you still sometimes refer to as *Mr.* Dawson."

"That's how we were introduced when I first moved here, remember? It's a slip of the tongue. It means nothing."

"How can you be close to a man you refer to as mister?"

"It's easy. I've known him for longer than I knew you before we got engaged—"

Logan balked at her words.

"I'm sorry. That came out more harshly than I intended."

He backed away.

She stepped closer. "I'm sorry—"

Before he could respond, a constable dashed by into the dining room, delivering an ominous message. "Rustlers on the McIver ranch!"

The music stopped. A hubbub of voices filled the air. Women moaned in brief terror. Men took a moment to adjust to the news, then raced out the door, some faster to respond than others, clomping down the stairwell. Logan's gaze flew to Melodie's.

Shock flooded her body.

How could he leave her? Now in her time of need when they were opening up to each other, he couldn't possibly!

As other policemen ran past them, Logan struggled with an inner torture he knew she'd never understand. He made a most agonizing decision. He brushed his lips across her soft cheek then ran down the stairs and out the door, joining the others.

ANNABELLE RIDGEWAY WAS the first to break the silence. Her words came like an echo, chipping into Melodie's wall of icy numbness.

Would Logan survive this time? Would he return safely? Would he return at all?

"We should continue eating this fine dinner," said the superintendent's wife to the dozens of women seated before her. "The cooks have outdone themselves and I know they're planning a table of fine desserts."

Several women murmured, but few could stomach another morsel. With all the empty seats around them, the loud clink of cutlery echoed against their plates, like swords against armor.

What if he never came back? What if the last words Melodie had said to him were those spoken in anger?

Superintendent Ridgeway's daughters, Henrietta and Charlotte, stood by the window peering down at the open square below. "Where do you think Papa will send the men? How many do you think he'll send?"

The Mounties had left to chase away danger and the women had stayed behind to...*to pray.*

Stumbling from her place beside the wall, Melodie tried to remember...had she brought a cloak? Had she brought her reticule? Where was it? How had she gotten here? It was by carriage, yes, a rented, golden horse-drawn carriage. No, no, she'd come by her own buggy. Or had she walked?

"Melodie," said Annabelle, coming closer. She wrapped an arm around Melodie's shoulders. "Come sit with me, dear. You're so young, sweetheart, you're like another daughter to me. We'll wait this out together.''

"I don't think I can wait…not by the window…not again.''

"We won't wait by the window. We'll sit and have coffee. We'll listen to the musicians. I've ordered them to play something uplifting.''

"No Christmas carols, please.''

"I promise.''

"How do you manage, Annabelle? How can you take this? Is there a secret?''

"Some wives can take it, my dear. And some never will. The secret is…the secret is you decide ahead of time the type you want to be.''

CHAPTER SEVEN

DRESSED IN standard-issue buffalo-skin coat, Logan ran up the stairs. He didn't see Melodie so he raced to Annabelle's side. His shoulder holster, heavy with the weight of his Enfield revolver, slapped against his ribs. "Where is she?"

"She's not here."

Panic seized him. "Where then?"

In a room full of watchful women, Annabelle stepped to the window and pointed down. Melodie was seated in her buggy alongside an elderly couple. The gentleman was holding the reins while the women sat solemnly in the back with a blanket over their knees.

Logan ran outside. "Melodie!"

She peered around her conveyance. Her face looked pale and drawn against the colors of her calico bonnet and burgundy wool coat. Her eyes flickered in the warm lighting of oil-lit streetlamps. "I'm going home."

"We have to finish our talk." His hot breath came out in frosty white clouds.

"I stayed until I saw the men and horses returning

through the gates. I spotted you in the square, safe and unharmed, then I couldn't take any more.''

"I didn't ride with the others. I was ordered to prepare the mounts and stay on guard till the others returned.''

"Sutcliffe!'' cried the commander. The thunder of horses' hooves in dirty snow echoed against pine buildings.

"Melodie, please,'' begged Logan. "Stay.''

"Officer Sutcliffe! We need you here!''

"You had better go.'' Her mare neighed, then the buggy left.

Logan raced to the commander's side. "Yes, Superintendent?''

"For those of us with wives, I do understand your dilemma. But you're on duty, dammit, until I say you're relieved.''

Logan nodded.

"Of the six culprits involved with the cattle rustling, four escaped our grasp tonight. I understand they've captured two. You're needed in the jailhouse for identification.''

"Were they killed, Sir?''

"They're unharmed.''

Logan strode past the men across the square to the jailhouse. Due to a paid informant at the bank, the Mounties had kept careful watch on two ranch houses in the district for the past six months. The informant had told them there had been a lot of money exchanging hands around the same time cattle had been disappearing. Who had they caught?

When the door opened, a staff sergeant and two constables were guarding the captives.

"On your feet," called the staff sergeant to the men in handcuffs. When they turned around to face Logan, they were dirty and grimy as if they'd been on the trail for months.

But God help them, Logan recognized one. He'd never forget that twisted chin.

"Do you know either of these men?" asked the staff sergeant.

Logan stepped to the taller of the two, the broader, more muscular one who wasn't afraid to look directly back.

"This one."

"I've never seen you before in my life," the man spit back.

Logan cursed through thinned lips. "That's because I didn't look like this before I met you."

The greasy black brows came together in a frown. "Are you speakin' riddles?"

"No, Sid, I'm not." Logan stepped closer until he smelled the salty stench of perspiration. Raising his hands, Logan yanked on his own sleeves until he exposed his scarred wrists. "You shackled my wrists. You chained my feet. *You put a bullet through my face.*"

Sid Grayveson stumbled back. "Uh, I thought I'd left you for dead."

''That's enough.'' The staff sergeant stepped between the two men. ''That's enough, Grayveson, until you speak to a lawyer. The judge will appoint you one.'' Then he turned to Logan, who'd fallen against the wall. ''Sir, are you all right?''

''THEY'RE GOING TO TRIAL,'' said Donald as Melodie pinned the jeweled snowman to his lapel.

Engulfed by the orchestral sounds of the dozen musicians behind her in the town hall, Melodie hesitated for a brief second then continued pinning. ''Yes, I heard.''

Behind them, a hundred couples were already dancing in the biggest Christmas event of the year, sponsored by the Businessmen's Association of which Donald was the president. Both of them had locked their stores tonight, December twenty-third, not to be opened again till after the holidays. She felt a blessed relief with all the time ahead of her. Was it enough time to make her decision?

''They say he'll get twenty-five years in prison for attempted murder of a police officer.''

She nodded. And the other man would get ten for his involvement with the thefts. Two Grayveson brothers were still at large, but the despicable one who'd shot Logan had been caught. The other two were apparently the American connection to the ring, but the Mounties were confident they'd be caught if they returned to this area.

Melodie had no doubt. From what she'd seen at

the fort three evenings ago, the police were sure-footed and focused. Despite her own grief, she'd witnessed the bond among men. Each one of them had laid his own life in harm's way in order to help Logan. The thought comforted her deeply.

And so did the realization that she'd also survived that traumatic night.

Donald fingered the pearl necklace around her throat. "You look lovely in my beads."

"Thank you." She was also wearing the home-spun gown she'd intended to wear the evening Logan had reappeared. Made of burgundy velvet, and heavily brocaded with beads around the square neck-line, the buttery fabric shifted around her legs, ta-pering to a prominent bustle in the back. It had taken more yardage than she'd expected, but sewing it had filled her spare time with pleasure for the entire month of November.

"Logan is a good man." Donald tipped her chin to the light. "Despite our differences over you—and I still intend to wed you—I hope you know I say it honestly."

"I believe you." She repositioned herself slightly out of his grasp. His hand fell to his side.

"Donald!" shouted the mercantile owner as he came striding toward them. "I've got those adver-tisements set up for the *Calgary Herald,* and I need your advice."

Donald touched her hand. "Excuse me a mo-ment."

Before he pulled away, however, Melodie saw him glance past her shoulder. His jaw snapped shut and his face clouded.

When she spun around, Logan was standing there. More handsome—*yes, handsome*—than she'd ever recalled, he was dressed in his scarlet uniform, muscles firm beneath the cloth. Her heart jumped in response.

Freshly shaved and hair groomed back at the sides, he reached for her hand. His fingers were warm and strong over hers. "I've come to ask for a dance."

Donald stepped forward. His waistcoat twisted around his frame. "She declines."

Logan's expression shifted for a moment, but he didn't release her trembling hand. He pressed it once more, possessively, making it difficult for her to let go, difficult for her to hide her tension.

"If you'll dance once with me tonight, Melodie, then I'll give you an annulment…if that's what you wish."

She had the wildest urge to run away from danger.

"How difficult could one dance be?" His voice held a thick challenge.

Very difficult, she thought.

"You'll give us the annulment?" Donald's tone changed. "Well then, perhaps you should, my dear." He pressed his hand between her shoulder blades and gave her a slight push before joining the other businessman in discussion.

She felt as if she were being tossed into the jowls

of a hungry panther. Donald didn't know how difficult this was for her. She hadn't been in Logan's arms since their wedding night. She opened her mouth to object, but Donald was already being pulled away by the other man.

Logan's gaze was direct. "You have nothing to fear from me."

She had *everything* to fear. Her security, her sense of balance, her control over the situation.

When Logan stepped back and bowed on the dance floor, he held out his arms and waited for her to come to him.

Resolving to maintain her composure, she inhaled a deep breath of cedar-scented air then pressed her palms into his.

"That's nice," he whispered into her hair, causing a shiver to rise over her skin. He gathered her against the warmth of his body and she closed her eyes for a moment. *This was what it had felt like. What she had missed the most about losing Logan.*

He led her about the dance floor to a waltz, graceful on his feet, in complete control of every movement.

She gripped the length of his back and felt his muscles harden beneath her touch. "How do you feel now that they've caught the outlaws who did this to you?"

He grinned in the irresistible way she remembered, carefree and jovial for the first time since he'd returned to Calgary. His load had lightened. "Like a new man."

"I'm so happy for you," she said softly, conscious of his breathing.

He pulled her away to look at her face. "I can feel it. Thank you."

What could he feel? The hot and heavy pounding of her arteries against his? The clamminess of her palms? The catch in her lungs?

They followed the music in rhythm with each other. "Do you recall the last time we danced?"

"It was on our wedding night."

"I was wearing this uniform and you were in your breathtaking ivory gown. I remember it was beaded with tiny pearls up the front and I couldn't wait to unbutton each one. I thought about you in that gown for the first six months I was gone."

"Logan, don't—"

"Your gown is beaded again tonight."

The silence between them rushed in her ears. He slid his warm hand up her back. His blue eyes flashed. "Why did you agree to marry Donald?"

She felt a flurry of nerves cascade up her spine. "Had I known you were alive—even for a second— I never would have allowed him to court me."

He nodded slowly. "But it's done now, isn't it? And he's such a safe choice."

There was that description again. *Safe.* She stiffened and tried to put an inch of space between them.

He wouldn't allow it, keeping his grip firm. "Despite what you may think, I don't harbor any particular grudges against Donald Dawson. When we lived here together, I thought he was a fine man."

It would be easier on Melodie if Logan said something nasty. To be frank about Donald's good qualities threw her off-kilter.

"But Donald Dawson isn't a policeman, now is he?" Logan continued, holding her close. "As far as his work goes, how much safer could you be than to live with a man who sells platters and spoons?"

"He's an astute businessman."

"Indeed. He makes a fine living and would provide well for you. He's much to be commended. But the woman *I* knew used to enjoy adventure and unpredictability."

"That was before my husband was snatched away from me, before I was told he'd been killed. Adventure and unpredictability no longer thrill me."

"Is there that much to be said for predictability and boredom?"

"You're deliberately taunting me."

He shook his head in objection. His eyes grew misty. "Does your new...*husband* share the same dreams and hopes as your old one?"

She gasped for air. "Logan, don't do this."

"Dawson already has two grown children. At his age, is he eager to start a new family?" Logan's forehead lined with concentration and a devilish look came into his eyes. "Or perhaps you no longer want children?"

Her temper began to rise. "Of course I do. And Mr. Daw—*Donald* says he'd be happy to have more children for my sake."

A muscle in Logan's jaw flicked. "Now there's the difference between us, I suppose. I would have them not only for your sake, but for *mine* as well."

She opened her mouth to give him a sharp reply but decided to hold her tongue. She just had to get through this dance.

He tightened his hold on her waist and twirled her through the crowd. "One more question, Melodie."

Her composure was being bombarded. Shaken by his words and his touch, she begged him, "You're taking this too far. No more questions, please."

"Ah, but you promised. One full dance in exchange for an annulment, remember? It's a small price to pay for your freedom."

She willed the music to stop, but it kept going. The violins began, then the piano.

"Here's the thing I'd like to know. It's hypothetical, of course, but it's a question that consumes my mind. Pretend for a moment that Donald is a police officer. Entertain the notion for a moment, please. If he were a policeman, too, would you still choose him over me?"

"Well, that's a silly question." This time, she stopped dancing. The music was thankfully beginning to fade, as if close to ending. "It's hypothetical and there's no reason to think about it."

"It's a question I want you to answer. *Need* you to answer."

The song ended, but they didn't move off the crowded dance floor.

Would she marry Donald if he were in the force? She wasn't sure.

She heard the orchestra begin another song. "Silent Night" wafted from their guitar strings, two stirring male voices resonating through the air.

A musician addressed the crowd. "Most of you will recognize this next song, but you may not know the story behind it. Now we sing it in English but it was originally written in German on December twenty-fourth, 1818, when the clergyman of an Austrian parish took the poem he'd written to his choirmaster. Their organ was broken but both men wanted music for their Christmas Eve service, so this is the beautiful carol they composed for two solo voices and guitar accompaniment. Here goes."

No one was dancing, all standing as still as wheat in a windless sky, listening to the beauty of the lyrics. Melodie hadn't heard it since *that* night.

Logan brushed the wisps of hair from her forehead. His fingertips grazed a path down her cheekbone. All the longing she'd buried deep within her for two wretched years came welling to the surface. He'd once unlocked her heart and she weakened at the searing memory.

He watched her with silent expectation, riveting on her face, then down lower to her mouth. His fingers rolled over her lips and she froze, breathless with anticipation.

Deliberately and confidently, he wrapped one of his large arms around her waist and another at her shoulder, then pulled her into the safe circle of his arms and lowered his mouth to hers.

His kiss deepened and she responded with the urgency of her own need. An explosion of excitement filled her pores. Wrapping her arms around his neck, she pressed against his body as if no time had ever come between them.

Logan.

She felt his body responding to her touch.

This was who she needed. This man, forever.

He whispered her name in a fevered tone she'd fought hard to forget. She ached with the realization that if he ever disappeared again, it would break her into a thousand pieces.

When someone yanked her arm and pulled her body out of Logan's grasp, she fought to catch her bearing.

Donald tugged her to his side. "You mock me at my own event."

Logan swayed at her unexpected withdrawal. Steadying himself, he rubbed his mouth. His body flexed with the anger that seemed to ripple just below the surface. "Your head may want to marry him, but your heart doesn't. Which will rule your life, Melodie, your head or your heart?"

Stunned by Logan's words, she struggled for an appropriate response.

"That's it," said Donald. "We want the annulment."

Furious with Donald for treating her like a child, and embarrassed by the curious glances of the crowd, she shoved his arm off hers and stalked away from both men.

CHAPTER EIGHT

"I CAN'T MARRY YOU." Standing inside her kitchen beside the back door, Melodie looked at his glum face. Her stomach swirled at the difficult words she'd had to say.

They'd just arrived from the dance a minute ago and were dressed in their coats. The inside air was chilly, for no fire burned in her stove.

Donald leaned against the doorjamb. "You received a terrible shock when Logan returned. You haven't had time for it to sink in. You've known me for longer than you've known him. Haven't I proved myself devoted to your happiness?"

Her temper had simmered at both Donald and Logan, and her feelings were clear to her now. For the first time since Logan's return, she was honest with herself about her pending marriage to Donald. Logan's questions had hit their mark. She *wanted* an adventurous life, full of many children whose father wanted them as much as she did. She *loved* Logan.

"Devotion is a wonderful thing. So is friendship and taking care of one another in our daily lives. I'll always thank you for that, Donald. But love is a totally different thing and when it has a hold on you, nothing compares.''

Donald tapped his gloves on the wall, then the counter as he walked around the room, glancing at her shelves full of imported china and the shiny knickknacks he'd given her.

She grasped for soothing words. ''You've been a great friend in my time of need. We can continue to be friends.''

''Perhaps friendship is all I really needed.''

''What do you mean?''

Despite his outer calm, a pink stain crept into Donald's throat. ''I don't think you've ever kissed me the way you kissed Logan tonight.''

Melodie blushed and fingered her coat buttons. She and Donald had never taken it beyond a light kiss or peck on the cheek. He hadn't pushed her, and she'd never stopped to think why. But saying so would only chafe the rawness of Donald's wound. ''I'll always have the deepest of respect for you.''

Donald pondered that for a moment. ''That means the world to me. I suspect I saw this coming. As soon as I saw you look at him that first night at the Police Ball.''

Melodie unclasped her pearl necklace, tucked it into his hand, then focused on his gentle expression. ''You shouldn't be alone for Christmas. You could spend time with me and—''

''No.'' He raised a hand in the air to stop her from continuing. ''No, I'll—I'll take the train to Regina to see my sister. The doctor says she's getting stronger, and I imagine seeing her little brother might do her some good. One of my daughters lives there as well.''

''Always the gentleman.'' Melodie stepped closer and ran her hand along the side of his bristly cheek. ''Thank you for making the last two years bearable.''

''I'm a widower myself, remember?'' His smile lit up. ''But you aren't a widow, Melodie. You never were. Merry Christmas. Now go find Logan.''

MELODIE HAD PLEDGED her marriage vows to one man and she desperately assured herself she would keep them. If she could only find Logan.

Trudging through the light, new-fallen snow, she headed down the hill toward the river and the superintendent's home. Maybe they had seen him.

She passed a couple walking home from the big party. Buggies on the road wove by her.

Carrying a small lantern with her to light her way, she felt its weight bear down on her wrist. Stopping for a moment to rest, she peered up into the night sky from beneath snow-fringed lashes. Stars glittered. She picked out the North Star and watched it sparkle, wondering where Logan was.

She'd already checked at the fort but the corporal said no one had seen Logan there since before the party. That sent her racing back to the town hall, but there'd been no sight of him there, either. A visit to the private town house of Dr. Calloway and a chat with the neighbor next door confirmed that neither man had returned there.

Melodie's heart was bursting with things to say to her husband.

Like how much she adored him. How much she'd missed his smile and his easygoing banter. How much she loved watching him simply saddle his horse, his deft hands working lovingly over the animal to make it feel wanted and well cared for and special. With all the attention Logan poured on every living thing, be it animal or person or plant, what had he gotten in return? He'd been torn out of the comfort of his life and all those who wanted to cherish *him*.

Her empty, outstretched arms had ached for two long years to hold her precious husband.

A train rumbled on the distant tracks, startling her. Surely he wasn't going anywhere. No, of course not. He had a duty to fulfill at the fort. A policeman couldn't up and leave when he got upset.

Had she caused him a lot of distress in leaving him standing at the party, believing she wanted the annulment?

She'd make up for that, too.

Reaching Annabelle's door, her velvet gown frozen with snow from the knees down, Melodie rapped loudly. After what seemed like ages, the houseman answered with Annabelle behind him, dressed in her night robe.

"My dear, please come in. You look frozen to the bone."

"I'm sorry I've disturbed you. Is Logan here?"

"Logan? Why no." Annabelle peered down the outside stairs to see if anyone had accompanied her, then opened the door wide. "Please come in. It's half-past eleven. I'll make us a pot of hot tea and you can spend the night."

"I can't. I need to find Logan." Melodie turned around and raced away.

"But my dear, it's snowing! Wait and I'll get our houseman to accompany you!"

"I'll be fine!"

Fortunately, Melodie's tall boots kept the ice on her petticoats from touching her legs, and her woolen stockings kept her legs warm right to the top of her thighs.

Where was Logan? Breathing deeply and clutching her lantern, Melodie tried the boardinghouse. Not there, either.

Her fingers felt rigid. Fatigue from lifting her legs through the weight of the snow caught up with her. She should go home, dry off and think where to look next.

Reaching her kitchen door, she saw a flicker of light shift beneath her curtain. Was someone inside?

CHAPTER NINE

THE WALL CLOCK CHIMED midnight.

Logan opened the hatch of Melodie's kitchen stove and placed another quarter log onto the orange flames. Still wearing his uniform, he straightened, rubbed his hands over the heat and listened to the twelve strokes of midnight. Hearing the door latch click, he spun around in alarm.

Releasing a startled cry when she caught sight of him, Melodie slid through the door, huddled in her thick coat.

He hesitated in the stilted air between them. Her dewy eyes and moist lips swiveled to his face.

Apprehension coursed through him. Had it been presumptuous of him to come? "I hope I didn't alarm you. It was cold in here and I couldn't imagine you coming into a chilled house. I've stoked all three fires. They were almost out. You've worked too hard already, all day on your feet, to tend the fires yourself."

If they were married in every sense of the word and he were living with her, he'd make sure to keep the house warm. "I knocked but only Rufus answered, and the back door was unlocked."

Rufus nudged his way to her side. She patted his furry white head but kept her questioning gaze on Logan. "I never lock the back door."

"Where have you been?" He forced dignity into his voice. "You look frozen."

"Oh, Logan." Her solemn expression mellowed, and he felt something between them he hadn't felt since his return. It was the warm and pliant nature of her gaze. It made him tingle with a sense of promise.

"Come in, please," he said. "Maybe it was wrong of me to come, but…is…is Dawson with you?"

She shook her head.

"He let you walk home alone? This late at night?"

"He did walk me home, then I—I left again."

Logan glanced to the fire, certain she was about to tell him that it was finally over, that she'd taken offense by Logan's forward kiss on the dance floor and his insistence that she make a choice there on the spot.

"I suppose you're wondering why I'm here." He should tell her then be on his way. He had no intention of forcing his company on her, nor his kisses— no matter how desperately he wanted to hold her again, to feel those soft caressing lips upon his own. "I wanted to give you something. For Christmas."

In two long strides, he reached his heavy fur overcoat. Parting one pocket, he removed a gift wrapped in silver packaging.

When he handed it to her, she stared at it but didn't take it. Sliding out of her woolen coat, she stood in a circle of frozen burgundy velvet, capturing his attention with her softly trembling chin. He saw her throat tighten as if she were trying to suppress a sob. "I don't need any presents from you."

His chest squeezed with the ache. She didn't want anything to do with him. It *was* a mistake to come.

Gingerly he placed the rectangular gift on top of her pine table. "I'll put it here in case you want to open it when I leave. If you don't want it, then please…just donate it to the local charity." Lifting his fur overcoat off a hard-back chair, he made his way to the door. "I promise I won't bother you anymore."

"Logan."

Her voice was satin smooth, more alluring than he remembered. Quiet, breathless, unassuming Melodie.

He stopped as she lifted the package. Untying the ribbon, she unwrapped his gift.

It was a music box, silver on the top and pine around the sides. Carved onto the silver lid were several Christmas trees. The sides were simply pasted with black-and-white postcards of various scenes of snow and mountains. When she lifted the lid, it played the tune of "Silent Night," in the same way as when he'd picked it up from the salesman in Montana Territory, four long weeks ago.

"This is what jogged your memory."

"It's a pretty song, that's all. I wanted you to have it. With no pressure this time."

She set the box down. Breathing heavily, she

turned to look at him. A shock ran through him at the emotion he witnessed in her face.

He groaned.

And then she came running, stretching out her arms and wrapping them beneath his.

Soft laughter escaped him as he was pushed back by her unexpected embrace. "What's this? Do you like your gift that much?"

"No, silly. I mean yes, I love it. But it's not the gift, it's you, my love."

My love? Had he heard correctly? He burrowed his face into the clean scent of her hair. A hot ache grew inside him. This was much more than he could hope for.

"What does this mean, Melodie?" His voice crackled with the strain of possibility.

She answered him with another question. "Do you know what day it is?" She placed her chin on his chest as she focused her brown eyes on him.

"The clock just chimed. It's December twenty-fourth."

"We were married on this day."

"I remember," he said, as soft as a night caress. He hadn't thought she'd noticed the time.

"After Donald brought me home this evening, I went out again because I was looking for you."

"Why?"

"Because I wanted to tell you how I feel."

He groped for words, stumbling again. He wasn't at all as smooth and confident as he wished to be, because her closeness was like a drug that affected his thinking. "And how…how is that?"

"You were right to ask me those questions about Donald. I wasn't being truthful to myself and that's why I got angry with you tonight." He felt her arms trembling as they squeezed around him. "When I asked myself would I marry Donald instead of you if you were both Mounties, the answer was no. No, I'd never choose Donald over you."

He'd never asked for much in his life, but to be whole, he needed this woman.

"It was torture for me when you disappeared," she continued. "But it would be worse to keep my distance now that you've returned. If you ever disappeared again, it would break me to pieces, but I'd rather risk everything I have than to be with any other man."

He couldn't believe he'd heard right. The shadows from his heart lifted. "You'd like to remain married to me?"

She nodded and smiled and he was filled with a sense of bottomless joy.

"I love you," he whispered into her ear, already kissing the sweet skin along her temple.

She exhaled a long sigh of contentment. "I could never stop loving you."

When his lips came down on hers, a moan broke at the back of his throat.

She struggled to explain her feelings while he kissed the pulsing at the hollow of her throat. "And something Annabelle told me a few days ago… I've decided that I'd like to be the type of wife who chooses to survive.''

''Annabelle is a smart woman.''

''I've already told Donald how I feel.''

Logan sobered for a moment. ''It must have been difficult news for him to hear.''

''He took it better than I thought, and he gave me a gift as well.''

''What was that?''

''He graciously stepped aside and told me to go and find you.''

''I'll have to thank him when I see him next.''

''It won't be for a few weeks. He's gone to visit his sister and oldest daughter in Regina.''

''So he won't be alone for the holidays. That's good.''

She held him at bay for a moment. ''When you walked into my shop that first day, were you confident this would work out?''

''I could barely keep from shaking. I wasn't at all sure...''

''And then?'' she prompted.

''When you brought me into your parlor that evening, I spotted our old rocking chair. When I saw it, I thought there might be some hope left.''

She smiled.

''Why did you keep it?''

''When we were alone, we used to curl up together on it, remember?''

He nodded.

''That's where you first proposed…one Saturday evening in late November.''

Swallowing hard, he stroked the hair at her temple.

''Sometimes when I missed you most, I'd sit in that chair. It felt like you were there with your arms around me. The chair and the memory of us in it was the only thing that kept me going in my darkest moments.''

''I'll try to make sure there'll never be any more moments like that again. They're setting us up with partners. When we go out on a call, we'll work in teams of two.''

Her face brightened. ''You'll watch out for each other.'' Sighing, she ran her tender fingers down the scarring of his left cheek. ''Did this cause much pain when it happened?''

''I'm grateful I don't remember much of it.''

''Does it give you any other problems?''

''Headaches at times, but they've nearly vanished.''

Her eyes sparkled with sympathy, but he didn't want her to feel remorseful.

''It's all right. It's over.'' Logan's lips recaptured hers, more demanding this time. Both hungry for each other, they pressed their bodies closer. When his tongue explored her lips, she parted for him and responded with a soft moan of her own.

''You feel good to hold.''

''I'm going to hold you all night, my lovely wife. I'm going to make love to you for hours.''

"I don't think it can get any better than the happiness I feel at this moment."

"We'll see."

He loved the way she blushed at his promise.

Rufus whined at their feet. When they looked down, the dog was licking the water off her boots.

"Your gown is dripping. The ice from your skirt is melting." He studied the velvet fabric and the way it clung to her curves.

"You've stoked the fire in here too hot," she teased.

"You'd better get used to this temperature, especially if we're going to have all those children we talked about."

Eager with the anticipation of holding his wife for the first time within the privacy of their marriage, he ran his hands up the back of her pinned hair. Sliding out the hairpins one by one, he wrapped his fingers into the silky black strands.

"I've waited so long for this moment, sweetheart." His hands grazed her shoulders and worked their way toward her velvet waist.

"I never thought it would be possible to make love to you, Logan." And then she spoke more shyly. "It'll be my first time."

A surge of pleasure had him brushing his mouth against her hot throat. "It's as if you waited for me."

She planted sweet kisses along his neck and he felt a swelling of desire. Running his fingers down the dozen buttons of her bodice, he tore himself away from her mouth long enough to ask, "May I unbutton this for you?"

"Please…"

Lifting her off her feet, he carried her to the parlor, swooping up his fur overcoat as they passed the chair. The parlor doubled as her bedroom, and he'd already restarted the fire in there. When they got there, the room glowed golden.

Setting her to her feet, he closed the door so that Rufus would remain in the kitchen. When he spread his coat on the floor before the flickering flames, he laid Melodie down gently on the soft brown fur.

They both removed their shoes. He yanked off his tie with wild abandon, rousing another smile from her gorgeous lips.

Her skin was warm beneath his touch as he un-latched the beading from their buttonholes. As she tumbled out of the velvet, he kissed the nape of her neck.

"Let me look at you."

Her breasts, round and swollen beneath her corset, shifted as she moved, causing his flesh to tighten in response. With two swift strokes, he untied her pet-ticoat, sliding it off her bountiful hips. Next came her cotton bloomers.

She was lying in the buff from the waist down, her corset half-slid off one shoulder. Her thighs and calves glistened in the firelight and made him catch his breath.

"I don't ever want this to end," she whispered.

"It never will."

When he slowly unclasped her corset, it was sheer heaven and utter agony to wait for the fabric to drop. When she was finally fully unrobed, he admired her naked glory, dipping his face close to hers and lowering his mouth to one succulent pointed breast.

"I can't believe you're mine. Everything about you makes me hunger for more. When I thought I'd lost you, it made me realize that I never used to stop long enough to inhale the beauty around me. I was always dashing off to work on one thing or another, always concerned about the next step in my life. Impatient with everything and everyone. This time, I promise to take the time to share the moments we have together."

"Now I know why I married you," she responded.

Their soft laughter echoed against the log walls, dimmed by the thick fur beneath them.

Big, soft nipples arched to meet his craving mouth. She moaned, and the most wonderful wave of satisfaction rolled through him.

He didn't bother with his shirt buttons. After unclasping his collar, he eagerly tugged his shirt over his head as she hastily undid his pants.

Together, their nakedness contrasted like rich, deep cloth—her light golden skin next to his deeper olive.

"I don't believe I've ever used my coat like this before," he said with amusement. The fur enveloped his backside, feeling heavenly pressed against his skin.

"I like it, inside out." There was humor in her

tone too, although the profile of her face and jawline grew serious once more.

Stroking the underbelly of her breasts, he watched her through half-closed lids, marveling at the tremble he caused when he touched her.

"I haven't gotten you a Christmas present yet." Melodie nuzzled her shoulders into the thick pile of fur beneath her naked body. "I'll have to think of something perfect."

"You *are* the perfect gift."

When he nibbled on her earlobe, he was cocooned by the splendor of her love. Finally, after two torturous years of waiting, they united and bonded as husband and wife, *timeless lovers.*

"We'll speak no more about regrets," he whispered.

When the night ended, and the early morning dawn filtered through the window, their lovemaking began again.

For Logan Sutcliffe had finally come home to his beloved wife.

* * * * *

If you've enjoyed
"The Long Journey Home,"
don't miss THE SURGEON,
by Kate Bridges.
Available from Harlequin Historicals
in December 2003.

Forrester Square

LEGACIES . LIES . LOVE .

*Award-winning author Day Leclaire
brings a highly emotional and
exciting reunion romance story to
Forrester Square in December...*

KEEPING FAITH
by
Day Leclaire

Faith Marshall's dream of a "white-picket" life with
Ethan Dunn disappeared—along with her husband—
when she discovered that he was really a dangerous
mercenary. With Ethan missing in action, Faith found
herself alone, pregnant and struggling to survive.
Now, years later, Ethan turns up alive. Will a family
reunion be possible after so much deception?

*Forrester Square...
Legacies. Lies. Love.*

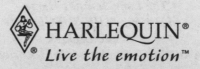

HARLEQUIN®
Live the emotion™

Visit us at www.forrestersquare.com

PHFS5